ASHBORNE

BOOK ONE OF THE DAUGHTER OF THE BURNING THRONE

JAYCIE REID

Cover Design by:

Miblart (www.miblart.com)

Map Design by:

Jonathan Stueve (@stueveastray)

Edited and Formatted by:

Samantha Miland (@soulfyre_sanctuary)

www.soulfyreeditorial.com

ISBNS:
Hardcover: 979-8-9934459-0-8
Paperback: 979-8-9934459-1-5
E-Book: 979-8-9934459-2-2

For those I love, and those who loved me through this journey. This book belongs to you, too.

NOTE FROM THE EDITOR

There have been a lot of questions in the book community around em dashes. AI did not create them. Please remember that AI learned it from somewhere— by it being fed so many different works from tons of different authors. With that in mind, Author Jaycie Reid LOVES her em dashes, deal with it. AI was not used in any way, shape, or form in this novel.

Samantha Miland, Editor

Soulfyre Editorial

CONTENT WARNINGS

Ashborne contains many adult themes, ranging from talk of mass genocide, cannibalism, traumatic loss, adult language, jokes, and romantic scenes.
Reader discretion is advised.

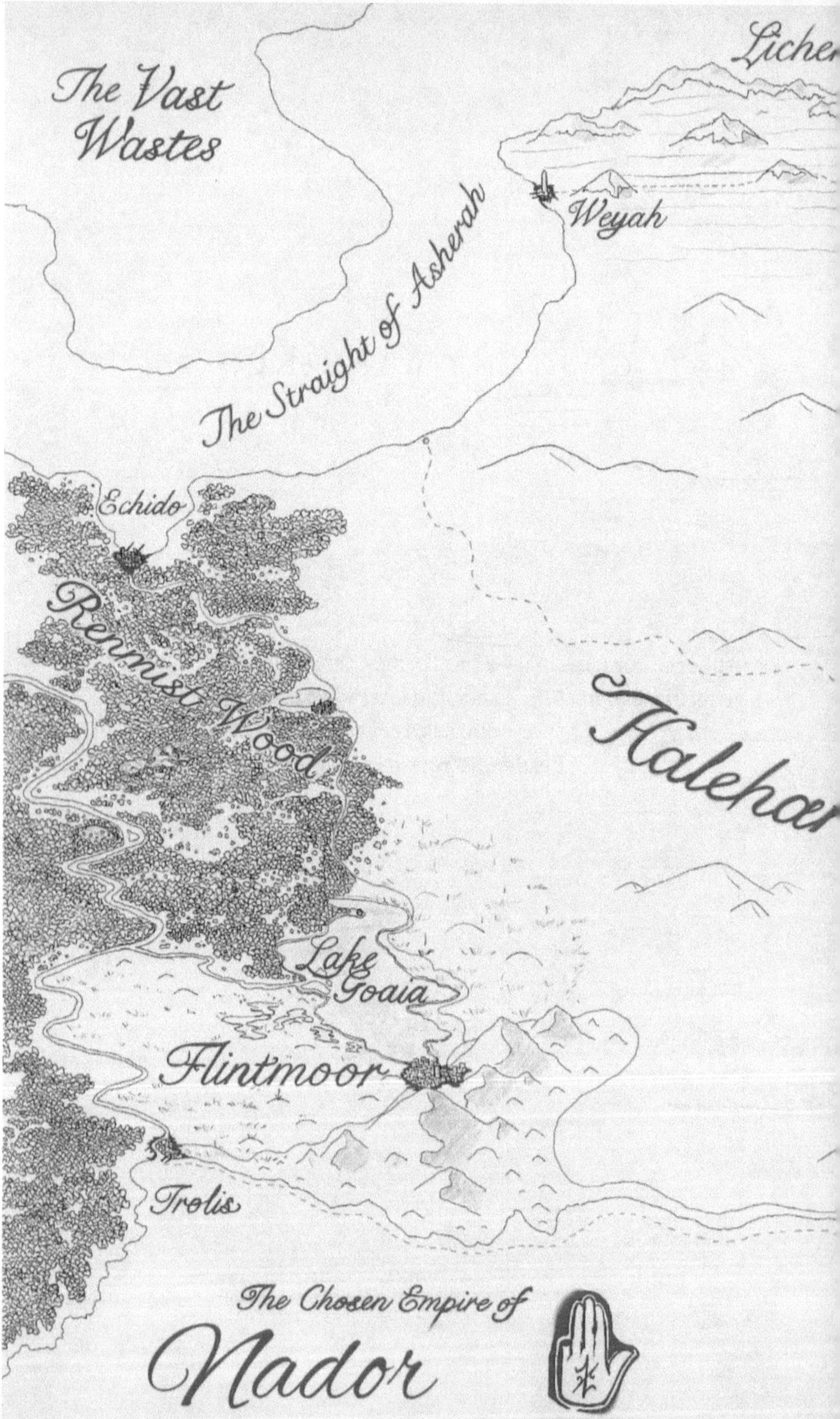

The Vast Wastes
Licher
Weyah
The Straight of Asherah
Echido
Renmist Wood
Halehar
Lake Goaia
Flintmoor
Trolis
The Chosen Empire of
Nador

Draconia

Sea of Itsaso

Eldridge

Fyrsire Forest

Serpantongue Mt.

Caverns Pass

Aeronjaw Cliffs

Crille

Suirith

Atheria

esert

of

ad

le for

Kirios

Kuolburgh

Kalimeda's Gate

Ocean-Halimeda

RHEA

T he night air crackled with energy as the warm early summer air erupted into screams of excitement and wonder. With my hood over my head, no one paid me any mind as I side-stepped further into the village, the squeals from children's mouths carried on the wind, their voices like music to my starved soul.

Chaos ensued all around as vendors handed out their goods, everyone with a drink in hand, and if not a drink, food. The smell of fresh-baked bread, chocolate, and roasted meats made my mouth water. When was the last time I'd been to Flitmoor?

I did my best to navigate the bustling village square. The quaint buildings, all one or two stories, were adorned with ribbons and flags in the symbolic shade of deep emerald, for which Flitmoor was known. I jumped in line for the most popular vendor, the line snaking through the crowd of people, causing a divide in the square. I made sure to keep my eyes downcast and my hood pulled tight around me. Little bolts of lightning crossed my skin as the excitement built and the real-ization of what I had done set in.

I was *outside,* and no one knew.

A central bonfire cast a warm glow on the shops that lined the village square, where vendors and patrons chatted merrily. Music erupted from the other side of the square, and suddenly, any open spot was filled with couples dancing, shouts of glee lost in the crackles of the bonfire. Tension built in my chest, like a knot being pulled taut. I *wanted* to be one of them. No, no, *needed* to be one of them.

I stepped to the back of the line of the busiest vendor in the square. Every patron left the stall with the same thing: a steaming mug of mulled wine and a fresh chocolate pastry. I swallowed the saliva that pooled in the back of my throat. The hot mulled wine sounded so wonderful, but right now I had to keep a clear mind. I couldn't risk being seen here on a night with so many extra eyes and ears that could see and hear rumors which could be shared with those who would happily see to the end of my life.

I moved along with the line, keeping myself as small and discreet as possible. I didn't have long in Flitmoor, but the determination of needing to enjoy every second outweighed the fear of discovery.

Just as I was about to step forward with the line, I was sent tumbling into the grass, the wind ripped from my lungs, and a stabbing shock of pain shot through my back where I crashed on the grass. My hair, free from the confinement of the hood, was in a messy disarray, covering my face and obscuring my vision of the two men who stood above me.

"All the levels of hell, I'm so sorry! " A voice shouted from above me as I was pulled back to my feet so fast, stars danced in my vision. "I didn't see you there. I was walking backwards, which I shouldn't have been doing, you know, with so many people out tonight," he continued, stuttering apologies and explanations.

"Don't worry about it," I muttered while pulling my cape tighter around my shoulders and throwing my hood back up. I kept my gaze down, just as I'd been taught. Instinctively, I scanned the crowd, waiting to see if anyone saw me— the strange red-headed girl with unusual eyes that would have me killed on the spot if the wrong people knew I was here.

"I think you need to lay off the drinks, Bastian," a second man said, his voice deeper than his friends. It reminded me of midnight walks to the library under the watchful protection of the full moon, wrapped in the comforting embrace of the twilight. When I looked at him, I was met with the most enticing pair of earthy green eyes. The stranger's gaze lingered on me for a moment, then back to his friend, who was still sheepishly fretting over me.

"Don't accuse me of being drunk, Haedion, when I am certain you've had at least twice the amount I've had tonight." Bastian sent a pointed look at the second man before he directed his attention back to me. "Again, I'm sorry to have knocked you over." His cheeks were a flushed pink, highlighting the splatter of freckles on his sun-tanned skin. Whether from embarrassment or alcohol, I couldn't tell. Perhaps both.

"And he's going to pay for you, at the very least," Haedion, the dark-haired one, said and pointed behind me, where it was clear that I was holding up the line. The disgruntled worker cleared his throat impatiently, arms crossed across his chest.

"What do ye want?" He asked, his accent short and gruff, the classic sign of a Flitmoor native.

"I, uh," I stuttered. The words slipped from my mind until the warm, heavy scent of chocolate and baked bread once again enveloped me in its warm embrace.

The man's beady eyes narrowed in impatience as he sighed through his nose.

"Chocolate!" I blurted. "Whatever your most popular chocolate pastry is."

He moved quickly, throwing a pastry I couldn't see into a small paper bag and thrusting it over the counter into my hand.

"And for you?" He looked over my head to Bastian and Haedion, who towered behind me.

"We'll have the same," Haedion replied.

Within moments, they had their pastries, and I wasted no time ripping apart the fluffy layers of bread. Melted chocolate leaked from where I took a bite— the warm, sweet taste erupted across my taste buds.

"Thank you," I said to Bastian. He was nearly finished with his treat, devouring it in two bites.

Bastian shrugged, tossing the last piece of bread into his mouth. "Ain't no problem. Hey," he started, the music pulling his attention away from us. "There's an open bench over there. Will you come join us?" He pointed to the largest bonfire that sat next to the village center, where the band and dance floor are filled with laughter, smiles, spilled drinks, and full bellies. It's more people than I'd seen in years.

My mind screamed at me, and heat coursed through my veins like small embers. It was a chance for more people to see me. To know what I was. But I had made it this far. A little fear wasn't going to stop me from enjoying my time tonight. No matter how brief it might be.

"Sure," I said against my better judgment, before finishing the last bite. Melted chocolate stuck to my fingers, and I discreetly popped one in my mouth and licked it clean. Or, I thought I'd been discreet. When I looked up, Haedion was watching me, with a devilish look in his eye that sent shivers down my spine.

My cheeks burned, and I hurried ahead, leading the way to the bench, praying to the Kirios that I could get through the rest of the evening without embarrassing myself further.

Haedion and I settled down in front of the roaring bonfire just as the stars began to shimmer across the night sky. The music quieted down, and the band announced a short intermission. In the absence of music, voices rose across the village, filling the void the band left behind.

"I'm going to get us something to drink," Bastian said. "I'll be back."

Before I could say anything, he disappeared into the crowded city square where villagers mingled and drank their fill before the band returned. My heart longed to feel the same as people smiled at one another, and the way they absently touched. When was the last time I'd been *seen*?

"I'm not sure we got your name before." Haedion's voice pulled me back into my body.

"Rhea," I said, fiddling with a loose thread on the hem of my cape that I keep tucked around me tightly.

"Rhea." Haedion repeated my name slowly, like a prayer on his lips. "Are you from Flitmoor?"

"I am," I replied. Keeping my head low, I watched the flames dance alongside the simmering embers as they floated into the night air.

They showcased their beauty in warm hues of red, orange, yellow, and gold, with echoes of blue at the very center of the embers, calling to me.

Here we are. We see you. We see you. We see you.

"Where are you from?" I asked, but my voice muffled in my ears, like I'm trapped underwater.

"Atheria," Haedion replied. My skin prickled where I felt him watching me. "Or at least Bastian is. We travel around the country collecting rare items for our employer."

"It doesn't pay much." Bastian reappeared, thrusting a warm cup of mulled cider into my hand and thankfully breaking the alluring grip the flames had on me. The aroma rising from the steam smelled heavenly with hints of orange and earth.

It wouldn't be so bad to have just one cup now, would it?

"But we do get to travel to some of the most remote places. We've been to the Caverns Pass, the coastline of Eldridge, the Library of Mordino, to Atheria, and everywhere in between." Bastian sat down next to Haedion, drinking deeply from his cup, his blonde hair reflecting the warm light from the fire.

"Are you just here for the solstice?" I asked before taking a sip of the warm liquid. Flavor exploded across my tongue, citrus and spice melded together to form an intoxicating combination. Haedion shifted slightly, his knee bumping against mine. Sparks ignited across my skin at the touch, and I stifled a gasp into my drink as I gulped down another sip.

It wasn't just a small feeling, but one that left pockets of energy as goosebumps formed where our skin had met. I couldn't resist when my eyes lifted to his, and I found him studying my face. I kept my eyes hidden in the shadow of my hood, the cover of night concealed whatever glimmer of red he might see.

"We were in the Renmist Wood for work and thought we'd stay around for the solstice." Haedion took another sip from his cup, his eyes never leaving my face.

"What types of items do you collect for your boss?" I asked, steering the conversation to keep them from asking prying questions and to satisfy my curiosity.

When was the last time I freely spoke with a stranger?

"Jewels, cloths, vases, books, scrolls, anything really." Bastian sat back, crossing one foot over the other. "Our boss, who would skin me, I'm sure, if he heard me—"

"He probably can hear you," Haedion cut him off.

Bastian rolled his eyes before finishing. "— Has the most eclectic taste. Never know what he's going to request we bring to him."

"Any exciting stories?" I asked curiously. Their life was so beyond anything I'd ever experienced. To be out there, traveling the continent, seeing things, and finding treasure. I ached with a pain I was all too familiar with. *Desire. Need. Want.*

"We have plenty of stories. If you hang with us for a bit, I'm sure we can impress you with one or two." He sent me a flirtatious wink.

My mind started buzzing. The cider, the fire, and the energy wrapped me in a warm cocoon of euphoria. I tilted my head back and looked up at the glittering stars in the sky and imagined floating away in them. The freedom, the laughs, the excitement— all of it. The taste of it was something I didn't know how badly I needed until now.

"What are you thinking about?" Haedion asked, his head tilted slightly as he studied me. His dark hair fell onto his forehead, where it met his eyebrows that pulled together, waiting for me to reply.

I wasn't thinking about anything, just enjoying the moment. As I opened my mouth to explain, the band picked up their beat once again, and the open village square was immediately flooded with bodies ready to resume their dancing.

That is when I noticed a beautiful, brown-haired girl looming behind Bastian. She bit her lip, hesitating, and she shifted her weight as if building the courage to approach. Behind her stood a group of girls whispering encouragements through bouts of giggles.

"Bastian," I whispered, keeping my voice low enough that she couldn't hear. "I think that girl wants to ask you to dance with her." I jutted my chin toward her. He flashed a coy smile and turned, startling her back a step.

"Hey, beautiful," he said as he climbed to his feet. "Wanna go dance with me?"

From my position on the bench, I could see the excitement light up in her eyes as she nodded, a wide smile growing across her petite face. Both Haedion and I watched as they disappeared into the flurry of bodies all twisting and spinning together.

"To answer your question, I was looking at the stars," I said, drawing Haedion's attention back to me. My body leans toward his, like two magnets edging closer and closer together. "They look brighter tonight, don't you think?"

A slow, sinful smile formed at the corners of Haedion's beautiful mouth."I'd say so," he whispered. He picked up my hand and intertwined his fingers through mine.

"Come dance with me." It wasn't a question. He pulled me to my feet, the world spinning around me, and I stumbled, trying to regain my balance. Out of habit, my hand clamped on the hood of my cape, making sure it was still firmly in place.

"Don't worry, little Enya, I won't let you fall," Haedion murmured in my ear. I suppressed the shiver that ran up my spine as Haedion spun me around. His grip was solid, making sure I stayed upright. Giggles bubbled from my throat, escaping past my lips, and suddenly the world became a blur of faces, light, and music. My face became numb with a permanent smile, making my cheeks twitch with exhaustion. But I didn't care.

We bumped into others as Haedion spun me in circles, my laughs rang out. We conformed to the others, our bodies moved in sync until our chests heaved with exhaustion as the last note rang out— but only for a moment. Then, without missing a beat, the music continued. A new song that had the crowd cheering with elation.

Haedion lifted me by my waist and twirled us in a circle before setting me down. I buried my face in his chest, and I'm overwhelmed by the scent of smoke and leather. Haedion's fingers found the back of my neck. I pulled back just enough that I could feel his breath against my cheeks. He started to lean down, but hesitated. I had never experienced something like this. Never had I been held, touched, and danced with, without reprimand. Happiness, excitement, and want flowed through me as I closed the distance between us and touched my lips lightly against Haedion. His body tensed against me, and for a moment, I feared I'd done something wrong. I

inched back, rejection hit me like a hot knife in my gut, and something caught in my throat.

But then he took both his hands and cupped my cheeks. His skin
was rough, revealing years of hard work in just a simple touch against
my delicate skin. Then he kissed me. Deeply. His mouth enveloped
mine, sending sparks across my body, and flames flowed through my
veins. It's as if a dam had lived in my body, preventing a part of me
from opening and flowing without restraint. Now, without restrictions,
something new coursed through every nerve in my body.

My mouth opened, and he sucked in my bottom lip, gently biting
the soft flesh. His mouth concealed the moan that escaped my throat.
Gods, I wanted to live in this moment forever. Haedion's fingers
trailed the side of my face, down my neck, so delicately that goosebumps pebbled under his touch.

I was so lost in the taste of Haedion that it took me a moment to
realize people were yelling. Screams— not of glee, but fear— pierced
the night air as smoke began to pour into the village center. Haedion
tore his lips from mine, and that's when I saw. The forest was engulfed
in flames around us. The bonfires raged, their flames streaming so high
that the tallest branches on the centuries-old conifers burned to ash in
seconds. Smoke and embers rained down from above while the
screaming intensified from alarm to pain.

Fear widened in Haedion's eyes as he grabbed my hand.

"Bastian!" His voice boomed across the chaos. His hand locked
firmly on mine as he pulled me behind him as we frantically searched
for Bastian. We dodged and maneuvered around villagers as they
darted every which way, calling for loved ones or running in a blind
panic. People flashed by me, their looks of terror permanently seared
into my mind. My lungs burned as smoke quickly overtook us, and I
coughed with the need for fresh air. Each breath was like a red-hot
iron down my throat.

"Cover your mouth, Rhea," Haedion commanded while he
continued to move forward, not bothering to look back at me. His
head swiveled as he ran until he stopped so suddenly that I was thrown
into his back. I followed his line of sight, where Bastian stood on an
abandoned cart, catching young children as they jumped from a home

where the roof was ablaze. Their cries of fear lost in a mix of voices around us.

"Shit!" Haedion cursed under his breath as he led us, dodging men working together with buckets filled to the brim with water to douse the flames.

"Where did this come from?" I coughed, covering my nose and mouth with my arm. It did little to protect my aching lungs from the onslaught of smoke.

"No clue, but we need to get out of here."

We skidded to a stop at the cart where Bastian stood, chest heaving, sweat streaming down his temples. Men from the village had successfully reduced the flames on the roof to a soaked, charred mess. It would be a painful mess to deal with tomorrow, but they'd managed to save the integrity of the structure.

Haedion dropped my hand to offer Bastian help. I stepped closer to the home that just ten minutes before had held a happy celebration. A family lived here. Children. I lifted a finger and ran it down the cold, wet siding of the building. Water ran down in rivulets that reminded me of tears.

Tears welled in the corners of my eyes in response. Disappointment, frustration, and anger rushed through me with such force that I had to brace my back against the building. Why couldn't I get a moment to myself? To enjoy life? To live?

"Rhea?" Haedion called, his tone calm, but the alarm was clear in his wide eyes and half-outstretched arm. He wasn't looking at me, but transfixed above me.

I turned on my heel, slowly, like I might startle whatever he was seeing. From where I'd been leaning against the building, lightning bolts of fire ran trails up the siding away from my silhouette. *Oh, no.* The epiphany cascaded down on me like a boulder crashing down a hill.

This was my fault.

This was my magic.

No, no, no, no.

I stifled a cry with my hand. I didn't think this was possible. No, this couldn't be possible. I was *half* fae. *Half!* No magic, no powers. But as the realization washed over me, I knew it was true. I could feel the power coursing through my veins with every beat of my heart. It hadn't been my imagination earlier when the embers spoke to me as they burned in the bonfire.

Nausea churned in my stomach.

"Hey, it's okay." Haedion took a hesitant step toward me, as if I might bolt like a feral animal.

"I'm sorry," I whispered before turning and running from Flitmoor. They both called after me, but I didn't slow down, didn't even check to see if I was being followed until I hit the thick covering of the Renmist Wood.

2

RHEA

I stumbled through the heavy wooden doors of the castle, not bothering to stop them as they slammed shut, sending a ripple of vibration down the corridor, rattling the portraits fixed to the walls. My nose and throat burned from where I vomited into the bushes just outside the gray washed stone walls concealed with climbing ivy. I'd attempted to return the same way I'd left, through the supply entrance in the kitchen, but with the commotion down in the Flitmoor, the area was swarmed with people. Calix would certainly have come to check on me and noticed that my chambers were empty.

I was going to be in *so* much trouble. I raced down the halls and prayed that Calix had been called out to help the villagers and that by some miracle missed my absence.

But like always, my prayers had gone unanswered. When I opened the door to my bed chambers, Calix waited, arms crossed, leaning against my desk. He stood there, so casually, as if I hadn't broken the most important rule I had— the one that kept me alive. And safe.

He didn't move, didn't speak as I slipped off my shoes and untied my cape, tossing it across the armchair in my small sitting area. A fire simmered, low and warm, in the hearth, casting a warm glow around the room. But that warmth didn't reach Calix's eyes.

"Where in all the realms have you been?" His words were so soft, so calm, but laced with a dangerous edge. His auburn hair was amiss, as if he'd been running his fingers through it.

Oh, he was pissed. Beyond pissed.

"I was in the library—," Calix held a hand up, cutting me off.

"Stop before you try to sell me some bullshit story that you were in the library. I checked the library. Don't you know that would be the first place I looked? So don't lie to me. Where the fuck were you, Rhea?"

"I was here." I crossed my arms, determined to talk my way out of this mess. I needed him to leave me alone so I could process what happened to me and what I had done. My heart thundered in my ears, the magic filling every vein in my body. The unmistakable feel of it had me clenching my fist in response. Not only that, but my lips tingled with the ghost of Haedion's pressed against mine. His intoxicating scent clung to me like it didn't want to leave me either.

How much had Haedion and Bastian seen or pieced together? That would be something to deal with later.

"No, you weren't." He pushed off from the desk, striding over to where I stood. Calix grabbed my cape and brought it to his nose, where I knew the unmistakable hint of smoke was laced into the fabric.

"You were in the village for the solstice." It wasn't a question. And just like that, Calix knew where I had been. He'd always been able to figure me out. No secrets between us.

"Do you have any idea how selfish and reckless that was?" He demanded, throwing the cape at me. The smell of smoke washed over me with the hint of Haedion shoving its way up my nose. Heat burned in my cheeks, both from the reprimand and the memory that replayed in my mind. Of the way Haedion's lips had felt against mine and the stolen moments where I forgot who I was.

"You sit in here for twenty-five years and tell me that wanting one night to yourself is selfish." I snapped back.

"It's for your safety, Rhea. Or do you not understand that?" He replied through gritted teeth. "Is the threat of execution not real enough to you? Do you know what could've happened if the wrong person had seen you tonight? You'd be dead, your parents, your sisters, all dead and probably half of Flitmoor."

Each of their faces flashed in my mind. My mom, who was always calm, was capable of soothing any situation she found herself in, the perfect balance of my intense, overbearing father. And my sisters, who could not be more opposite if they tried. Ari, the elusive one— quiet, wicked, and smart. And Gwen, like a torrential storm, forced into one small body. My stomach soured at the realization of the danger I'd put not only myself in, but them—the ones who had sacrificed to keep me safe.

"Just get out. I want to go to bed." My vision clouded with shades of red. Out of the corner of my eye, I saw the flames in the hearth growing higher in response.

"What aren't you telling me?" He asked, his amber eyes narrowing on my face, searching for the answer in my expression.

"I don't owe you an explanation for every choice I make, not anymore." I hissed, taking the chance to skirt around him and dash for my wardrobe across the room.

"This isn't about *us*," he emphasized the word like it was bitter in his mouth. "You've made it abundantly clear that there is no us. All I'm concerned about is keeping you safe."

My hand flew to my mouth, as if the kiss I'd shared with Haedion was written on my lips. Could Calix see the blush that stained my cheeks or the way I buzzed with energy? I felt it. And if he'd truly known me so well, could he also see it? Was he sensing the change I was going through?

"I am sure you have better things to do than sit here and argue with me," I said, choosing to ignore his jab. Absently, I ran my hand across the hanging nightgowns, all various shades of bright jeweled colors, their fabric satiny smooth against my feverish skin.

"I do, actually. That's another reason I came looking for you." His tone shifted in a way that had me turning toward him. I'm startled at the dark circles under his eyes and the way his uniform was disheveled. How had I not noticed before? Calix was never anything less than perfectly put together. Something wasn't right. There was more than just the fire in Flitmoor.

"What is it?" I asked, the tension gnawing at my stomach.

"Ka'an is coming for a visit and bringing the guard," he replied.

Fear, like melting ice, ran down my spine. Nausea worked its way back up my throat.

"Why?" I sputtered, trying to reel back the panic that threatened to send me into a spiral.

"His letter gave no reasoning, but he is set to arrive tomorrow evening."

Tomorrow.

"And in Ka'an-like fashion, requested— which we all know means we better have— a ball. A lavish, masked ball with every member of the royal household and the villagers of Flitmoor in attendance," he barked out a bitter laugh. "Can you believe that? A masked ball? With a guest list of 2,000 people, with just 24 hours' notice." Calix exhaled a long sigh out of his nose. "Your mother and sisters have been working non-stop since the letter arrived, making the proper arrangements."

"Everyone?" My brain churned his words slowly over in my brain. A ball. Here, tomorrow. Ka'an's entire armed force, known for their brutal nature and soul dedication to his wishes. Men I'd witnessed butcher villagers, servants, and even each other at the chance to be able to serve their master. They'd expect me to be in attendance. It couldn't be a coincidence that the events of this evening weren't related to Ka'an's arrival. It just couldn't be.

You're right, you're right, you're right. The flames called to me where they burned hot and bright, reacting, once again, to me. *He knows, he knows, he knows.*

Calix cocked his head to the side as he watched me. I fixed my expression into something neutral, unreadable. He opened his mouth like he wanted to say more, his cheek twitching in annoyance, but stopped himself.

"Goodnight, Rhea." He dipped his head, the movement too rigid, too formal for the exchange we'd just had, then excused himself from the room. The quiet click of the latch felt like the first nail in my coffin that would hold me down.

Sleep was elusive. Every time I'd closed my eyes, I felt the way Haedion's had danced with me and the laughs we'd shared. I couldn't remember the last time I'd laughed like that. Fire licked their flames along the walls of my soul, acting as a constant reminder that they're here now to stay. Their warmth was so comforting, as if they'd been a missing part of me filling a hole that was just their size. But their heat seared fear into my chest.

How were they here? The question loomed like a cloud over my head. The full-blooded fae had magic; everyone knew that. And they were long since dead. After Ka'an's massacre of the fae royalty and subsequent genocide of their bloodlines, I was perhaps the only half-fae left in the realm. The rest of my kind had been effectively hunted down and slaughtered.

Ka'an's arrival in Flitmoor couldn't be coincidental— there had to be a reason. The sadistic self-proclaimed ruler of Nador had successfully wiped out the fae twenty-five years ago, and since then, he'd gained immeasurable strength and used it to rule with an iron fist. He'd been the star of my nightmares more than once. His black eyes, framed by sullen grey skin and long dark hair that seemed to move with a mind of its own on a phantom wind. My own personal demon who would stalk my dreams, with a chill-inducing laugh that would replay in my head long after I woke up in a sweat.

There was a soft knock at the door just as the light began to filter into my room through the soft cream gauzy curtains that framed the floor-to-ceiling windows.

"Rhea?" Ari cracked the door open and popped her head through.

"Come in," I moaned, throwing back the plush, feather-filled blankets of my bed. I shot a quick look at the fireplace where the embers sat extinguished, not even a whisper of warmth emanating from the coals. I sighed in relief, one less thing to worry about this morning.

"What did you do to piss off Calix? He's been acting like a tyrant all morning and snapping at anyone who comes close enough to bite." She shut the door behind her and strode across my room, an ivory gown bag laid over her arms.

I cringed internally. Calix, a fierce and intense soldier, also had a temper and a desire to *always* be right. To a fault. It was the downfall of any romantic relationship that could have been.

"He didn't get his way," I replied as I stretched my arms over my head, shaking out the weariness from my limbs. "You know what that does to fragile men."

She laughed, head tilted back, the high-pitched tone of her voice echoing off the stone walls of my bedchamber. Her icy-blue eyes crinkled in the corners as she smiled. "Yes, especially him."

Ari hands me the gown bag. "This is your outfit for tonight. Mother had your mask altered to add a covering over the eyes so you can see out, but no one will be able to see in."

I untied the bag that held the dress and revealed the long-sleeved emerald gown adorned with gold accents. The sweetheart neckline, shimmering with golden thread that dipped just low enough to still be modest.

"Where did Mom find this?" I asked, holding up the gown, letting the full-length skirt fall to the ground. It was beautiful and so *formal*—certainly not the normal dress code. The hairs on my arms stood on end.

Ari shrugged, the ends of her chocolate brown hair resting on her shoulders. "Not sure, she had Marie pull out gowns for each of us. Gwen was wailing when I left, saying that hers is red and how it 'clashes with her eyes!'." Ari draped her hand on her brow in a fainting motion, mimicking our sisters' flair for the dramatics. "She desperately wanted your dress, but Mom insisted that you have the green one. Said it would complement your red hair."

I forced a laugh, the pin prickles crawled up my back, leaving me uneasy. I couldn't place the feeling. It wasn't the dress, my sisters, or my mother. The unmistakable, uncomfortable gnawing in my gut was like a constant ticking of a clock. With each tick of time, a new rush of dread was released. I pushed it down, forcing myself to be present in the moment with my youngest sister.

"Anyways." Ari handed me the black laced mask with its soft satin ribbon. "With so much extra activity going on, she suggested you remain in here today. Too many leering eyes, and with Ka'an coming, too many eager to please him."

"Of course," I replied, running my fingers over the velvety material of the dress. The supple material was tight enough to hug every curve, but loose enough to let me dance and move without restraint. Dancing tonight would be nothing like dancing with Haedion the night before. Tonight would be strict. The equivalent of tiptoeing on eggshells, and praying no one drew Ka'an's attention.

"I've got to get back to helping with setting up. I'll see you tonight." Ari retreated toward the door. "I'll be in the pink dress!" She added before she slipped out. Before the door could click shut, Marie waltzed in. In her arms, she balanced a tray that held my breakfast along with a steaming pot of tea.

"Good morning, Rhea," she said as she set down the tray on the small vanity table, arranging the pot, teacup, and saucer in front of me. "Did you have a nice evening last night?" Marie sent me a knowing look, the corner of her mouth turning into a mischievous grin.

"It was uneventful," I replied, hiding the smirk behind a perfectly hot cup of tea I hadn't hesitated to reach for.

"Although I heard that someone left the servants' entrance in the kitchen unlocked last night. Not sure who that could've been."

With a gasp that was so perfectly executed, I would have believed it to be real if Marie hadn't been grinning ear-to-ear. "Goodness gracious. I can't believe someone would be *so* careless."

I covered my laugh with a sip of tea; the warm liquid soothed the ache in my throat from the onslaught of events from last night. "Thank you, Marie." My gratitude came out in a whisper. She had risked her position within the castle for me.

"Did you have fun?" She replied, her tone just as hushed. "Or at least before half of the village went up in a blaze?"

"It was better than I could've imagined." The cup clicking on the saucer sounded too loud when I returned the cup to the tray. "I was there for the fire, but got out easily. How is the damage?"

"It is reparable. The trees and vegetation will need time to regrow, but nothing that can't be fixed with time," she replied, rubbing her hands on her perfectly pressed white apron. "I must be getting back; your mother and sisters have the castle in an uproar preparing for Ka'an's arrival."

"What of my father?" I asked.

She nodded, understanding my silent question. "He's preparing his men and doing his best to keep his head about himself. You know how he is when it comes to his daughters."

I do. And I'm even more grateful when I remember I am not his by blood, but something deeper.

"I'll see you tonight." She gave a quick wave before she too left me alone with my thoughts.

❦ 3 ❦

HAEDION

"These jackets are uncomfortable and impractical, Haedion. How are we supposed to grab her and get out of here if I can't move my arms over my head?" Bastian whined as we melded into the crowd of party-goers being ushered into the ballroom of the castle.

Chandeliers hung from the ceiling, dripping with crystals that reflected the light from the brilliant candles and lit sconces lining the walls. The energy made my stomach roll, and the spot between my shoulders itched with the need to protect myself from a danger I could not yet see. He was here, I could *feel* him.

"Would you be quiet?" I glared at Bastian, who was gaping wide-mouthed at the feast laid out on two large tables that ran the length of the ballroom. Villagers, and presumably some of the castle staff, picked carefully at the food, nervously waiting for the guest of honor to arrive. I was keenly aware that he was here, somewhere. Surely reveling in the growing tension that was festering by forcing us to wait, all of us dreading which form of him we'd see this evening. Would he be the incredible performer, singing praises to his adoring subjects, or the malicious king ruling as he pleased, lawlessly and bound by his fury? Or both. I'd seen both, more than once. That one seemed to be his favorite.

"Thank the Kirios, there's food." Bastian's shoulders sagged in dramatic relief and made a beeline for the closest opening, his previous discomfort forgotten.

If there was one thing that could fix the bastard of any ailment, it was food. Giggles erupted from a group of women who eyed Bastian with flirtatious smiles.

"Hey, ladies." Bastian winked, sending the women into a fit of squeals and laughs, fanning themselves and covering their mouths with their hands.

"Would you behave yourself?" I chided, ignoring the inviting looks. Sure, they were beautiful, but that didn't matter. Human women, females, whoever— I wasn't interested, not really. Not past one night of blowing off steam, to forget who I was. Last night had been a moment of weakness, but it had been serendipitous that Rhea was the one I found.

I scanned the crowd, looking for her golden red hair. She was here somewhere; she just had to be.

"Haedion, you've got to try these little pies." Bastian shoved one at my face, nearly forcing it down my throat.

"Oh, realms, please save me," I muttered under my breath before accepting the pie. I took a bite to satisfy Bastian, who, pleased with himself, turned back to the table to look for his next treat. The dessert turned to ash in my mouth.

I could feel him a moment before the doors of the hall swung open, like a cloud blocking the rays from the sun and sending the world into a dimmed light. Ka'an strode into the room, tenebrous cape billowing out behind him like he was walking on a dark wind. Instantly, the hall went silent. His movements were so familiar to me that they could be my own. My fingers found the edge of my mask, making sure it hadn't magically disappeared. I sent a short prayer to the Kirios that the little bit of material would keep me hidden.

But the god didn't listen to things like me. Not anymore.

Bastian returned to my side to watch as Ka'an easily commanded the room with his presence. The crowd shrank back as he passed, and despite the distance, I could see a wicked grin pulling at the corners of his mouth. He relished in this control, his superiority. Anger darkened the corners of my vision.

The room remained quiet as Ka'an neared the dais, where King Agnar and his wife, Carina, stood side by side with their three daughters, whose beauty shone through despite the masks shielding half their faces. Two dark-haired women and one with golden red hair and a mask so dark that her eyes seemed to disappear within it.

My heart dropped into my stomach. *Rhea.*

I elbowed Bastian in the ribs and nodded with my head in her direction, hoping he wasn't too busy sneaking bites of food to understand. She was right there, hands clenched together in front of her so hard that her knuckles were turning white. So close but so far away.

It was already going to be a feat to get her out of here unnoticed. But the princess of Flitmoor? That was going to be borderline impossible. The Necroscythe had developed an interesting sense of humor after spending centuries locked up in that damn library in the middle of the desert. No wonder this retrieval came with such a substantial reward attached to it. I was an idiot for not having inquired further.

"What is she doing up there?" Bastian mumbled as he chewed, low enough that I had to strain to hear him.

"Agnar, Carina, thank you for hosting such lavish festivities in honor of my arrival!" Ka'an's voice carried across the room. "You didn't have to do such a thing." His voice was just as serpentine as I remember. The same one I'd spent years listening to, one that still plagued my nightmares from the last time we spoke.

"It had just been a mere suggestion." Ka'an clapped Angar on the shoulder as he stepped on the dais. He towered a solid head above the King, who kept his eyes perfectly level, gazing out at the crowd of people. Villagers, dressed in their best, created a rainbow of color amongst the dark uniforms of his soldiers that radiated such tension that it was palpable. No one moved. No one dared to breathe.

"Of course, your Most Esteemed. Your wish is our command." King Agnar's voice remained monotone, as if any inflection in his tone might trigger a catastrophic response.

"What wonderful examples you are to the other cities and villages around Nador. Respect and loyalty are the two things I value the most." Ka'an faced his audience. "Now, let us continue with the festivities!" He clapped his hands twice, and soft music from the band started.

"She's going to sit at the end table with the royal family," Bastian said as we watched Rhea keep her head down and sit in her spot between her sisters.

"What's the move, Haedion?"

"Watch and wait for an opening," I replied, frustration biting its way into my words.

"Does he know you're here?" Bastian asked, hesitantly, watching Ka'an with a mixture of both curiosity and fear.

"No, he doesn't." If he did, I'm quite certain this room would've been reduced to rubble already.

"Can you feel hi—," Bastian started. I shot him a glare, begging him to ask another question. I was already on edge; I didn't need more prodding to push me over.

"Sorry," he apologized sheepishly.

The room started to settle into a rhythm. A few brave souls found the dance floor and began their formal routine of twirling and dipping, switching partners, then finding their way to each other again. Minutes passed, and the tension ebbed to a tolerable level. A few laughs began to rise above the noise, and tentative smiles slowly appeared.

I hadn't forgotten about Rhea, though, who had yet to touch her food. Ka'an had leaned back in his seat, wine goblet in hand, as he watched the party unfold. He swirled the wine in the cup as his eyes darkened, narrowing in on something across the room. Nausea churned in my stomach. I'd seen that look before.

Shit.

We needed to get out of here, right *now*. Before I could grab Bastian, Ka'an threw back his chair, slamming his cup on the table. The music cut off in a horrible shriek of strings and clamor of cymbals. Silence rippled through the hall, as if everyone had sucked in a collective breath and held— waiting for what was going to unfold next.

"You!" He shouted, pointing a knobbled finger at a petite woman near the back of the room. She held a serving tray in her arms, stacked high with empty plates teetering precariously on top of each other. She didn't blink as Ka'an stalked down the dais and across the room. Lightning illuminated the room, followed by a crack of thunder so loud the building shook under my feet. The crowd cowered against the walls, muted shouts of terror through mouth-covered hands. They trembled under the power radiating from Ka'an. Invisible arms held the woman in place, her arms pinned to her sides, the tray and plates clattered to the ground, sending cascades of broken porcelain across the floor.

"Haedion, we need to get out of here before he sees you," Bastian whispered, tugging my sleeve. I hadn't noticed that we'd sunk to the ground. Bastian strategically placed himself in front of me, just out of sight of Ka'an.

No, we couldn't move, not now. Any movement would draw his attention.

I shook my head subtly. His eyes softened— an understanding.

"What is your name, maid?" Ka'an demanded as his shadows wrapped tighter around the woman. She kept her expression impressively steady, her eyes the only giveaway of her fear.

"Marie," she answered, her voice quivering. She had a young face, but the streaks of grey woven into her chocolate brown hair reflected the maturity of her age.

"Ah, Marie." Ka'an rubbed his chin. "Tell me, why do you wear the shield of the fae, which is strictly forbidden by law?"

Marie visibly paled. "I'm not sure what yo—, you mean, Your Excellency."

Ka'an cocked his head to the side, as if she were his prey. He began to circle her then, eyeing her up and down.

"Oh, I think you do. The shield of the fae. It is the depiction of their gift from the Kirios. The *stone*," he emphasized the word, as he slowly pulled his sword from the scabbard on his hip. "That they foolishly decided to preserve as knowledge rather than use it to its full potential." He held the sword up, admiring the craftsmanship.

"Do you know what this stone is on the pommel, Marie?"

I hadn't noticed he carried the sword until the Prismara of the Vesperian caught the light, its shimmering hues of red, orange, and gold like liquid magma, trapped within the confines of the gem.

"No, sir." Marie shook her head, voice warbling. "I do not know what it is." But the way she fidgeted with her hands in front of herself revealed to me that she knew exactly what she wore.

"Let me tell you then, Marie. And let's use this as a teaching moment to remind everyone why the shield of the fae is a banned symbol in this country." Ka'an brought the handle toward himself, stroking the stone under his thumb.

"This stone is the birthright of my bloodline and my kind. With it comes power, knowledge, and untapped potential. The vesperians, when gifted their stone, used it to conquer, expand, and grow. My ancestors had it placed in this sword as a representation of our values. And what did the fae do when they received theirs?" He laughed bitterly. "They kept it in the raw form, giving it to their dragons in the catacombs for safekeeping. To study and keep protected. What an embarrassing *waste*," Ka'an hissed with a wave of his arm. "And then, they believed themselves to be gods, overpowering my kind when we were at our weakest, treating my kind like livestock." He spat on the ground.

"So tell me, why would you carry their shield around your neck?" He pointed to her chest, where a small golden chain hung with an arch pendant barely visible under the neckline of her dress. I didn't notice it at first, but Ka'an had always had a keen eye for details.

Her hand flew to her neck, as if she could cover the pendant—undo the broken law and make it disappear. She opened her mouth, but all that came out was a guttural gasping sound. Marie's other hand joined the first, trailing up toward her neck where purple crept into her cheeks, her lips turned blue, and her eyes bulged with the pressure on her throat. One of Ka'an's longtime favorite party tricks... killing from a distance, without lifting a finger. The excitement on his face was sickening, like punishment and death were his favorite hobbies.

"Shit," Bastian cursed under his breath. "He's going to kill her."

I couldn't— wouldn't watch him kill another innocent human. Like the coward I was, I looked for Rhea instead, who stood with the rest of the royal family. The look of horror was etched in the visible features of her face, from her mouth that hung open to the worry lines etched in her forehead.

Rhea mouthed Marie's name silently, shaking so hard I could see the strands of her golden hair tremble with her. But I was so lost in the way her soft mouth moved that when Bastian suddenly hit me in the gut, a curse was ready on the tip of my tongue, but it dissolved quickly.

Fire rained down from the lit sconces and candles adorning the chandeliers like a midsummer thunderstorm. Shrieks rose from the crowd as people scattered about, doing their best to avoid the firefall. The linens on the tables and emerald flags of Flitmoor shimmered and danced as they were eaten by the flames. Smoke rose quickly in the room, and with it, the panic. We both shot to our feet to avoid being run over.

"It's Rhea," I yelled to Bastian over the chaos. "She's doing this!"

"How?" He asked, as I dragged him out of the way of a ball of fire that landed right where he'd been standing.

"I'll explain later, let's just grab her and get out of here before Ka'an notices."

Between dodging the fire still streaming from the ceiling and people scrambling in the smoke-filled room, it quickly became harder and harder to see— and breathe. My lungs recoiled when I took a deep breath, my chest spasming into a cough.

When we finally made it to the edge of the dais, Rhea was no longer looking at Marie, but at her hands, where lines of fire crawled up her hand and wrist, then disappeared underneath the sleeves of her gown.

"*Oh, little fae,*" Ka'an's eerily sing-song voice amplified across the room.

"Fucking hell," Bastian mumbled, glancing at the smoke-filled air above us.

Fucking hell was right. I had hoped, even sent a thought to the Kirios, that we might be able to get out of here before Ka'an realized that Rhea was a fae— the fae he'd dedicated his life to eradicating. Fae, that until last night at the solstice, I thought he had been successful in eliminating.

"*I know you're here, darling little fae. Come out, come out, let me see you.*"

"There's a door back there." Bastian pointed to a small servant exit behind the dais, tucked into a decorative alcove that had gone unnoticed at first glance.

I nodded. "Okay, let's move."

The smoke provided enough cover that we crept up the steps unnoticed. Rhea's sisters had left her side; they now cowered behind their parents, tears leaking down their cheeks from behind gilded masks.

"*Little fae*," Ka'an said, irritation leaking into his snake-like voice. "*How did you come to be here? Come share with me.*"

Rhea's head snapped up, looking for Ka'an in the mayhem, and instead found herself looking at Bastian and me. Her head cocked with confusion, then recoiled with recognition.

"Don't say anything, we're going to get you out of here," I snapped, more harshly than I intended, but we didn't have time for her to argue or ask questions. I grabbed her by the arm, dragging her backward toward the door while Bastian used his body to shield us from view.

"Move, Haedion," Bastian urged, ushering us around the corner of the alcove. Ash clung to his blonde hair, turning it a smoky grey that matched the color of the air around us.

I reached for the handle, finding it unlocked, and I shoved Rhea ahead of me with Bastian right on my heels.

"Don't stop, keep going," I encouraged. Ka'an wouldn't stop looking for her. He couldn't, not now that he knew there was a fae in the world. One he missed. One that could, with the proper knowledge, be his downfall. He would be angry.

No, not just angry.

Murderous.

4

RHEA

We didn't stop running. Not when we hit the fresh night air, or even when we made it through the village to the edge of the Renmist Wood, where the trees still smoldered from the night before. Limbs blackened and bare.

Every time my pace began to slow, Haedion was there, his encouragements harsh but true. If Ka'an caught up to us... I didn't even want to consider the atrocities that he'd commit.

We ran for hours, or maybe it had just been minutes. I wasn't sure. The vision of Marie's hands pulling at her neck, gasping for breath, and looking to me for help was forever burned into my mind. It played on repeat, and with every footfall, her name echoed in my mind.

Marie. Marie. Maire.

She was dead, I knew she was. When the dam of fire finally cracked, and it came crashing down in a cascade of flame, I had lost sight of her. By then, I knew it had been too late anyway.

Bastian, ahead of us, finally slowed to a walk, straying off the path into the thick vegetation of the wood. Just as we got close to where he'd disappeared, he popped back onto the trail with three supply bags. He tossed one to Haedion, one to me, and slung one over his shoulder. Where in the realms did those come from? When I cocked my head, clearly confused, he replied through heavy breaths, "Don't worry about it."

They'd known they would be leaving Flitmoor with me tonight. The all-consuming fear I'd felt that led me to follow them without question out of Flitmoor was replaced by a new dread. Was I being kidnapped? Had I willingly let them rescue me only to be walking into a new nightmare? Had this been a ploy since the moment Bastian crashed into me the night before? Or had they orchestrated that as well?

"Wait," I said, my mind reeling. The moon, now fully risen in the star-scattered sky, lit the dirt path ahead of us.

"Rhea, we have to put as much distance between Flitmoor and us —," Haedoin started to say before I lifted a hand to cut him off.

"Stop."

My head swam, not only with fear and anxiety, but confusion. I'd been so desperate to escape the castle unseen that when they'd shown up and whisked me away, I had allowed it.

Oh, realms, my lungs burned. The combination of the smoke that I'd spent the last two nights inhaling and running for gods know how long was catching up to me.

Haedion's dark eyebrows narrowed as he studied me, his jaw ticking.

"What is it?" Bastian took a drink of water from a canteen tucked into the side pocket of his bag.

"Where are we going? Ha-have you been planning this?" I instinctively took a step backward, hoping the separation would give me some clarity.

It didn't.

"Why would you think that?" Bastian said at the same time Haedion said, "Yes."

I didn't miss the flabbergasted look Bastian gave Haedion, who just stared at me with an infuriatingly neutral expression that was impossible to read.

"Great, she's never going to trust another word I say. Thanks, Haedion." Bastian threw his hands in the air, exasperated.

"We can't lie to her, she's too smart," Haedion replied. "She's pieced it together already. Between last night and us being there at the right time tonight. Not to mention, you just came out of the woods with not just two, but three bags. Right, little enya?"

It felt like I'd jumped headfirst into a tub of ice water. I was right, they had been planning this. Scheming to get me out of the castle, and I'd been so stupid to trust them. Haedion felt or sensed my need to escape and leaned into it to gain my trust, so tonight I'd go with them without question.

Anger, confusion, frustration, fear, and something else... sadness? I couldn't tell as they all swirled around in my mind faster and faster, all fighting to be felt first, to be the one in control.

"Yes, that was it." I hear myself say, but my voice sounds distant. "But why me?"

"We were sent for you," Haedion answered.

"Who sent you?"

"Our boss," Bastian chimed in. "He told us there would be a girl in Flitmoor who burned with fire. That was our only hint."

"I just didn't realize he'd meant that we'd be looking for the only living fae in the realm," Haedion said, crossing his arms across his broad chest. "I would've asked a few questions first, such as, oh, I don't know, how are you alive?"

"I was always led to believe I was *half* fae," I shot a glare at Haedion. "I was told my birth mother was a healer, and my father was a fae soldier who died at the Massacre of Draconia. No one knew about their affair, except my parents, who were their friends. My mother died giving birth to me, so the midwife brought me to Flitmoor." An uncomfortable knot that I couldn't swallow away formed in my throat. My parents. I didn't even think about what would happen to them when the smoke cleared and their oldest daughter was gone. Or my sisters. Oh gods, my sisters. Calix had been there, behind us, when the chaos began. I knew, deep in my gut, that despite his anger at me, he'd protect my sisters. He would've gotten them out of there.

"It's a tragic story, but it's untrue," Haedion said. "You've realized that by now, haven't you?"

"I came to that conclusion last night, thank you," I hissed. The fire itched inside my veins, begging to be released once again.

"Is that why you're wearing a mask that also hides your eyes? And also wore a cape last night?" Bastian asked, unbashfully pointing to my face covering.

The mask. Hell, I'd forgotten I had been wearing it. The feel of it suddenly became unbearable against my skin, like sand rubbing on an open wound. I ripped the mask from my face and tossed it to the ground. No reason to pretend anymore, they both knew what I was, perhaps even before I had. They had noticed my cape that I had worn every day for my entire life. The same one I missed so terribly now that I'd almost asked them to turn around for it.

"It is the reason," Haedion noted, his eyes locking with mine for the first time. Bastian's jaw slacked, studying the burgundy orbs of red that gave me away as inhuman.

"How did you not know?" Haedion asked.

"How should I have known? I had no reason to believe I was anything other than what they told me I was."

"Your eyes are fae eyes," Haedion said, then pointed to my ears. "And you were able to hide those behind hair and the hood, too. Did you really, truly believe you were only half?"

"As you know, there hasn't been anyone with fae blood running around for the last 25 years. I didn't exactly have anyone to ask." I replied, my words clipped.

"You had access to a library, didn't you? Or are you illiterate?" Haedion hurled the insult that hit me like a smack in the face.

"Did you forget that Ka'an burned the books? *He* eliminated the entire history of the fae. Please don't insult me like I haven't done everything I could to survive." Anger won over, and I threw the bag I'd been holding at him, putting as much force into my throw as I could. Red crackled in the corners of my vision as heat worked its way up my throat.

Haedion caught my bag with far too much grace for my liking and casually dropped it onto the ground. "If you were so concerned, then why did you go to the solstice party last night? Where *anyone* could've seen you."

"You should be thankful I did, I made your job easier. *I found you*," I seethed, my jaw clenched so hard my teeth ached under the pressure.

"Well, *you* should be thankful you ran into *us*." A slow, calculated smile spread across Haedion's face.

"And why is that?" The urge to smack that pretty smile off his face was overwhelming.

"Because we were paid to bring you to The Necrosycthe. The creature—,"

"— Monster," Bastian cut in.

"He might be a monster, yes," Haedion agreed. "But he's the monster that operates the most untouched library in Nador. The only comparable collection would be the catacombs underneath Draconia. The one personally protected by the dragons."

"If you come with us, you could get answers," Bastian offered, looking at me hopefully.

"You think I'm going to come with you after that? Hell no, absolutely not." I took two more steps back to give myself a moment to think. A library, untouched by Ka'an? I didn't know something like that still existed in Nador. Or at least one that was accessible. The dragons incinerated anyone who came close to the catacombs since the elimination of the fae— everyone knew that.

But I didn't want to go with these *strangers*. That's who they were to me by any definition. Strangers who had been hired by a mystery boss who knew what I was, who I was, and paid them to find me. It didn't matter the way Haedion had made me feel last night, the kiss we shared, or the undeniable way I craved to experience it again. There was no way they could be trusted.

And I couldn't run; they would surely chase me down. And I didn't want to test my newfound abilities, even though my fingers twitched with anticipation at the idea. Still too new and unpredictable.

"Where are you going to go then? Back to Flitmoor? Ka'an has his soldiers combing the castle grounds and ransacking Flitmoor for you. He's got you figured out by now. Everyone will have been accounted for, except *you*." Haedion pointed at me, and the magnitude of the situation came crashing down around me.

He was right. I couldn't go back to Flitmoor. I couldn't go home.

"You're freaking her out, you insensitive asshole," Bastian said, stepping closer to me, hand extended cautiously like I was a frightened animal ready to flee.

"If I were you, I wouldn't want to go with us either. But listen, will you at least come with us tonight? We have a campsite not too far from here where we can lie low until the morning, then we can discuss what to do after we've all had some time to rest. How does that sound?" The crease between his brows softened, his eyes widened, pleading with me to listen. I didn't miss Haedion standing behind his friend, arms crossed, looking so much different than the man who'd flirted, danced, and kissed me last night.

I weighed my options, but it didn't take long. The answer was obvious, and the need for self-preservation and curiosity outweighed my desire to tell them both to go straight to hell.

"Fine, but just till the morning."

Bastian's mouth curved into a gentle smile. "Let's get going then. We'll all feel a little better when we are under cover." He scooped up my bag from the ground and handed it to me.

"Under cover?" I asked, securing the bag over my shoulder.

"There is a small lake just off the trail up a ways that backs up to a cave in the hillside. It's a shallow cave, perfect for overnight camping trips."

Great, a camping trip in a cave. Exactly where I wanted to be.

Haedion didn't say a word to me or Bastian as we continued down the path at a pace that still forced me to work to keep up with them. They barely spoke, but when they did, they spoke loud enough for me to hear what they were saying. The simple gesture soothed the tension that had wrapped its tendrils around my chest.

They didn't seem like they wanted to hurt me or turn me over to Ka'an. I couldn't imagine the lavish reward they'd get for me if they did. Money, status, power.

Whatever this Necrosycthe offered them to bring me to him, it had to be enormous.

"Ah ha, here it is." Bastian pointed to a small trail that strayed from the main dirt path. It was hardly more than shoulder-width in diameter, easy to miss, especially in the shadows cast in the dark moonlight.

"It's just around the bend in the path up there," Haedion said as

Bastian took the lead down the narrow path with me on his heels. "We aren't far. I'm sure you're tired." His voice was softer than it had been earlier.

"I know I am!" Bastian said through a yawn, stretching his arms out wide.

As we rounded the path, a large clearing came into view. Just as they'd said, a lake sat in the center, fed by a gentle waterfall rolling off the sloped hillside. The moon reflected off the water, bathing us in a silver aura. Shishermi flowers sat near the water's edge, thriving in the wet grassy lakeside with their petals open, the aqua-blue glow on full display.

"Let's just get settled down and quiet, just in case Ka'an does decide to send his men this far from Flitmoor tonight," Haedion said as we entered the mouth of the cave.

"Do you think they will?" I asked.

Haedion and Bastian moved quickly, pulling items from their bags and setting up camp for the night. Bedrolls, blankets, food, and canteens were all set out in an organized fashion, with the supplies in the center and their beds at an angle in front of the mouth of the cave. I watched them so carefully that I didn't miss the side look Bastian sent Haedion when he didn't answer my question.

"Will he?" I asked again, this time I couldn't suppress the edge of panic that laced my words.

Haedion's head snapped up, his eyes meeting mine, unflinching. In the past, even those who knew what I was struggled to look me in the eye. Marie and Ari were the only two who'd accepted it, who hadn't shamed me for being different. But Haedion, he looked at me— really looked, and didn't shy away.

"He could." He shrugged. "Even if they do come this way, it's nothing Bastian and I can't handle."

"Yeah, and even if worst comes to worst, you can just burn down the forest with them in it!" Bastian said as he took off his shoes and stretched out on his bedroll.

Nausea churned in my stomach at the thought. The magic felt so familiar to me and foreign at the same time. When it appeared, the power filled a gap in my soul I didn't know was empty. But now, I was so consciously aware of it, the newness of it, and the way it had a mind of its own scared me in ways I didn't know I could be fearful of myself.

"Sounds thrilling," I muttered under my breath.

I sat down and flipped open the bag. On top, folded so neatly and tucked in with care was my cape. The same cape that I'd slung over my chair in my room back in Flitmoor.

When I looked at Haedion, he was watching me carefully.

"Is this my cape?" I asked, but I already knew the answer. The loose thread on the hem and chipped button at the neck told me as much. How did he know I'd want this?

"It is," Haedion confirmed.

❧ 5 ❧
HAEDION

Rhea barely slept that night, and I didn't blame her. She had pretended to fall asleep quickly, tucking her cape around her and nestling down into her bedroll. I couldn't erase the look she had given me when she'd realized we'd retrieved her cape for her. Something akin to awe and confusion mixed with gratitude as she'd secured the cape around her neck and pulled the hood over her head like a second skin. A small comfort in her world that had just been flipped upside down.

Even though I knew last night what she was, I still couldn't believe it. She reminded me so much of the fae I knew from Draconia, and I cursed myself for not realizing it sooner. The grace with which she moved, the stillness in how she stood— all small signs, but signs nonetheless. I had forgotten in the twenty-five years since I'd lived among them.

As Bastian and I talked in low tones, I kept my eye on her. Her back was too rigid, and she flinched at every unexpected sound as the forest came to life just outside the cave. She was frightened and untrusting, and with how I'd spoken to her earlier, I didn't blame her. The dread had been eating away at my resolve since I saw Ka'an walk through those doors in the hall— the first time *seeing* him in over two decades. I'd treated her unfairly.

"You sleep, I'll take the first watch," I told Bastian, who thankfully didn't fight me. He was asleep before his head hit the pillow. Rhea, however, lay there until the night slowly turned into a morning glow, and her body relaxed into gentle sleep.

This was my chance to get out while they both slept. I stood slowly and moved on silent feet across the cave floor, careful not to wake them. The fresh air of the clearing hit my lungs, and the muscles in my back twitched in anticipation as I aimed for the treeline. Once out of eyesight of the cave, but still close enough to hear, I removed the mental lid I had on the shadows roiling around inside my mind.

Instantly, I'm plunged into darkness, the shadows stretching and moving, as if they were a muscle begging to be worked. As the shadows leaked from my hands, the tension eased with each passing second. And for the first time since setting foot in Flitmoor, I felt the crushing anxiety that had sunk its claws into my chest loosen— even if it was just a bit, it was something. I was sorely out of practice using the shadows to my will, but the release, if nothing else, was a relief.

Then the itch began. At the corner of my mind, where the dream-space I'd spent years building sat like an abandoned box left to gather dust.

No. Dread sank like a knife to my chest, the air whooshing from my lungs.

The itch turned into a gentle knock, like a rapping on a doorway that led to only one other mind. Then the gentle knock turned into a consistent pounding that grew with such intensity that my head ached from the pressure.

Boom, boom, boom.

If I didn't answer, my brain felt like it might implode.

I cracked the door an inch, peering inside the mental doorway. There, waiting for me with the same serpentine grin that I'd seen in person hours ago, was my brother.

"Hello, Haedion." Ka'an said, standing on the threshold of my mind.

"What do you want?" I couldn't hold back the bitter edge of hatred that burned the back of my throat.

"Is that any way to talk to your brother after so long?" He placed a hand on his chest, as if my words injured him. But we both knew he didn't care. There was a reason he was breaking a decades-long silence between us; he needed something.

Desperately.

"Spare me the theatrics. You need something. What is it?"

He took a long sigh out of his nose, as if my refusal to play his game irritated him. He'd become used to his position of power, of having his subjects cater to his games. But not me, never me.

"Did I feel you tonight?" He began to pace on his side of the doorway, watching me with cold precision that sent cold chills up my spine. Ka'an couldn't know I was with Rhea and that I had been in that room with him tonight. My features stilled into neutrality— a skill I'd become adept at.

"Feel my magic? No, I seldom use that now," I lied.

"No, in Flitmoor," he hissed, his eyes narrowing. I could see his composure slipping, his shoulders tightening.

"You were in Flitmoor?" I kept my voice even, forcing a hint of boredom into my tone. I had to keep him unaware of my whereabouts.

"Obviously. I could have sworn I felt you there."

"No, you must've been mistaken." At that, something darkened in his soulless eyes.

He clicked his tongue. "Hmm, *I must have. But that is not the reason I decided to reach out now, brother. I need your help."* The muscle in his jaw ticked as he spoke.

"What could you possibly need from me?" Memories bubbled up from the depths of my mind. The sting of betrayal, loss, and grief opened like newly stitched wounds.

"There is a fae in Nador. One I missed. I need your help locating her and bringing her to me."

"Why me?" I asked.

"Because you are the only one in the realm that I can trust to help me get done what needs to get done." A wicked grin spread across his face. *"I want the Prismara of the Fae. I want you to find her, take her to the catacombs, and have her retrieve it for me."*

I clamped my hands behind my back to hide the trembling that took over my entire body. The Prismara of the Vesperians *and* the Prismara of the Fae in Ka'an's hands would have catastrophic consequences. Untapped power and potential in the hands of the male who single-handedly, under the guise of wanting to mend relations, carried out the mass genocide of an entire people. He could travel the realms, split the earth, and do whatever his twisted mind could make up.

There was no way he could have both stones.

"What's in it for me?" I pressed, wondering what in all the realms he could offer me in exchange.

"I'll give you the one thing I know you've wanted since the moment we got here." I felt the invisible knife slip between my ribs. Curse Kirios, he knew me. *"I'll send you home."*

My heart skipped a beat, then two, then three. The thing I'd wanted most in the world, but hadn't let myself think about for a long time.

Home.

"What do you propose?" I detested the words even as I spoke them. But *home*. I could weep at the thought, could almost smell the mossy earth of the cliffside cottage my mother raised me in.

"Find her, bring her to Draconia, and have the dragons turn over the Prismara to her. I will take it from there." Ka'an's wicked grin turned into a full-blown sadistic smile.

I hated myself, but I couldn't bring myself to care. Not when the one thing I hadn't even allowed my mind to dwell on. I could get away from Nador, bring Bastian with me, and be away from Ka'an and the constant reminder of my failures.

"Deal."

❀

The sun shone through the canopy, streams of warm orange light accompanying me on my walk back to the clearinh. Bastian stood at the mouth of the cave, his shoulders sagging in relief when he saw me. A pit formed in my stomach at the sight.

"Where did you go?" Bastian asked when I was within earshot.

"I needed a moment." I forced as much nonchalance into my tone when my thoughts were racing a million miles a minute. How would I convince her to travel to Draconia? Could I really willingly hand her over to my Ka'an?

"A vesperian moment?" He whispered, looking at me, then the forest, and back to me.

"Something like that," I pushed past him into the cave. If I had to look at him one more moment, I might vomit.

Am I really no better than my brother?

Since the moment I left Kayar, a piece of my soul had been ripped from itself. The air and the way the sun bounced between the two moons plunged us into brief darkness, only to flood us with warmth once again. My mother, and the tears she had shed when I told her Ka'an and I had been chosen, and how she'd promised she would wait for me... no matter how long.

I squeezed my eyes shut tight and forced a deep breath into my lungs. *Bastian, home, Rhea, Ka'an.* How was I going to worm my way through this mess? Ka'an could not, under any circumstances, have both prismaras. But home called to me, begging to return and stitch together the bloody mess I'd been for the last half-century.

"Are you okay?" Rhea asked, startling me from my thoughts. She sat on the dirt floor, her bedroll already packed with her cape folded neatly on top. She studied me intently, the red in her eyes was nearly glowing in the dim light of the cave.

"Yeah, fine." My words were too clipped, too short to be fine. I'm grateful when she doesn't press.

"We need to get going if we are going to make it to the borderline by nightfall," Bastian said, coming into the cave. "Rhea, would you mind filling up our canteens for us while Haedion and I get our stuff packed up?"

"Sure." She stood with a fluid grace and picked up both of our canteens and left without another word.

"What the hell is with you? Is it Rhea?" Bastian shot under his breath, his hand clamped on my shoulder. I hated lying to him; his genuine kindness was like no other person I'd met. Despite his losses and the pain he'd fought through, it didn't make him bitter or mean. It made him better. He'd never once used it as an excuse.

"No, it's not her," I lied, again.

Curse the realms, I hated keeping the truth from him.

"I'm just thinking of how we are going to move across the desert with an extra person that the Sandwraiths would kill to get their hands on." The first bit of truth sprinkled in with a lie. It was something to be considered, the logistics of moving across the desert with Rhea in tow.

"You haven't said a kind word to her since leaving Flitmoor, but I can see the way you've been looking at her. You are working through something, and I suspect it has to do with last night— and I get that. *And*," he enunciated the word. "Despite drinking more than I have in ages, I don't think I'll be able to scrub the memory of you two at the solstice. I can see the spark, so work it out, man." He winked at me.

I rolled my eyes and looked out of the cave toward the pond where Rhea knelt at the edge. She filled the canteens one by one, setting them next to her. Suddenly, she flew back, seeing something under the surface. Bastian and I both watched, too slow to reach her, as she peered back over to the edge. I yelled at her to get back just as two webbed hands burst from the water, dragging her under.

"Oh shit!" Bastian exclaimed as my heart jumped into my throat. Without hesitating, we raced over to where Rhea had disappeared under the surface. She was gone. Pulled deeper into the water, where not even the light from her fire would be visible. We both dove in, the cold water rushing past me as I swam against the unexpected current in the lake.

I could sense Bastian next to me in the water as we both chased after a trail of bubbles until Rhea's dark shadow appeared. She was fighting against the unknown creature, dragging her deeper and deeper into the murky waters. Sediment and churning whirlpools of water distorted my vision, but then I saw it: the long, dark hair, streaming behind the creature.

A rusalki.

Rusalkis drown their victims, pinning them to the bottom of whatever body of water they lived in. My heart pounded in my ears, and my lungs burned with the need for air. What if we didn't get to her in time?

When we hit the bottom of the lake, we were alone. Bastian and I swiveled in the water, looking for Rhea and the rusalki, but they were nowhere in sight. If I couldn't find her in the next few moments, I'd have to go back to the surface for air.

Bastian smacked my arm, pointing to a cloud of disturbed silt like a tornado spinning upward in the water. Ugh, thank the Kirios.

The Rusalki didn't sense or feel our approach. She was too focused on Rhea, who was fighting with every ounce of strength, eyes narrowed in a battle of determination against the creature that had her pinned to the muddy bottom. Rhea stilled, her brows furrowed in concentration. She grabbed hold of the Rusalki's forearms as her hands began to glow red-hot. The Rusalki lurched back in alarm, but Rhea didn't let go, didn't relent an inch as the creature began to scream, the sound getting lost in the water.

Bastian took advantage of the distraction, kicked over, and thrust his knife through the Rusalki's spine. The creature flew back, neck moving at an unnatural angle before twitching and then going still.

Rhea went limp, the fiery glow slowly flickering out, swallowed up by the cold water. I grabbed her, locking my arm around her middle, and used the bottom of the lake as a pad to launch. I pushed off toward the surface and just hoped we weren't too late.

❄ 6 ❄

RHEA

"God Dammit, Rhea, breathe!" A strong voice commanded—
a familiar voice, one that I wanted to come back to. It
reminded me of feeling free and alive. The words were
muffled, and the darkness was so peaceful. There was no pain there,
and no struggle. No Ka'an, no death, no persecution. Then something
jarred my body, and I broke the surface between the light and dark.
Life seeped into my skin again, and with it whispered in my ear to
fight.

Something pounded between my shoulder blades, and with each
strike, the voice said,

"Wake." *Pound.*

"Up." *Pound.*

"Do." *Pound.*

"Not." *Pound.*

"Die." *Pound.*

With the last strike, a wave of water erupted from my mouth. My
lungs screamed for air, and my lungs ached with the need to expand.
Each breath cut like knives down my throat, but the cool air tasted so
sweet.

I'm alive, holy shit.

"Thank the realms," Haedion gasped, catching his breath. I sat up and leaned forward, bracing on my hands and knees, letting the water come up with each spasm of my chest. The taste was a repulsive mix of murky pond water, mud, and bile. My eyes burned, the pressure behind them sent red-hot spikes through the very center. Goosebumps rose across my skin as a steady breeze passed through the clearing, sending shivers across my core.

When my lungs were finally cleared of water and I could inhale once again without the urge to vomit, I sat back on my heels. Haedion looked murderous, his mouth pressed into a thin line, staring at the same spot I had been dragged under.

"Since when do rusalkis go after females?" Bastian asked from behind me. "They're man hunters."

Haedion just shook his head; a dark aura surrounded him like an ominous cloak.

"Where did she go?" I croaked out, my throat hoarse and raw. I had blacked out after I willingly called— no, not called— begged the fire to come to me. Prayed that it would find me in the depths of the lake where the weight of the water was so intense I thought I would be crushed. It had obeyed; my arms and hands grew hot as fire raced across my skin. The last thing I remembered was the shock in the rusalki's soulless black eyes before my vision twinkled out, and I drifted off into the comfortable nothingness.

"She's dead." Haedion's tone was short, but there was something else in those two words. Fear, maybe? The thought made me tremble. That creature had died down there on the floor, left to rot and decay alone.

"Get her cape before she freezes to death," Haedion said to Bastian, climbing to his feet. He extended a hand and pulled me up with him. The world spun around me, in a whirl of color. I released Haedion's hand as fast as possible and stumbled a few steps toward the cave. My toe caught the edge of a rock half concealed under the grass, and then I was headed face-first into the ground. A warm hand around my waist kept me from completely smacking into the earth.

"Are you incapable of walking?" Haedion snapped, but his hand stayed glued to my waist.

"I'm just fine." Frustration boiled under the surface of my skin. He'd done everything to keep me safe, but was it all transactional to him? If he didn't deliver me to his boss safe and sound, would their financial deal be forfeit?

I opened my mouth to snap at him just as Bastian reappeared.

"Here you go!" Bastian said, my cape in hand and all three bags in the other. He slung my cape around my shoulders, fastening the button for me with a warm smile that reached his eyes. He patted my shoulder reassuringly when he was done.

"Ready to get going?" He asked, as if they hadn't just saved me from a near-death experience. Was this their normal day in their lives? Maybe I'd gotten more than I bargained for when I wished to live like them at the solstice. The Kirios must have a sense of humor.

"I still haven't decided if I'm coming with you," I replied, between chattering teeth. Sleep had not brought clarity, as I had hoped, and my need to escape and find answers was at odds with my unwillingness to trust these two strangers.

But they *had* got me out of Flitmoor, saved me from the rusalki, and, as much as I might want to ignore it, I can't forget the night of the solstice. The freedom, excitement, and... *Haedion*, ugh. Despite his clipped words, biting tone, and offhand insults, I could feel there was more to him.

If they'd wanted to cause me harm, they'd had their chances, and instead they chose the opposite. So no, it wasn't them that I should be focusing my concern on, it was their boss. This Necroscythe. A collector, library protector. What could he want with me? How did he know what and who I was if I didn't even know myself?

"Where would you go otherwise?" Haedion ran his hand through his wet hair, pushing it back to keep the water droplets that clung to the ends from falling in his eyes.

"Look, I know you're scared, Rhea. I would be, too," Bastian said gently. "But your best, safest option is with us. Once word spreads among civilians that Ka'an is looking for you, everyone will be hunting for the pretty, red-haired fae." He tries to give me an understanding half-smile, but it falls short.

"The Necroscythe, if that is what you're worried about, has no intentions of harming you either," Haedion added, as if he'd crawled into my mind and followed my train of thought. "He's fiercely protective of his collections. If he wanted us to retrieve you, it's for a good reason— and maybe one we are not even aware of yet."

"Well, if the Necroscythe hadn't sent us when he did, there is a good chance you would've died in Flitmoor yesterday," Bastian pondered, and he certainly could be right.

"Who is the Necroscythe?" I asked, trying to conjure an image in my mind of what he looked like. An old professor? A young healer?

"That will be easier to explain after you two are introduced." Haedion sent Bastian a sideways look before he could get a sound out.

"That sounds ominous," I muttered, rubbing my hands together, coaxing the warmth to return to my numb fingertips.

"He is ominous, but trust us, you want to meet him," Bastian declared. "Let's get going. The closer we get to the desert, the warmer it's going to get."

The hours passed slowly as we walked. Bastian tried to ask questions to pass the time, but as the sun climbed higher in the sky and the heat pressed down, the conversation died, and my mind ran wild. The landscape, the trees, and the wildlife— all the things I'd spent years just reading about in the Flitmoor library, I'd thought of as my playground. I couldn't get enough. With each new smell, noise, and curve in the path, I was sprinting to investigate. I didn't care about the insufferable heat or the sweat like fresh morning dew on my forehead. I was out. I was free.

When my sisters would spend their summers swimming in the lake and walking through the flower gardens, I'd be in *my* library. I had longed and silently prayed to the Kirios for a life outside the walls of the castle that protected me. I was grateful for it, truly I was. But I couldn't begin to count the times I sat and watched from the window and watched people come and go and longed to be among them.

And for the first time, I was able to experience it. But never in a million years would I have thought that this would be how my prayers would be answered—two strangers, my life an undeniable lie, and a vesperian tyrant out for my head.

We walked until we came to a fork in the road. At the center, two arrows pointed in each direction, one toward the desert, the other in a script I didn't recognize. Directly behind the sign, off the paths, sat the largest fir tree I'd ever seen, the tip disappearing into the canopy above us.

"How do you feel about stopping for lunch?" Bastian asked us both, brows raised in a silent plea.

"You'll complain that you're starving if we don't stop now, and then you'll start praying to the Kirios to give you strength." Haedion sighed loudly, stomping off toward the shade the trees provided, where small rocks littered the ground. He settled himself down on the one nearest the base of the tree and propped his feet up. I felt his stare as I carefully avoided loose rocks outside the trail— I wasn't eager to recreate my scene from this morning.

"You make me sound like I'm a whiner, Hae," Bastian said, finding his own boulder, food already in hand, his bag discarded on the ground next to him.

"Do you not believe in the Kirios?" I asked Haedion as I sat down on the flattest stone I could find. The bag they'd packed for me had everything I needed, including food that I found wrapped with such gentle precision I couldn't help but notice the touch. Meats, cheeses, and bread were separated and individually packaged for ease. I started with the dried meat, chewing slowly.

"Oh, he does," Bastian answered for Haedion, as he chewed. "He just doesn't think highly of—,"

"I am capable of answering for myself," Haedion said, cutting Bastian off mid-sentence. A stilted, awkward silence stretched between us through bites of food, and the gentle wind that shook the large branches overhead."It's not that I don't believe in the Kirios, I do." Haedion said at last, when I'd started to think he wasn't going to answer. "I just don't think you abandon your children after handing them cosmic power. The fae and vesperians had fundamental differences to begin with and struggled to work together. Then the Kiros handed them both a stone with enormous power and responsibilities, and then left them to govern themselves. It led to conflict, and death, and ultimately, the vesperians left the realm."

"And now we have Ka'an," Bastian whispered, giving Haedion a sideways glance.

"And now we have Ka'an," Haedion echoed.

It was a story I'd heard pieces of from Marie and my mother. Marie knew the necklace was the symbol of the fae, and knew that Ka'an had deemed it an executable offense to own or wear one. I'd been wracking my brain trying to figure out why she'd chosen last night of all nights to show blatant disrespect for Ka'an and risk her life. And for what? Ka'an hated the fae. A deep-seated, burning hatred of my people. Marie understood that and still made her choice anyway, and then died for it.

"The vesperians wanted revenge, and they got it in the form of Ka'an." Haedion threw a piece of bread to a small group of birds that edged closer and closer to us, just waiting for a crumb to drop. They swarmed the offering, chirps and twitters between each other as they battled for the last bite.

"Rhea, what do you know of the desert? Have you heard of the sandwraiths?" Bastian asked. The quick change of subject was not lost on me. What knowledge did they have that I did not?

"I know of them. Despite what Haedion thinks, I did have access to a library and frequented it often." I narrowed my eyes at Haedion. "But I have no experience with them firsthand. Flitmoor made a point to not trade with the cities near or across the desert to avoid the confrontation."

"They're as nasty as the stories make them out to be," Haedion said, standing up to stretch. Sweat marks marred his cream color tunic that clung to his skin.

"Bloodthirsty cannibals that only want what's best for themselves. If they hear that the fae Ka'an is looking for is in their territory, we will have a new challenge on our hands. They're greedy, savage little creatures."

"So, task number one. Avoid the sandwraiths." My gut roiled—another unknown. I kept my face as neutral as possible when, on the inside, alarm bells rang.

"That would be preferable. I've had to rescue Bastian from them more than once in the last five years that we've been working for the

Necroscythe." Haedion said, a devious smirk on his undeniably hand-
some face with his sharp lines, strong jawline, and high cheekbones.

Bastian laughed, the sound ringing out, startling the group of birds,
sending them into flight. "If I recall, you have also been a prisoner with
me before, too."

"Yeah, yeah, only because I let myself be captured," Haedion
chuckled, rising to his feet. "We really should get moving again." He
stretched his arms over his head, and I couldn't help but stare at the
way the bottom of his tunic rode up, revealing the hard lines of his
stomach. When my eyes finally reached his face, I found him watching
me. Heat flushed across my skin, and I quickly looked away.

I bit back a curse. I *had* to push all thoughts and feelings of whatever Haedion and I shared between mulled wine, heightened emotions,
music, and dancing. And since then, he had made it evidently clear it
was nothing more to him than a one-time fling at a solstice celebration.

"I'm pretty sure he's trying to kill us," Bastian sighed, his pants
exaggerated and heavy, but a toothy grin spread across his face.

"If I have to go, you have to go. Get up," I giggled, smacking
Bastian on the shoulder as I stood.

"No, he's most definitely trying to kill us," Bastian wheezed, his
chest heaving. "I can feel myself melting into the ground." He sprawled
out on the mossy dirt, his limbs bent in awkward directions. "Just leave
me here," he let out another gasp. "Save yourself!" He dramatically
tossed his arm over his face, going still. A laugh escaped me as I yanked
him to his feet.

Bastian was Haedion's opposite in every way, from the freckles
splattered across his golden, tanned skin to the humor he tried to
insert every chance he got.

He threw an arm over my shoulder. "You're going to have to carry
me, Rhea."

"You two together are going to be insufferable," Haedion rolled his
eyes, but there was something else there— a twinkle, a light fighting
against the dark.

We continued the journey toward the desert. As we walked, the
landscape changed. Sand seeped in, mixing with the damp, fertile soil

of the forest, replacing the green plant life with an arid landscape. It wasn't until the sun started to set the following day that I began to realize how close we truly were to the desert as our footfalls found more sand than dirt.

"We are almost to the edge of the desert." Haedion pointed to something hanging on a large coniferous tree. As we neared, I realized it was a sign, ropes dangling from the bottom.

"Are those—?" I started to say, then stopped mid-sentence, bile creeping into the back of my throat.

Bodies.

Bodies were hung from the sign by their necks, picked dry by the elements and wildlife. Bones bleached by the sunlight, cracked in the dry air.

"Beware of the sandwraiths. Travel at your own risk," Haedion read the sign aloud. Underneath the text, the same phrase was written in half a dozen languages, some of which I have had a general under-standing of. Some, I couldn't even begin to guess where they originated from.

"Isn't it uplifting?" Bastian said, faking a cheerful tone. "The desert sure knows how to roll out a welcoming committee." He trudged ahead, leaving Haedion and me behind. He eyed the sign as he passed, the hanging bodies blowing gently in the wind like a sick, perverse wind chime.

"Tell me what you're thinking, Rhea," Haedion whispered, closer to me than he had been. He had moved with such silence that I nearly jumped out of my skin at his question.

I whipped around and came nose to nose with him. He didn't falter at our proximity, but instead leaned into it. The sweet, smoky leather scent wrapped me once again in its intoxicating embrace, making my head swirl.

"I, I—," I stuttered. *God damnit, Rhea*, I cursed myself. *Pull yourself together. Remember, he's been nothing but cold and transactional since they saved you. The night of the solstice was nothing more than a way to blow off steam. There is nothing more to it.* And I truly wanted to believe it.

"I think you've been an asshole," I blurted, the thought rolling off my tongue faster than my brain could think to shut my mouth. My hand flew to my lips, as if I could shove the words back inside. Heat crept into my cheeks as mortification rolled over me. I wiped my palms against my pants, wiping away the clammy sweat.

But he had asked.

Haedion cocked his head, studying me with his unnaturally earthy eyes, which reminded me of looking into a kaleidoscope of the forest.

"I'm an asshole?" His tone was flat. "I'm just being realistic."

"Do you know something I don't?" I asked.

"No, I'm just thinking about all I've seen with Ka'an and the lengths he will go to get what he wants. I know about his magic, and I've seen the cruel mayhem he can cause," Haedion replied, shifting his weight uncomfortably.

"Do you not think I'll escape him?" Something catches in my throat, and the fear I'd had a firm grip on since this morning wiggles free of my hold. He'd been confident, and Bastian had reassured me that they were capable. My heart began to pound uncomfortably against my ribcage.

"No, that's not it." Haedion lifted his hand like he was going to touch my cheek. Before his fingers could brush my skin, a crunch of leaves in the sand signaled Bastian's return.

"Hey guys, something is going on out there. Haedion, you need to see this." There was an edge of concern and urgency in his voice that sent alarm bells off in my head. He waved at us to follow him.

Haedion wrapped his hand around mine and silently pulled me behind him, following the path Bastian had disappeared. As we approached Bastian, semi-hidden behind a tree, I could see the horrific scene unfolding before us. The tree line disappeared, and the desert opened up, a dozen or so paces in front of our hiding spot, where a small crowd had formed within the sandy dunes. We watched helplessly as three humans were forced to their knees; their hands bound behind their backs. All men, from what I could see, were pleading for their lives with hooded figures.

"Are those sandwraiths?" I muttered to Haedion, my fingers still intertwined with his.

"Yes," he confirmed, his hand tightening on mine.

Some carried swords and spears, while others carried bows. One hooded figure stepped forward out of the bunch, armed with a long scimitar. He raised the blade above his head and swung down cleanly, severing the first man's head from his body. The next man in line vomited in response, and the third slumped over, passing out.

A sandwraith, dressed in all red, differentiating himself from the others— the leader, perhaps, stepped out from the group. He took a long moment to circle the men, kicking the disembodied head of the dead man away like it was nothing more than a stone in his path, and I nearly vomited. He finally made a quick motion across his neck, and within seconds, the group of sandwraiths rushed the other two humans. They stabbed, kicked, and punched anywhere they could make contact on the vulnerable men whose screams echoed across the desert as the sand started to bleed red.

"Shit," Haedion cursed under his breath.

My stomach rolled as we helplessly watched the massacre. The men disappeared underneath the mass of bodies, their screams turning into gurgles, then into silence. Just as I turned my head away from the bloodshed to ask Haedion what we did now, a figure jumped down from the branches above. A gloved hand covered my mouth, and a sharp kiss of a blade pressed against my throat. The pressure was strong enough that my skin warmed as beads of blood bubbled from the wound.

My heart thrummed in my ears, drowning out the squelching sound of the knives meeting the flesh of the dead men on the sand. Panic started to rise in me as a quiet, curt female voice commanded, "Do not scream."

7

RHEA

"You're not going to scream, right?" The female whispered in my ear. I couldn't move my head to see Haedion or Bastian, but with how oddly quiet they were, I suspected their predicament was the same as my own.

With the blade still firmly against my neck, the tendons pulled so taut that opening my mouth to speak was a struggle. I managed to utter a small "right" under my breath.

"Good, come with me." She removed the knife and grabbed my arm in a vice grip, guiding me back over the sand-covered forest floor towards the thicket, away from the gruesome scene unfolding on the dunes. She snapped at her companions in Skarneic, a language hailing from the northernmost islands of Nador.

A small voice of doubt inched its way into my mind. If this woman, whoever she was, was able to get the jump on me so easily, how in the Kirios was I going to be able to escape Ka'an? What use was my magic if I was so quickly overpowered?

"They were going to be next. Make sure you disarm these idiots," the woman hissed, her nails digging into my skin. She patted my sides, then my legs, searching for weapons I did not have. The two other men quickly followed her lead, pulling multiple weapons from Haedion

and Bastian. Haedion stood still, a stony look on his face, while Bastian kept giving his captor lewd looks and sideways comments.

I wanted to snap at the woman and tell her that we weren't planning on walking straight into the group of Sandwraiths— we'd been observing the horrific scene. Instead, I focused on keeping my expression neutral and listening to their conversation.

"I'm sure they didn't know, Nafre. Cut them some slack. They didn't actually walk out into the desert. And these two seemed to be properly armed." The burly, dark-haired one was leading Bastian by the arm to stand next to us when they both tripped over a root hidden by the sand. Bastian tried and failed to regain his footing, crashing in a heap on the ground and pulling the other man down with him. Bastian swore as he pushed himself into a sitting position.

"For fucks sake, Eiran." The female, Nafre, let go of my arm and stomped over to where her companion watches Bastian on the ground. A second male guided Haedion over to stand beside me. His eyes locked with mine, and a silent understanding passed between us. Stay quiet, see who these people are and what they want. If they had wanted us dead, they would've slit our throats already.

"Nah, don't worry about me, guys, I'm fine!" Bastian laughed at himself as he clambered to his feet. He dusted the sand off his front as he tried to ease the tension with his humor. Nafre and Eiran returned his humor with a deadpan, unamused glare.

"Idiotic travelers," Nafre mumbled under her breath. She turned, her glare landing on me as she stalked back to where Haedion and I stood. Her thick, long braids bounced against her back, the golden hoops and beads woven into the strands clanked against each other with each step she took.

Haedion shifted his weight ever so slightly closer to me as if he wanted to position himself between Nafre and me. She didn't miss the adjustment and narrowed her eyes at Haedion. Nafre cocked her head with an almost predatory nature, scanning him from head to toe. Haedion, in response, arranged his expression to appear bored and unbothered under her scrutiny. The same face that had infuriated me more than once over the last few days. But I had a feeling she could take Haedion on, and laugh as she did.

"What is your business in the desert?" Nafre asked in the common tongue, Nadorian. Her accent was thick and heavy on the vowels, typical of the Northern Isles.

"It really isn't any of your business." Haedion's tone was passive, dismissive, but after spending the last few days together, I could start to see his tells. His hands were clenched under his crossed arms, and he had positioned himself with his left foot slightly in front of his body — ready to throw a punch if needed.

He was ready to fight out of this if he had to.

"Don't be fucking rude." The blonde man, who still had a grip of Haedion's upper arm, hissed. This man was different than the other two Northern Isle natives. He was leaner, taller, and paler in complexion, and his voice lacked the characteristic accent of the island. I was almost certain that Skarneic was his second language— Nadorian his third.

"Relax, Silas." Nafre waved the man down as she said, "Our business is to try to prevent travelers from getting themselves killed by the sandwraiths. I couldn't care less where you're going, I only care if you plan on passing through the desert. We offer our services to those who might need it, and who can afford it, of course."

"We do plan on passing through the desert, yes," Haedion offers the barest of answers. I catch myself rolling my eyes at his passive retort.

"We are capable of getting ourselves through, thank you," I added.

"Straight through, no straying from the road?" Nafre, while quite shorter than both Haedion and I, still seemed to assert power and control—the clear leader of their group, and someone who could cause issues for us.

"We also plan on stopping at the Library of Mordino." As soon as the words were out of my mouth, Haedion turned on me with a glare.

Yeah, I should leave the talking to Haedion.

Nafre barked out a humorless laugh. "I've never met travelers who *wanted* to go to The Library. That's interesting. What for?"

"No concern of yours," Haedion replied, his voice monotone with an edge of darkness that prickled against my skin. His bullshit facade was beginning to fade.

Nafre paused for a moment, taking her time to look at each of us individually. Haedion didn't move a muscle, and Bastian gave her a smile and a wink that she quickly moved past with a disgusted tsk. She saved me for last, starting with my barely worn leather boots, then the tight form-fitting pants, and the lightweight tunic I was wearing. As she reached my eyes, my mistake hit me as her gaze widened with surprise, then excitement. Oh shit, I wasn't wearing my cape. It had been too hot. I had tucked it into my bag hours ago and tied my hair in a knot on the top of my head. My eyes were on full display now.

"Good news travels fast, you know. Bad news travels even quicker." A wicked smile crossed her face.

"I'm not sure what you're referring to," I replied. I needed to keep my head, even though I felt like the ground was slipping out from under me.

"We were at a trading post last night, just east of here." She began to circle us. "And just before we left, a hawk arrived with the royal Atheria seal. Ka'an is looking for someone— no, not just someone. A fae. Dead or alive. Although the reward for being alive is significantly higher."

Bile burned the back of my throat. By now, the whole country knew there was a fae alive and what I looked like.

"This fae's last known location was Flitmoor, three nights ago. That is the exact amount of time that it would take to walk from here to Flitmoor, isn't it?" She looked to Eiran for confirmation.

"What did the note say this fae looked like, again?" She asked him, a knowing smile plastered on her beautiful dark face.

"Golden red hair and red eyes," Eiran replied, understanding written in the slow smile that slithered across his face.

"Ah, that's right." She came back to me. Nafre fingered a piece of my hair that had come free from the knot I'd tied on the top of my head.

"Silas, we'll need to get a hawk out as soon as possible," Nafre said, not taking her obsidian eyes off of me.

"Yeah, that's not going to happen." Haedion ripped his arm free from Silas. With one hand, he pushed Nafre backward, and with the other, he wrapped a protective hand around my waist and pushed me behind him. He kept me there, pressed against his back, leaving no air between us.

The unmistakable whine of blades being pulled from their sheaths rang out.

"Wait, wait, wait!" Bastian threw himself, hands raised in between us.

"Bastian, get the fuck back now," Haedion growled. A blade suddenly appeared in his free hand.

"We'll pay you," Bastian said, ignoring Haedion.

"Ha!" Nafre laughed, flipping her blade menacingly in her palm. "I don't think you can match the amount of money that Ka'an would reward us with if we turned her over to him." She pointed the end of the blade at me.

"He'll kill you first," Haedion said. "He won't give you anything. Ka'an will string you up and kill you for sport. I've seen it before."

"How do you know?" Silas spat, his icy blue eyes bore into Haedion like daggers.

"He just knows," Bastian cut in. "Listen, we will pay you."

They're quiet for a minute, contemplating what Haedion warned and what Bastian offered. Haedion's hand squeezed my waist reassuringly as tension thrummed in the silence.

"I highly doubt you have the amount of money that we'd get from Ka'an, and that's a gamble I'm willing to take. We'll take our chances with him," Nafre said.

"I have that much, and more. But you have to come with us," Haedion replied.

"Come with you where?"

"The library. You've never been— and few have. It'll be worth your time," Haedion said.

"We've always talked about one day making the stop there, but—," Nafre trailed off.

"But what?" Haedion pressed.

"The Necroscythe," Eiran answered for her.

"We haven't wanted to cross paths with him," Silas added.

Haedion's grip relaxed just a fraction. "If you come with us instead of alerting Ka'an to her location, we will take you to the library, pay you, and keep *you* safe from the Necroscythe."

"You're friends?" She pressed.

"He doesn't have friends, but close enough," Haedion replied through gritted teeth. His patience was beginning to wear thin.

Nafre let out a contemplative hum as she thought. "Fine, it's a deal."

"Wonderful!" Bastian threw his arms up in victory. "Now that we've got that all figured out, why don't we put all the sharp, pointy objects away. Please? No need to get all stabby right at the beginning of our newly formed alliance."

"Is he always this annoying?" Nafre asked Haedion, who sighed impatiently, his hand still warm against my waist.

"You have no idea."

❋

H aedion, Bastian, and I made our camp a small distance away from Nafre, Eiran, and Sillas. They'd agreed, after a short argument with Haedion, that the best course of action would be to stay here for the night. The nearest shelter was too far away, and traveling in the twilight would make us easy targets for the sandwraiths. The group we'd witnessed butcher the humans were nowhere to be found when we ventured back out to the line where the forest met the desert.

As night began to fall and the moon rose, the thorn forest came alive with noise. Crickets, hoots of owls, and something that eerily sounds like a hoarse scream carried on the wind. The cheese I just swallowed sours in my gut, thinking about where that scream could be coming from.

"They're speaking Skarneic, right?" Bastian asked as he nibbled on a small portion of dried meat. We arranged our bedrolls in a triangle shape tonight, all of us within touching distance. Haedion seemed uneasy and barely touched a bite of food. When I tried to talk to him while we set up our camp, he avoided conversation with short, one-word answers and nods of his head.

What an ass. The hot and cold was going to give me whiplash.

"They are," I confirmed, answering Bastian's question. "They aren't saying anything of importance, though. Just talking about what they could do with the money they get from us."

"You speak Skarneic?" Bastian sounded surprised. Haedion raised his eyebrows and gave a nod of approval— the most he'd acknowledged me in hours.

"I speak three languages and can understand at least five with decent enough comprehension." I shrugged. Growing up, I read anywhere and everywhere I could in as many languages as I could. It was my escape when I felt like I always had to hide. That library was the place I could be me.

"What other languages do you speak?" Haedion asked as he scanned the forest for the hundredth time since we sat down for the night.

"I also speak Borvik, Skarneic, and, of course, Nadorian," I replied.

"*Who do you think they are?*" Eiran asked Nafre. I caught his eye over Nafre's shoulder. In the past, I would've looked away, embarrassed, timid, and unsure. Now, I held his stare, letting him see me. Magic stirred under my skin, boosting confidence through every nerve.

I was a weapon. Just as powerful as if I were a swordsman or archer. My weapon was my power. I just had to learn how to control it before it controlled me.

Eiran was the first to break our stare.

"*The girl is watching us,*" he said, lowering his voice.

"*I'm sure they're just as curious about us. We did threaten to hand her over to Ka'an.*" Nafre lay down on her bedroll, and both Eiran and Silas followed her lead.

"*And she's a fae. How is she alive?*" Eiran asked.

"*If we stick with them for a while, I am sure we will find out.*" Nafre rolled over, her voice muffled by the bedroll.

The night was quickly in its darkest, and the muggy air clung to my skin when I bolted awake hours later, my clothes damp with sweat. The nightmare of rewatching the three human men being torn apart and mauled by the Sandwraiths replayed over and over in my night-mares. Instead of watching it from the safety of the forest, Bastian, Haedion, and I were the three human men. The coarse sand bit into my knees, and the unforgiving wind that blew across the desert burned my eyes, causing tears to roll freely down my cheeks. I was helpless to watch as Bastian's head fell to the ground, his body slumping over as blood poured from his neck. Haedion screamed next to me, the sound so real that my ears were still ringing as I took deep, steady breaths to try to calm my racing heart. My chest ached, and my lungs refused to inflate. Nausea swelled in my gut, and I could feel the contents of my stomach working their way up my throat.

I needed to move.

As quickly and quietly as I could without waking anyone, I slipped from my bedroll and bolted from the campsite. I made it as far as I could before doubling over and hurling, the bile and acid burning my nose. Weakness spread through my limbs, and my knees hit the ground as another wave of nausea churned in my stomach. I braced on my hands and knees and prayed the sensation would pass quickly.

It was just a dream. I was safe. We were safe.

A minute passed, then another as I focused on my breath. When my lungs finally filled with air, I focused on pushing the terror from my mind with each exhale. As the weakness ebbed and the nausea subsided, I sat up and propped myself against a tree. The cool ground was inviting against my clammy skin.

"Here," a quiet voice said, and I nearly jumped out of my skin; my heart rate skyrocketing once again. Haedion crouched down next to me, with my canteen in his hand.

"Fucking realms, Haedion. You scared the shit out of me." I settled back down, gratefully accepting my canteen from his outstretched hand. I rinsed my mouth out and spat the water onto the forest floor.

"I heard you get up and take off. I was worried." He sat down next to me, pulling a torn cloth from his pocket, and handing it to me. I wiped my mouth with it, the familiar scent of Haedion hugging the fabric.

The forest sounded alive. Across from us, a Shashirmin Beetle glowed an iridescent purple as it ascended the trunk of a dry deciduous tree. We watched as it twisted and turned and eventually disappeared into the bare branches.

"Do you want to talk about it?" Haedion asked, finally.

"No." I don't want to talk about the murders that haunted my dreams— vile, vivid, and real enough that they caused my stomach to purge.

"Fair enough." He paused, as if contemplating his next words carefully. "Tell me something else, then. Tell me about you."

"How about you tell me something about you for once?" I shot back, tiredness, helplessness, and the emotional toll of my new reality eating away at my resolve.

"What would you like to know?" He replied with gentle patience.

"Where are you from?" I rolled my head over to look at him. Haedion's head was tilted back, eyes closed. His forehead crumpled with my question, his mouth pressed into a thin line as if resisting the urge to say something more than he should.

"Next question." As if sensing my stare, he opened his eyes and looked at me. "I promise I'll answer that one later." A tired smile played on his full lips, and I had to resist the urge to reach out and touch them— to trace them with my fingertips. This was the Haedion from the night of the solstice. Not the short, curt, abrasive man I'd seen the last few days.

"How did you and Bastian meet?"

The corners of his eyes crinkled as he smiled. "That's a funny story. It was about five years ago. I was in Atheria on an errand from the Necroscythe. Bastian ran the streets of the city, surviving by pickpocketing and stealing from the vendor stalls in the black market in the Nadorian underground. He tried to pickpocket me, I caught him, and we've been inseparable ever since." He smirked at the memory, a mischievous twinkle in his eye.

"And now you two travel around the country together?" I asked, the idea so far beyond anything I could have ever imagined— until now.

"Yeah," he replied. "We travel all over on errands. Sometimes it's hard not having a home to go back to, but I don't think I could stay in one place anymore. Not after," he stopped himself. "Never mind." He cleared his throat. "The library is as close to a home as we need. Tell me something about you now. Was the solstice truly the first time your magic appeared and you realized that you weren't just half fae?"

I forced a sigh out of my nose because I'd been racking my brain, wondering how I didn't realize it before. How had I gone so long not knowing who I was or what I was? "You have to understand that I spent very little time outside the walls of the castle in Flitmoor. Yes, I had access to the library, but you know as well as I do that Ka'an had all the books regarding the fae and histories burned. I had no reason to believe the story I was told was anything but the truth, and I couldn't research even if I'd wanted to. And yes, to answer your other question, the solstice was the first time." I looked down at my hands, which looked so ordinary, so plain, and were capable of such destruction if I let them get away from me.

Haedion slowly stood, pulling me up with him. "We should try to get a couple more hours of sleep." He said, his eyes straying from mine to my lips.

"You're probably right," I murmured, looking down at our intertwined fingers. The rough calluses of his hand scratched against the soft skin of mine.

Haedion gently tucked a stray lock of hair behind my ear; his hand lingered on the delicate spot between my neck and shoulder. The tension in the air was palpable, and I had to stop myself from leaning into him and pressing my lips against his.

"We should be getting back," I whispered. "Like you said."

Haedion took a step back just out of my reach. Without a word, he turned away, back toward camp, leaving me alone in the dark.

8

HAEDION

I was in such deep shit.

If this had been anyone else, *anyone* but Rhea, this would've been easy. I'd done everything in my power to keep my distance from her since I made the deal with my brother.

I did my best to stay out of her conversations with Bastian. I'd kept my mouth shut when I saw her grappling with the connections she's tried so hard to make about who she is and where she came from. I knew all the answers, even to the questions she doesn't even know to ask.

I couldn't help myself tonight when I heard her tear out of her bedroll and into the forest. I'd followed. I told myself it was just to make sure she wasn't leaving. Certainly not because I cared.

I couldn't care about her. I had a chance to go home. Something I hadn't let myself hope for in decades. But I had lived through enough nightmares that I recognized that haunted look in her eyes when she finally stopped retching.

The way she talked to me, her honesty, and her curiosity just made those feelings I'd tried so hard to keep buried resurface, whether I want them to or not.

Tonight, when I pulled away and left her standing behind me, I could feel her hurt and confusion. If she could just understand that it wasn't her. My resistance had nothing to do with who she is. I would've kissed her again thoroughly, just like I wanted to. But if I had let myself, I don't think I'd be able to break the connection.

Just as I started to doze off, hoping to catch just a few minutes of desperately needed sleep, Nafre, Eiran, and Silas were up and out of the campsite. When they returned, they informed us they found no signs of the sandwraiths, other than the blood-soaked sand. The bodies of the three human men were gone as well.

Nafre and Eiran led our group into the open terrain of the desert. Bastian and Rhea followed closely behind, with Silas walking next to me, taking up the rear. As far as I could see, there was nothing but sand. The forest was long since behind us, and there was nowhere to go but forward. The sun was nearly blinding as we trekked on. But this was familiar territory; it wouldn't be long until we were safe at the library.

Then all I had to worry about was getting her to Draconia.

"They eat anything," Nafre said, her voice muffled by the cloth she'd tied around the bottom half of her face to prevent inhaling the tiny sand particles. Rhea had been asking her troupe about their knowledge of the sandwraiths and the desert as we walked. I couldn't tell if she's genuinely interested or if she's looking for a distraction from the blistering heat. I could see the smile on her face by the crinkles in her eyes above her mask. And despite the slick sheen of sweat that glistened on her exposed skin, I knew she was truly enjoying talking to these additions to our group. Even though they'd threatened to turn her over to Ka'an just hours ago.

She continued to amaze me.

Curse the realms, I would be going straight to hell— but I was half convinced I was already there.

Our walk continued in silence, with occasional interruptions by Nafre to Silas or Eiran, or Rhea with another question to the group. The sun was all-consuming, and the uncomfortable pressure of the intense heat made the shadows in my mind crawl into the deepest parts of my being where they loved to hibernate.

Rhea slowed her steps till she was next to me. Her hand gently brushed mine in an ever-so-soft caress. Then it was gone. Almost like it had been an accident. But it wasn't, and I cursed the way my heart jolted at the sparks that had danced between our fingers.

I took a wide step away from her, putting some distance between us. If I was going to get through this, I was going to have to put up a rift between us. I just wish it didn't hurt so damn much.

Our destination for the night was a makeshift shelter maintained by brave travelers, created by the fae when there was peace in Nador. When we arrived just as the sun began to set, I watched Rhea's shoulders sag with relief. She ripped off her face covering that Nafre had given her and gave me a soft smile that I *wanted* to return, but I couldn't. Instead, I turned my attention to the sun's light as it fought against the horizon. It sank lower and lower, sending the sky into a magnificent collection of reds and oranges.

Our refuge is the familiar three-dome-shaped stone huts, all clustered together. It was a safe place that Bastian and I stayed at many times. Their openings all faced the center with a sad-looking fire pit in the middle. Nafre indicated that she, Eiran, and Silas would take the first hut and motioned for us to take the next one. We agree that we will depart when the sun is high again.

From the outside, the huts appeared to be small, but as soon as we stepped through the threshold, the sanctuary opened wide. A stone stairwell led down into the earth, and at the base separating the interior, was a thick wooden door. We descended the dozen or so steps and pushed through the door into a circular room. Candles were lit sporadically around the room, illuminating sleeping cots against the walls. Colorful rugs adorned the floor, bringing some life to the bland, colorless room. Some were threadbare with holes, the threads eaten away by the hundreds of feet to cross over them. Some were new, clearly donated by grateful travelers. In the center of the room was a worn, but solid-looking ashwood table and chairs.

"This is cozy, just how I remembered it!" Bastian marveled, coming in from behind me. He claimed the nearest cot, tossing his bag on the floor, as he flung himself down.

"Cozy?" Rhea questioned as she wandered the room, her head swiveling around, taking in our home for the night.

I sealed the door shut, and the latch clanged shut with a thud, locking us in from the inside.

"Hells yes, Rhea, cozy," Bastian groaned. "This is cozy! Have you ever slept on the sand? I was mentally preparing to wipe the annoying little grains out of my ass for a month!"

I sent Bastian an exasperated look as Rhea's laugh filled the domed space. The laugh, like music, slow beat against walls of separation I'd been fighting so hard to keep up between us. Fighting the obvious spark between us was getting more and more difficult to do.

"Don't encourage him, Rhea," I grumbled, sitting down at the table.

"Don't you remember sleeping on that course, thick sand, Hae? It takes forever to get rid of it!" Bastian exclaimed, arms spread wide with theatric-level dramatics to emphasize his point.

"Yes, and that's why we don't stay out there under the stars. I can't stand your complaining," I groaned as I bent over and pulled my boots from my aching feet.

"You weren't your cheery self when you had to clean the sand out of your—," Bastian started.

"Shut up," I growled, throwing my bag at him, who took the blow right in the chest with a smack. The man had better shut up before I made him. He was always cheerful and too damn happy, and gods, I don't know how or why.

"If I wasn't so gods damned tired, I'd kick your ass," Bastian yawned, as he lay back on his cot, letting my bag slump to the floor.

"Yeah, whatever. Let's just hurry up and get some sleep. I'm not sure about you both, but I didn't get much sleep last night in the forest." I stole a glance at Rhea, who was rooted in place across the circular room, her bag clutched to her chest. The pink in her cheeks from the heat and exertion was finally beginning to fade, but her eyes were wild with wonder.

"There is a basin in the next room where you can clean up if you'd like," I said to Rhea, pointing to the small cubicle covered with a color tapestry to provide some semblance of privacy. A grateful smile made her nose crinkle ever so slightly in a way I hadn't seen before, and my damn heart skipped a beat. Curse Nador and all the realms, even her fucking smile was too much. She was beautiful, wonderful, and reminded me so much of what I'd fallen in love with all those years ago that had been ripped away from me. I couldn't handle that pain again. I refused to.

"Haedion," Bastian barked under his breath after Rhea disappeared behind the curtain. "What the hell is your problem?" He gestures wildly between me and where I know Rhea is in the small adjacent room.

"What do you mean?" I asked. I knew exactly what he meant.

"You have been so hot and cold with her. What is wrong with you?" He pressed, a tone of disapproval in his voice.

"Nothing is wrong with me, I'm just trying to get the job done. We were hired to deliver her to the Necroscythe, not to be her friends." I countered, skirting around the obvious. After all these years with Bastian and the near-constant closeness, he knew me better than anyone in this realm.

"Okay, fine, don't tell me. But whatever your problem is, don't take it out on her. She's had enough to deal with, don't you think? Rhea doesn't need the brunt of your issues, too," Bastian retorted, his jaw set, eyes fixed on me like he could see right through me. "If you need to fight about it, fight me. I can handle it."

An uncomfortable itch prickled in the back of my mind, once again, and the door between my mind and Ka'an's rattled impatiently. I slammed my mental wall up, blocking out the sound, making my consciousness an impenetrable fortress. *Not now.*

Bastian's expression softens, the wrinkle between his brows relaxing. "Is it your brother?" He asked, lowering his voice to a barely audible level.

Fucking hell. My head spun as I struggled to maintain the conversation with Bastian, solidify the walls around my mind, and keep my expression neutral. "It's something like that."

Bastian gave an understanding nod. "Just stop taking it out on her."

Rhea returned moments later, her hair in loose waves down her back. She was barefoot, wearing a spare tunic that barely fell to the top of her thighs, and it was all I could do not to stare. Even standing there with her bag of filthy clothes clutched to her chest, she was the most beautiful thing I'd ever seen. She climbed on the cot farthest from the door and lay down.

"Night, Rhea!" Bastian yawned.

"Night, Bastian." She pulled a spare wool blanket around herself. "Goodnight, Haedion."

"Goodnight, Rhea," I replied, throwing a blanket over myself. I rolled to face the wall and squeezed my eyes shut. I had to get Rhea out of my mind and focus on the goal. I was so close to going home— the place I'd given up on seeing again many, many years ago. Her image burned into the back of my lids, of her standing there with her tunic that left so little to the imagination.

But sleep. I just needed to sleep. With the warm glow of the room dimmed low, I listened as Rhea and Bastian's breaths turned deep and steady, and finally, I tipped over the edge into my own unconsciousness.

Hours later, I'm viciously ripped from the oblivion I'd so desperately needed. A relentless booming sound echoed across the hut, loud enough that in my semi-conscious state, I believed I was back at the barracks and this was one of the horrible training exercises that prevented me from sleeping well for months.

But I was in Nador, and this was arguably worse.

"What the hell?" Bastian exclaimed. I was out of bed and across the room in seconds to the door where the hinges were shaking, fighting to withstand the pounding from the other side.

Rhea sat up in her cot, eyes wide with horror. I placed a finger over my lips, begging her to remain silent. The dagger that I'd stashed under my pillow was humming with energy and excitement in my palm. But just Bastian and I against a horde of, presumably, sand-wraiths, I would be forced to use my magic. I wasn't ready for Rhea to see that yet, and I was embarrassingly rusty.

The pounding abruptly cut off, and the same hoarse scream that I'd heard dozens of times rang out from behind the locked door.

"We know you're in there," a guttural voice followed the scream—each syllable like nails scraping against my spine. "And we will find you, Daughter of Fire. And we will take you to our master. The one who came, who set us *free*. It is he we serve and us who will be rewarded."

Rhea stifled a scream of horror behind her hand. My blood ran cold, like I'd jumped feet-first into ice water. Bastian blanched, eyes darting from me to Rhea, to the door. There was a distant sound of heavy shuffling that ascended the staircase, step by step, until it was gone. No one moved, and I wasn't sure Rhea was breathing in the eerie silence that followed.

"How did they know she was here?" Bastian finally broke the silence, his voice barely above a whisper. He looked to me for the answers, but I didn't have them. I wasn't sure how they knew Rhea was here. Unless my brother knew that she was already with me, and when I chose to ignore him last night, it was confirmation of what he'd suspected. So he sent the murderous creatures here.

Rhea sucked in a deep gasp. She wound her arms around herself like she might be able to contain whatever emotions were running through her body, her breath coming out in small pants.

Shit, she was panicking. The ends of her long hair began to glow red-hot, like embers from the campfires back on the solstice night. If she didn't calm down and quickly, she'd turn this hut into an oven and cook us alive.

"Rhea!" I shouted as I moved across the room till I was in her face. Her pupils were blown wide with fear, eating up the red of her irises. "Ka'an gave the Sandwraiths free rein of the desert when he took control. They are loyal to him. I'm not surprised he called on them to look for you. We will get through this desert together. They are gone. You are safe. Take a deep breath and get your control back."

"I can't." She shook her head, the embers glowing brighter.

"Yes, you can!" I gripped her shoulder and shook. Her skin was so hot that I had to fight against the urge to let go. And I don't; instead, I held on tighter, determined to ride out this nightmare with her. "Where is the magic coming from? Is it your mind? Or does it live in your gut? Where is it?" I shook her a little harder, willing her to focus.

"Wh— what?" She stuttered, her head cocked in confusion, trails of fire working their way up her arms.

"You can feel where it comes from, I know you can. Where is it?" I urged. This was a skill that those with the gift of magic were always eased into, were told stories about, so when the time finally came and their magic manifested, they knew how to reel it in. Rhea received none of it. She'd been dropped into the deep end with no lifeboats to save her.

"My, my gut," she said. "It's like a well in my gut. A never-ending well."

"Good job, Enya. Now, close your eyes and imagine that all the magic needs to come back to the well. Recall it, like water falling backwards in the well." I encouraged.

She thankfully didn't argue and squeezed her eyes closed. A few quiet breaths later, tears began to fall down her cheeks, sizzling as they went until they evaporated from the heat.

I cupped her cheeks with my hands, ignoring the blisters I knew were bubbling on my palms, and pulled my face within inches of hers. "You can do it," I whispered. "It will obey. Calm your thoughts, slow your heartbeat. Think about each breath you take."

I watched her cling to my words as she fought to gain control of the fire. Before my eyes, Rhea's shoulders began to sag, the muscles in her face relaxed, and the embers in her hair twinkled out one by one.

"Good job." I let out a sigh of relief when Rhea's eyes finally opened and the shimmering red of her irises stared back at me. My hands dropped from her cheeks, and the skin of my hands burned and fully blistered. I shoved them in my pockets before she could see. My pain wasn't another thing she needed to add to her list of worries.

Bastian, who remained rooted in place with his hands braced on the back of his neck, let out a low whistle. "Thank you for not cooking us in here."

She shot him an apathetic look. "Yeah, you're welcome." Her words were slurred, her blinks slow and groggy. The light left her eyes the second before her body went limp, and then I was catching her before she could hit the ground. With one arm hooked behind her shoulders and one behind her knees, I scooped her up and carried her to her bed.

"Is that normal? Passing out?" Bastian asked, standing next to me.

"It does happen," I muttered, my mind recalling the many times soldiers hit the ground after their magic drained them. But instead of being carried to bed, they were left, wherever they'd dropped.

"Do you think she is going to be able to get control soon, like you?" Bastian asked, tentatively. He knew he was headed into dangerous territory.

"Yes, she will." I glared at him, allowing the shadows to fill my irises. "It just takes time."

"We don't have a lot of that," Bastian said sheepishly, looking away.

"No, we don't."

9

RHEA

"This map is an example of years of dedication to collecting information about Nador separately, collectively, and through the first-hand stories of other travelers," Nafre said to Bastian as I climbed the steps from the hut the next morning. After the magic drained me, leaving me wrought with exhaustion, I didn't stir until Haedion shook me awake. And even then, I fought him till he nearly dragged me from my bed. The physical bone-deep tiredness was like anchors to my eyelids, begging me to stay curled up in the desert fortress.

On the ground, lying on the sand in front of Nafre, was a very detailed map of the desert. From the Renmist Wood all the way north, where the desert turned into tundra, to the Caverns Pass. There were small sanctuaries throughout the desert, similar to the one we stayed in last night, and other structures labeled in Nadorian. It was the most detailed map I'd ever seen. Ka'an had most of the maps of Nador destroyed as well. To have something like this was rare. And illegal.

"This is incredible." Bastian pointed to the small cities that lined the coast on the east side of the Caverns Pass. "Have you been to these places?"

"I'm sorry to interrupt, but we need to get moving," Silas said, tying a piece of cloth around his nose and mouth. "We can talk about this while we walk."

"Silas is right." Nafre nodded. She rolled up her map and stuffed it in her bag. "As long as we continue at yesterday's pace, we should easily make it to the library by sunset, right?" She looked to Haedion, who responded with a curt nod.

Nafre took up the front with Bastian, who said something to her to make her brace her hand on her stomach with laughter. I couldn't quite make out what he said, but how he smiled after she barked out a laugh, he was getting the response he was hoping for. Bastian threw a cocky smile over his shoulder at Haedion, who shook his head, a forced half-grin on his face that didn't reach his eyes. Eventually, I would have to clue Bastian in that I don't believe Nafre would ever be interested in him.

The poor guy.

"Rhea," Haedion muttered under his breath, just loud enough for me to hear him over the whipping of the wind. He hitched his bag higher up on his shoulders, taking a step closer to me.

"Hmm?" I hummed, noticing the new white cloths wrapped around Haedion's palms, with angry red welts peeking from underneath. Those were new. Was that my fault?

"I just wanted to make sure you were okay after last night?" His voice is hushed as if hoping to give us a hint of privacy in the exposed, open plains of the desert.

"I'm fine," I lied. Since I'd woken up, I'd tried to bury the memory of my panic taking control of my body, rendering my mind useless. The helpless, sinking feelings were like ghosts dancing across my skin every time I thought of Haedion's hands on my face as he begged for me to regain control. It doesn't escape me how easily I could have destroyed us all in the hut. The power that lies beneath my skin was powerful; I could feel it growing.

Haedion arched an eyebrow as if he didn't believe me. He opened his mouth, but his eyes jumped over my head, seeing something behind me.

Suddenly, I slammed into Bastian, his solid body unmoving as I ricocheted off him. "What the fu—" The curse slipped from my lips before being cut off.

"Do not speak," Nafre's sharp voice commanded. She motioned for us to crouch, and we all sank into the burning hot sand. The heat seeped through the thin fabric covering my legs. My muscles twitch uncomfortably, begging me to move. But I forced myself to remain still. Slowly, Nafre lifted her finger, and I finally saw what had us all frozen in place.

To the side of us, thirty yards or so away, a group of Sandwraiths stood with their backs to us, oblivious to our presence.

"What the hell are we going to do? Sit here like prey waiting to be spotted?" Bastian asked, eyes wide with fear, looking between Haedion, Nafre, and the sandwraiths.

"I don't know, but we can't go back. They'll see us for sure. We're stuck until they move on." Nafre flipped her hair in frustration.

"Or they spot us and kill us," Bastian grumbled.

We were silent for a heartbeat.

Then two.

Then three.

On the fourth heartbeat, as if sharing the same consciousness, the group of Sandwraiths all turned and faced us. Their almost mechanical, unnatural movements caused the hairs on the back of my neck to stand up on end. My stomach dropped in the moments that felt like we were suspended in an hourglass, waiting for the next grain of sand to fall. They saw us.

We were so fucked.

In unison, everyone began pulling weapons from hidden sheaths, Nafre wielding a particularly fearsome-looking double-edged sword that glistened in the sunlight. Where she had it hidden, I had no idea. Bastian holds short swords in both hands, the blades nearly the length of my forearm. Eiran and Silas were both equally protected with weapons in hand. Haedion unclips a short dagger attached to his thigh. I hadn't noticed until now that the weapon had been camouflaged, hidden in plain sight.

My breath caught in my throat, and a cold knot of dread formed in my stomach. All I had to protect myself was the fire. But with our relationship still so new and untested, I couldn't begin to contemplate it as an option to defend our group— especially after last night.

The same hoarse scream from the night before ripped through the air, and I resisted the urge to cover my ears. One scream turned into a choir of screaming voices, and then the group broke into a run, headed straight at us.

"There's at least thirty of them," Eiran said as he adjusted his grip on his fighting axe, sweat dripping down his temples.

"We've been in plenty of bad situations before." Nafre stood poised to fight. "Don't stop moving, or they'll pounce. They see one weak spot, and they will swarm you."

The adrenaline pumped through my veins, and my vision blurred as the sandwraiths neared. They broke into line as they ran, stretching lengthwise across the sand. As they approached, their pace slowed. They formed a circle around us, wrapping around until we were stuck in the center.

The tension was palpable. Haedion maneuvered himself in front of me, shielding me with his body. In his free hand, he held a small blade behind his back. He extended it out to me, handle first. As discreetly as possible, I took the blade and palmed it, feeling the razor-sharp edges before quickly tucking it into the pocket of my pants. I slowly twisted my head, looking around. We were surrounded. It was thirty on six, and even with my magic, we were outnumbered.

"We want the girl." A sandwraith stepped away from the group, a long wooden staff in its hand. It was the same voice as the night before. The one who found us in the huts. The memory sent goosebumps up my spine. Heat pushed out of my nostrils; the fire was asking nicely to come out. No, no, not yet. My magic would have to be the last resort. I couldn't risk it, not with the group so close to me and Haedion, who was close enough I could smell the distinct scent of smoke and pachouli.

Rust-colored stains covered the cloaks of the sandwraiths, reminding me of our first encounter with them just the day before. Perhaps this *was* the same group, the same leader who brutally slaughtered the three human men on the edge of the desert, cloaked in red.

"What girl?" Nafre played dumb, holding her blade up toward the approaching sandwraith. I could imagine seeing Nafre staring down the edge of her blade. Those dark, heavy-set eyes narrowed with determination. Even in the face of insurmountable odds and in the company of the country's most wanted, her confidence was unwavering.

The sandwraith stopped, cocking its head almost completely to the side as it examined us. Its face was masked by a heavy hood, but I could imagine the soulless black eyes that were hidden by the fabric. If it even had eyes. Who knew what they looked like under their coverings?

My skin itched listening to the heavy breathing from all around us. As if the Sandwraiths were salivating at the thought of getting to tear us apart, just like they did to those other men.

"Her." The leader lifted a knobby, sickly grey finger to me.

"Absolutely not." Haedion flipped the short sword in his hand, drawing the attention of the leader.

"Over my dead body," Bastian added, lifting his swords in challenge.

"We'd hoped you'd say that," the leader replied. He lifted the wooden staff and slammed it into the sand once. Five sandwraiths broke free from their circle and attacked Bastian with such speed that I barely had time to scream before he was on his knees, a blade pinned to his throat, his swords thrown across the sand out of reach. His neck was stretched so far back that I could see the veins constricting in time with his racing heart. The Sandwraith holding the knife to his throat wouldn't have to push hard to sever the artery. I bit my lip to hold back a sob.

No, no, no. My chest constricted, my breath caught in my throat. Nobody would die for me. Not today, not ever.

"If you don't give us the girl, he dies. And then we will continue this game until all of you are dead and she is alone. You are outnumbered," he hissed, knocking the staff against his head once, twice, three times.

"Do not let them take Rhea," Bastian shouted at Haedion as he struggled against the hands that pinned him in place. Haedion didn't acknowledge Bastian's words. Instead, he stared directly at the faceless Sandwraith. He shifted his weight, as if he were contemplating invisible options.

I wanted to vomit, but I shoved the nausea down that churned my stomach. If I didn't go with them now, the Sandwraiths would take pleasure in killing Bastian, Nafre, Silas, Eiran, and Haedion just to get to me.

I wouldn't let them die.

"Fine, I'll go with you." I stepped around Haedion and out of his reach before he could stop me. I walked, chest out, head high, until I was standing directly in front of their leader. The stench of rotting flesh rolled off of him in waves.

"Rhea, no!" Bastian shouted, panic lacing his words.

"I'll go without a fight, but first you have to let them go." I ignored Bastian's plea. I clenched my hand into a fist to hide my trembling fingers.

"I knew you'd make the right choice," the leader affirmed, smacking his staff on the ground again. Two more sandwraiths appeared at my side, each taking hold of one of my arms. Their bony fingers dug into my flesh, squeezing with such force I had to fight to remain still.

"We'll also be taking that one as well," the sandwraith said, pointing to Bastian. They yanked him to his feet and dragged him to my side.

"No, you will not, that is not what I agreed to!" I started to protest when suddenly something smacked the side of my head. Pain shot through my jaw and up into my eye. Flames danced in the edges of my vision.

"Shut up, you stupid girl!" he barked. Tears welled up behind my eyes from the pain, but I bit my cheek, holding them back. I would not show weakness in front of these monsters; instead, I took the time to commit each second of the pain to memory. This wouldn't be my end; I'd repay their brutality.

He looked over the top of my head, addressing the others. "Do not attempt to follow us. We will take pleasure in gutting this one if you try." He gestured to Bastian.

"I will be the one who will take pleasure in gutting you." Haedion's voice is deep, fury and promise fueling every word. I couldn't turn to see him, but I could imagine the darkness in his eyes and the white of his knuckles as he clenches his blade.

The leader began to laugh, but the sound was swallowed by the hoarse chorus of screams from the group. They all shifted and, as a unit, ushered us north, away from our path, and away from Haedion.

Fury burned along the edges of my veins as Bastian and I were led, hands bound, side-by-side in silence. As we walked, daylight turned into a golden afternoon glow. The sandwraiths chattered among themselves in a language of clicks and whistles— completely indistinguishable and nothing I'd ever heard before.

Not that I'd had much exposure to anything aside from what books taught me. But there was only so much life that could be taught through words on a page.

The cool night air was a relief from the grueling sunlight, but with it came the exhaustion. The muscles in my legs ached, and with every passing minute, I struggled more and more to press on, the sand holding on to my feet with each step.

The wind whipped my hair around my face, blocking my vision and tangling the strands into sand-filled knots. When I looked at Bastian, the bastard was smiling— but why?

"Why are you looking at me like that?" He whispered, taking a calculated step closer to me, his blonde hair falling into his eyes.

"Because you're smiling like a madman," I replied, my brows raised in confusion and curiosity.

On the horizon, little brown speckles came into view. "Because." He leaned in close enough that I could feel his hot breath on my ear. "You're going to get to see Haedion in action soon. And trust me, you're not going to forget it." His excitement, anticipation, and confidence sent shivers up my spine.

"What do you mean?" I kept my eyes glued ahead of me as more and more lights came into focus.

"Haedion could have, would have easily gotten us out of that predicament back there. He chose not to, for a reason." He jerked his head back toward the direction we had left our group behind.

I bit back a laugh. There had been thirty sandwraiths, maybe more.

How could one man take out a group of cold, murderous creatures that had outnumbered and out armed us?

A cocky grin etched itself on Bastian's golden, freckled face. "I can see that bewildered look on your face, trying to piece together how I could be so confident in one man's abilities. But, trust me, Rhea, he is more than capable, and he will have us out of here soon."

We walked farther in silence, and as we grew closer to the structures, it dawned on me that they were a camp filled with hundreds of tanned canvas huts. The chattering and whistles of the sandwraith's strange language created a background hum that rang in my ears. Smoke filtered around us from fires with meats strung across the flames, sizzling as the fat from the flesh dripped onto the embers.

There were hundreds of huts, each with different symbols and pictures depicting stories of violence. The paint they used was red, the same color that stained the robes of the dozens of sandwraiths that surround us. Out of the flaps of the huts, more and more of the sandwraiths popped their heads out, curious about the newest prisoners in their midst.

I placed my hand over my mouth to conceal the horror that dawned on me. The red paint was not paint at all, but blood. Many of the pictures are faded, the blood chipping away from old age. Some were new, the darkness of the blood from fresh victims. I found my feet before I saw something worse.

We *had* to get out of there, fast. Bastian better be right, and that Haedion would be here soon, because I wasn't sure how long we would last otherwise.

We didn't pass many additional sandwraiths milling about, but the ones we did stop and stared at us. I couldn't see their eyes through their hoods, but I felt their bloodlust as they watched us cross their camp.

"Sit," the leader's throaty voice cracked, pointing to the pole at the center of the circular room, when we were finally ushered into the tent in the center of camp.

Bastian sat, gesturing to his eyes to follow his lead. Without arguing, I sat next to him, my back leaning against the support beam running from the floor through the top of the canvas ceiling. Lanterns hung from additional support beams, bathing us in a warm glow. My magic stirred at the open flames, as if sensing its own and wanting to play. I let the power flow, just an inch as a test. It obeys, the edges of my vision rimmed with glowing embers under my command, waiting and ready for my orders.

The leader, the same one who'd threatened to slit Bastian's throat, followed us into the tent, knobbled staff in his hand. He hit it once against the ground, and instantly, my hands were secured to the pole.

"My command is sending our fastest hawk to Ka'an now. I am sure he will waste no time coming to retrieve you." The leader said as he pulled back his hood, revealing his face that was just as horrific as I'd imagined. Empty dark pits replaced where two eyes should have been, and his grey skin stretched so painfully tight across his face that it looked nearly translucent against his skull. Thin lips framed a grotesque smile with razor-sharp teeth shimmering in the firelight.

He looked down his nose, examining me, and then bent down till his face was level with mine. I suppressed a gag; his breath was rotten, like thousands of decaying corpses resting on his tongue.

"If you make any attempt to escape, or if any of your friends make a move to come to your aid, I will personally skin this one alive." He gestured to Bastian, who seethed back, anger smoldered in his honey brown eyes.

Before I could think better of myself, I leaned forward and spat in his face. "Go to hell."

"You stupid bitch," the leader hissed, wiping my spit from his face. "I will enjoy watching Ka'an torture and kill you." He stood and left without a backward glance.

"Don't worry, Haedion will come for us. You trust me, right?" Bastian whispered in my ear.

"I know," I breathed, trying to keep my heart beat steady and my thoughts clear. "That's what scares me."

"Why are you scared?"

"I don't want anyone getting hurt because of me." A horrible sinking feeling created a home in my stomach.

"You're not responsible for the actions that people around you choose to make." Bastian bumped his shoulder against mine. "Haedion and I make a choice every time we leave the library. This time, we said we would get you safely to the Necroscythe, and we will."

"Try to get some rest, Rhea," Bastian added, leaning his head back and closing his eyes.

I don't question, but my mind doesn't settle. Not even when I closed my eyes and did my best to relax the muscles in my back and slow my racing thoughts. I drifted in and out of consciousness, and the dreams that visited for brief moments were plagued with hoarse screams, soulless dark eyes, and the crushing, cold darkness of the lake.

❧ 10 ❧

HAEDION

The logical part of my brain kept me rooted in place as I watched my best friend and the girl I swore to deliver to the Necroscythe safely get dragged off into the rolling dunes. Fury raged, blurring the corners of my vision, but by a miracle, and the unending years of training, I was able to keep my cool.

This wouldn't be the first time that I'd rescued Bastian from the sandwraiths, nor the second. Each time I'd been able to sneak into their camps, the shadows kept me silent and hidden as I walked amongst their tents till I found Bastian. Then, under the cover of my darkness, we'd sneak out, no one the wiser that they were short a prisoner— and a meal.

But this time... this would be different. I could barely keep my skin from splitting apart on my shoulder blades, revealing to these three humans what I was. Our tentative alliance would inevitably be cut short.

"Do you have a plan, then?" Nafre glared at me, her arms crossed across her chest.

"Yeah, get them back and keep going to the library."

God dammit. I wanted to scream in frustration. Rhea had gotten under my skin, and the thought of her out of my grasp and in any amount of danger made my blood boil.

"And how are you going to do that?" Silas asked.

"You let me handle the logistics. We'll trail them till they hit their camp and then wait for the right moment." I picked up my bag from where I'd left it on the ground. The only thing easing the ache in my chest that was so unexplainably foreign was the fact that he had my blade in her pocket and Bastian was with her.

I'm grateful Nafre kept her mouth shut as they followed me in the direction where Bastian and Rhea disappeared with the sandwraiths. I use the time to slow my thoughts and keep my wits about me to prepare to open the mental pathway to my brother.

Before I even get to the doorway in my mind, I can sense him. He's irritated, but a smugness radiated from him before I could even open the door.

The grey, cloudy room framed Ka'an as he stood tall, waiting for me. Something in my chest cracked at the sight.

"*You ignored me last night,*" he said by way of greeting. That was when I realized I had been wrong. He wasn't just irritated; he was furious. The muscle in his jaw ticked as he fought to keep his words even. If we hadn't spent nearly every day together for what felt like centuries, he might've fooled me. But I knew him.

"*You caught me in a sensitive moment,*" I replied coolly, my eyes narrowed on the way he brushed his fingers over the blade strapped to his hip.

"*I don't care, Haedion. If I call, you need to answer,*" he shot back, his voice rising as his composure cracked.

"*You have me now, what do you want?*" I hissed, fighting to keep my breathing steady.

"*You found the fae, haven't you?*" His eyes twinkled with devious delight.

"*Of course I have.*"

"*Brilliant. I expected nothing less of your skills, but you know I had to send out other options just in case, right?*" He begun to pace, vocalizing his thoughts as he walked. "*I couldn't risk losing them now, so I sent out every-*"

one. The guard, sandwraiths, ravagers, and hawks to every outpost across Nador with a bounty attached. A million gold marks for the one who brought me the fae who can play with fire."

My blood ran cold. All of those horrific creatures were out searching for Rhea. Every leering eye would be watching for her and, with an amount of money so grand attached to her that even the most wealthy would be interested now.

"Well, lucky for you, I found her first," I said.

"Her," Ka'an said the word slowly, as if digesting the information. *"Interesting."*

"I've run into a slight issue, however. But don't worry, I'll be back on track soon." I regretted the words as soon as they were out of my mouth. Ka'an skidded to a halt and rounded on me so fast that I involuntarily took a step away from the doorway.

"What sort of issue?" He narrowed his eyes, taking a step closer to my mind. I couldn't let him enter my thoughts— not when I was struggling with how to deal with Rhea.

"Don't worry about it." I stepped up, challenging him to push me. It was a bluff; I was no match for Ka'an right now. I was sorely out of practice.

"Are you forgetting your place?" He said slowly, the words like a knife being dragged across my skin. *My place.* What had that been? Second, next to him. My thoughts, my feelings, my concerns were always subsequent to whatever Ka'an wanted.

"I have business to handle, and I will get in contact with you when I get it sorted," I bit out through gritted teeth.

"You work for me right now, Haedion. You give me the fae, I get you home. Simple as that, and if you have decided that you're unhappy with that arrangement, I'll make sure you're locked away here for the rest of eternity." Ka'an slammed his hand on the doorframe so hard that my ears rang. Out of the corner of my eye, where I kept watch on the world moving around me, I could see Nafre side-eyeing me.

I wanted to spit in his face. I wanted to drag him through the door and fight him— for real this time. No holding back, and no blood oath connecting us. Real and raw. Every pain he'd caused me threatened to rush back, egging me on to do it. Give Ka'an what he'd had coming for him for decades.

I couldn't, though. I would be on the losing end of that battle, and I was smart enough to recognize that. My fingers curled into a fist, and I squeezed them so tight that the bones in my knuckles popped.

Home. All of this was for the chance that Ka'an would send me home, I tried to remind myself. But would he really? Send me home? After everything, the seed of doubt took hold in my mind. I was beginning to second-guess myself.

"*I will keep you updated when my issue is resolved and we're ready to move forward.*" I grabbed the door and slammed it in his face before he could stop me. The mental lock clicked into place as my brain rattled with each fist pounding on the door.

He was going to be furious the next time we spoke, but I didn't care. I couldn't go back now. I couldn't simply slip away; he'd find me. He would batter at the mental walls that wrapped protectively around my thoughts until I relented. Ka'an would slice through my innermost thoughts and find our where I was, and Rhea. Even now, I knew he could sense me. I'm certain that's how the sandwraiths found us last night.

All I could do now was move forward, and right now, I was more than ready to devastate the entire sandwraith camp. The same camp I should've destroyed years ago. The complacency that grief and anger had lulled my powers into was embarrassing.

As we walked, I began working my magic internally, flexing it like a muscle. I pushed it away, drew it in, made it grow, and made it shrink. Over and over for hours as we trailed the sandwraiths at a distance that I was certain they wouldn't spot us, we walked, and I practiced.

Magic was a mental game. Always had been and always would be. It wasn't something you could pick up and play with, then store away until you were ready to play with it again. Magic needed to be worked and handled every day.

The day merged into twilight and then into darkness. The night brought a cool wind that soothed the rage radiating from my core.

We finally reached the sandwraiths' camp, the night in full glow.

"What do we do now?" Nafre asked, keeping her voice low.

Just hidden behind a dune, I watched as the camp bustled with life. Bonfires and lanterns lit the paths and tents through, illuminating and casting shadows as the creatures walked about.

"You three wait here, and I will be back with Rhea and Bastian," I replied, dropping my bag onto the sand next to them.

"How long will you be?" She pressed, looking from the campsite back to me. "What if something happens?"

I wanted to laugh in her face, then tell her to fuck off. But I resisted. I should have *some* manners. "Nothing is going to happen. I will be back. And worst case, you three go to the library. Tell the Necroscythe I sent you."

I didn't wait for a response as I turned my back on them and headed for the edge of camp. My footfalls were light as I hurried to get within proximity of the huts. Chirps and clicks grew louder as I circled the perimeter of the camp. Certainly, they'd keep their prisoners in the center of the camp. I just needed to get my eyes on it, be sure where they were before I unleashed the shadows that had been begging to be released.

By the third pass around the camp, I had a solid understanding of the layout, where they kept their weapons, and, more importantly, I was sure of where Rhea and Bastian were now being kept.

In the shadow of the night, I clung to the darkness as it poured from my fingertips, wrapping me in its embrace. With silent footsteps, I began my trek through the camp, keeping to the edges of the huts and avoiding the fires that illuminated the dark corners.

I was sorely out of practice. Before Nador, I could sneak through enemy camps in broad daylight, my magic creating shadows from nothing as an illusion to any wandering eye. That was a different world, a different lifetime. And I was here now.

It didn't take long to find where they'd put Bastian and Rhea. In the center of the camp, surrounded by a flurry of activity. If either of them so much as poked their head through the flap, they'd be spotted.

Behind a tent closest to theirs, I crouched down low, merging into the shadow the roaring bonfire cast. The smell of cooking meat assaulted my senses. I'd know that smell anywhere. It wasn't an animal.

It was human.

A gag worked its way up my throat, but I suppressed it. I'd seen worse. Been through worse.

At least fifty sandwraiths made themselves busy in the area, cooking, delivering food, and speaking in that indiscernible language. If it were just Bastian, I could sneak him out, no problem. But both of them, in a camp on high alert, would provide an extra challenge.

I wanted to kick myself then for letting myself get so bad. I was so out of practice it was embarrassing. Ka'an would certainly kick my ass if he knew what I'd allow myself to become. But even as I feel the magic move through me, and how I'd been forced to let it out yesterday, it was a foreign feeling.

I'd shut off that part of me so long ago and buried it under impenetrable layers. Then Rhea showed up and woke up pieces of myself that I didn't know I was capable of feeling anymore. A feral protectiveness that was different than the loyalty and friendship I'd cultivated with Bastian.

It hit me then, like a weight crushing my chest. I couldn't give Rhea to my brother. I wouldn't do it. Nador wasn't worth sacrificing for my desire to return home. Rhea wasn't worth it. And regardless of all of that, I didn't deserve it.

I couldn't move now and couldn't go back. So I waited, hidden within the folds of night, watching the tent where Rhea and Bastian were being held prisoner. I counted as the sandwraiths' numbers began to dwindle after they served their meal. Fifty turned into thirty, which turned into ten, and eventually only five remained.

Even at my weakest, I could handle five.

I called the shadows to shroud me like a cloak of night as I stalked closer to the remaining sandwraiths who stood guard. The sky had just begun to turn pink, a hint that dawn was not far off. I had to hurry.

Silently, I let the shadows down. They crawled across the sandy floor, searching for their victims. Without a sound, they crept up the backs and through the nostrils of the sandwraiths, who didn't realize they weren't able to breathe until I was in their lungs. The shadows filled the space till no air could enter.

They all collapsed on the ground, flailing and gasping until their movements grew sluggish and eventually stopped altogether.

When was the last time I'd choked the life from someone from inside their own bodies? I didn't know. Decades, more than that, maybe. I didn't have time to consider the ramifications of that on my soul. I bolted for the tent flap and prayed that we could get out of here unseen.

II

RHEA

Despite the hours spent traveling across the desert, the physical, bone-deep exhaustion began seeping deep into my resolve. Each sound caused my heart rate to accelerate with fear, just waiting for what horror could walk through the flap of the canvas tent. Dawn couldn't be far off, but I couldn't be sure.

My vision wobbled, becoming unfocused from the minutes that ticked by watching the entrance to the hut, convinced that at any moment Ka'an would waltz in and take me away, where I'll never see my family, Haedion, or Bastian ever again. That my death would be slow, agonizing, and drawn out. So, when Haedion poked his head through the flap, I believed I was hallucinating.

I shoved Bastian with my shoulder, and his eyes flew open. A huge grin on his face told me I wasn't losing my mind, at least not yet.

"I told you he'd find us!" Bastian said, his voice an excited whisper. "What took you so long?" He asked Haedion, who slipped inside the tent and began working to free our hands.

"Sorry, I waited until they went to sleep." He said as the ropes that restrained our hands fell to the floor. "Nafre, Eiran, and Silas are nearby, waiting for us. Despite the risk of being skinned alive, they wanted their money."

"Why didn't you cut yourself free? I know you slipped the knife in your pocket." Haedion extended his hand, pulling me to my feet. He didn't release my hand, instead pulling my wrist close to his face, examining the sensitive skin that had been rubbed raw.

"Bastian was confident you'd come for us," I quipped, yanking my hand out of his grasp, rubbing the tender spot. "And I wanted to allow you the chance to prove him right."

That was partially the truth. What I didn't voice was that I had been secretly terrified that the moment I cut us free, the leader would return and torture Bastian as punishment.

"You waited for them to fall asleep?" Bastian questioned, his brows pulled together in confusion.

"Yes, I waited for them to fall asleep." An ethereal gloom seemed to pulse from Haedion. "Then I took care of them." He replied, his voice low.

"What do you mean you took care of them?" I demanded, looking between them both.

"I'll spare you the details, but they won't be following us to the library. We shouldn't waste any time. I am certain they sent a hawk out the moment they returned with you." Haedion rested his hand on the small of my back, ushering me from the tent, Bastian close behind on our heels.

The moment we exit the hut, I'm immediately assaulted by the sun breaking on the horizon, ringing in the day. The warmth of Haedion's hand guided me through the maze of the sandwraiths' encampment, and the eerie silence brought me both comfort and concern. No leering eyes peering through tent flaps, and the campfires that burned high and bright when we'd arrived last night were now nothing but cold charcoals.

They couldn't all be dead, could they? Haedion, one man, a traveler errand-runner, certainly wasn't skilled enough or powerful enough to take on a camp full of sandwraiths. But Bastian had been *so* confident in his friend. I'm struck with the realization that I have never had what they had. No friendships, no connection with a level of trust that ran so deep that I could bet all that I was on it. A new wave of sadness washed across my soul, revealing a piece of me I didn't know was missing. A hole that I was so keenly aware of that my lungs struggled to breathe around it.

"Did you gut the leader like you said you would?" Bastian asked Haedion, a hint of knowing in the question, as we rounded a dune and spotted Nafre, Silas, and Eiran waiting for us in the distance. Nafre gave a short wave. They began walking to meet us, the three of them carrying our bags with them.

"No, I didn't, unfortunately. It doesn't matter now. Ka'an will be aware soon, if he isn't already, where Rhea is. Let's get ourselves to the library and under the Necroscythe's protection." Haedion's reply was curt, as if he didn't want to linger too long on the thought that Ka'an could be on his way anytime soon.

"I'm glad to see you both in one piece," Nafre observed, eyeing me up and down as she handed me my pack. "And you, how did you get them in and out so quickly— and unscathed?" She turned, giving her full attention to Haedion, her toned arms folded across her chest.

"I believe we can still make it to the library today." Haedion ignored the question altogether, his eyes squinting against the rising sun.

"How did you get them out of there so quickly?" Nafre pressed, stepping closer to Haedion. "I've seen groups of humans get carted off to their camps, and not one has ever returned. And you manage to get these two in and out in just a few hours. How the hell did you do it?"

"I'm better than the average human," Haedion retorted through gritted teeth, as if he was struggling to maintain control.

"He is," Bastian added, bumping his fist against Haedion's shoulder, a nervous smile on his face. "In and out completely unharmed."

Nafre narrowed her gaze, eyes bouncing between the three of us. "I don't know how you did it, but something isn't adding up with you."

"You're not entitled to answers for every question you ask," Haedion replied.

"Maybe we should leave you out here and contact Ka'an ourselves. Let him know where you're headed and collect his reward." Nafre hissed.

A slow, scary smile spreads across Haedion's face. "Please, try it. I'd love to see how far you get."

"I do not want to spend the night sleeping in the sand," Silas cut in, stepping between the two. "Nafre, drop it for now."

"Yes, Nafre. Drop it." Haedion picked up her bag and handed it to her.

"Shut the fuck up," Nafre snarled, ripping the bag from his outstretched hand.

"I'm liking you more and more," Haedion gave her a wink, side-stepping around her, grabbing my hand as he walked. Sparks bloomed in my stomach at the touch, and by the time our fingers slipped from each other, my skin grieved for the connection.

Hours passed the same as yesterday, the heat from the sun pressing down on us unforgivingly. My eyes stayed glued to the ground where my footsteps sank deep into the sand.

And just the same as the night before, I got to witness the sun slowly descend below the horizon. This time, however, I was safe. At least for the time being. No Sandwraiths, no Ka'an, no blades pressed to my throat just inches from where my blood pulsed through my veins.

"Ah," Bastian said at last, the sigh a breath of relief. "There it is." He pointed off in the distance where the library crept into view. The tall, tanned-stoned building framed by the stars and the night sky, candlelight illuminating the windows.

The moment I stepped through the threshold, into the foyer, the hair on my arms rose as if we stepped into an electrical storm. My skin prickled at the energy thrumming in the room, and I could taste the magic in this place and the ominous secrets it held. Heat flushed across my cheeks when I found Haedion looking directly at me. Watching me. I quickly looked away, desperate to fix my attention anywhere but him.

The foyer was giant, with a second level hidden behind large marble pillars. The room was empty, except for a podium in the center of the room perched on a small dais. No one dared breathe a word as we crept forward. The only sound was the sand scratching against the stone floor and Bastian's loud breathing were the only sounds.

Nafre arrived at the podium first, where an old, thick leather-bound tome reflecting names in all languages and dialects sat open, ready to be read. She drank in the sight of it all, the pillars and ten marble floors cascading high into the ceiling, wonder filling her wide eyes.

"It's like a sign-in sheet," Eiran said, peering down at the names over Nafre's shoulder.

"It is." A deep voice boomed, echoing across the empty chamber.

My knees trembled, looking for the source of the voice. I knew who it belonged to, but I couldn't see him. I spun in a circle, my heart pounding so fast my chest ached. I had been so focused on surviving my escape from Ka'an, surviving the rusalki, escaping the sandwraiths, and getting to the library that I didn't give a thought to what it would be like to meet the creature that paid to have me brought here.

"It's okay, Rhea," Haedion crooned softly, stepping close, the heat from his body seeping into my back. "You'll be safe here." His lips grazed the shell of my ear, sending shivers up my spine.

"Are you the Necroscythe?" Nafre asked.

"I am," the voice replied. From the corner of my eye, I saw a snake-like creature slither from the second level. It traveled down a pillar, wrapping its body around as it inched toward us. No book, no hours in the library, and no first-hand accounts could've prepared me for coming face to face with the Necroscythe. I could stand on Haedion's shoulders and would barely touch the top of its back. Its scales were a deep black with iridescent hues throughout. The flames from the lanterns reflected on its scales.

Pulses of vibration climbed up my legs as the Necroscythe slithered across the floor.

"What do you seek in the library?" It directed its question at Nafre; its forked tongue flickered out, tasting her fear. She had her shoulders back and head held high with confidence, but I saw her clench her hand into a fist to hide the tremors that wracked through them. She was terrified— rightfully so, I was too.

"They want money," Haedion interrupted, leaving my side and walking up to the creature.

"Money?" The snake hissed, lowering its head till it was level with Nafre— Silas, and Eiran behind her, hands resting on the weapons at their hips.

"It's a long story. They wanted the girl; we promised to pay them instead. Win-win for everyone. I'll go get them what they're owed so they can be on their way." Bastian walked toward a spiral staircase at the far side of the corridor, framed by two large ivory marble pillars that ran from the floor to the ceiling.

"Wait!" Nafre held up her hand, stopping Bastian in his tracks.

"Yes," the Necroscythe trilled smoothly, a distinct edge of humor in his tone. "You can trade."

Nafre's hand flew to her chest, jumping back in alarm. "How the hell?"

"Trade what Nafre?" Silas gripped her arm, pulling her to face him. His eyes furrowed in alarm and confusion.

"I didn't say anything; it was just a thought." She ripped her arm free from Silas and turned back to stare at the Necroscythe, jaw slack with disbelief.

"You can read thoughts?" She pressed.

"Hmm, no, not read, exactly, but almost. Feel your intentions though, your mood and feelings, yes." It replied. If it were a human, I would imagine him leaning back against one of the pillars, arms crossed, with a casual leg tossed over the other. "But yes, if you'd like to trade, you are welcome to it."

"Trade *what* Nafre?" Eiran growled, echoing Silas's question.

"She wants to explore the library. Study the maps, the histories that I have spent centuries cultivating and protecting so fiercely that very few individuals have even seen the inside of the walls of this very corridor."

"You what?" Eiran and Silas exclaimed at the same time.

"But the money—," Eiran said, his voice slow as he eyed the snake looming overhead.

"Think about it," Nafre said quickly with excitement at the idea. "The maps, the histories, who knows what is here that we would never have had access to before! It's worth more than gold."

Silas and Eiran remained silent, mulling over the idea in their minds.

"We trust you. If you want to stay, we'll stay with you." Eiran said, and Silas nodded in silent agreement.

"Wonderful," the Necroscythe said as his form began to slither, and for a moment, I thought they were retreating into the library. But I was wrong. It was shifting, shrinking, its scales disappearing, replaced by sun-tanned skin and black hair peppered with white. Where the snake was moments ago now stood a man, no taller than Haedion, dressed in a black form-fitted shirt with black linen pants. The eyes, though, his eyes were the same soulless onyx orbs.

"Holy shit," the curse slipped from my mouth. Instinctually, I reached for Haedion, finding his arm to steady me as the world tilted on its axis.

"You are free to roam about," the Necroscythe ignored my outburst entirely. "There are ten upper levels, we are standing on the first, and two lower levels beneath. If you head directly down this hall behind me, you will come to the stairwell that will take you in whichever direction you desire." His voice was the same as it was in his serpent form.

"I believe you three would be interested in a detailed map of the desert and the history of the Sandwraiths preceding the reign of the Fae and Vesperians I have here. It's on the second level. If you'd like, I can show you the way. As I understand it, you've been creating a detailed map of your own to expand your knowledge of the area. That is something I admire."

Nafre's mouth gaped at the praise. "We'd love to see anything you may have."

Their group set off, following the Necroscythe deeper into the heart of the library. Their voices grew faint as they ascended the steps to the second level.

"The mind-reading thing is kind of creepy. You could've warned me," I glared at Haedion once they were out of earshot.

"I think the Necroscythe finds his entertainment in reading people's minds, casting doubt, and causing chaos. When your life is infinite, I'm sure you have to get creative," Haedion replied, staring off where the Necroscythe and the rest of our group disappeared.

"Where are they going?" I asked, even more confused than I was when the giant serpent transformed into an ordinary-looking human. The Necroscythe wanted me here for a reason. Badly enough that he'd paid Haedion and Bastian, who knows how much, to retrieve me and bring me back here. And once I'm finally here, he barely acknowledges my presence. I bite my tongue to resist the urge to scream, "Here I am, what do you want with me?!" The thoughts that had plagued my mind about who this strange creature was and what would happen when we finally met melted away into anger.

"He'll talk to you later. For now, I can take you to the guest wing," Haedion said, gesturing to the stairwell.

"Wait, wait, wait." I dropped my back on the hard marble floors of the library, dust and sand scattering in the whoosh of air. "He just left me here? I thought he had paid you both to bring me to him, and now, he barely acknowledges me? What is going on?"

"It's just how he is." Bastian shrugged. "The Necroscythe want something from you, or to talk to you, or a million other things—," he paused, looking at the wide-eyed horror spreading across my face.

"But he doesn't want to hurt you!" He finished, rubbing his neck uncomfortably.

"What the hell, you guys!" I threw my hands in the air, heat rising to my skin in response. "I don't want to be dragged around like a collectible. I *want* answers. I *need* answers. This doesn't make sense that you both show up the night my powers decided to manifest. Then, you coincidentally save me from Ka'an, and take me halfway across the country to your shape-shifting boss— thanks for warning me about that, too, by the way— and now what? I'm not even important enough for a simple conversation?" A humorless laugh escaped my lips.

"You are important. Please, just let me show you to the guest wing and then I'll take you around the library until he comes and finds us." Haedion took my hand in his, squeezing tight as if he could force reassurance into my body through his fingertips.

"You're safe here, Rhea. I promise." Haedion breathed, stepping even closer till our chests nearly touched. "Nothing can get you here. Not the sandwraiths, not Ka'an, no leering eyes or dangerous creatures. So please, let me take you so you can get settled. Maybe even bathe and eat, and then I'll show you around. How does that sound?"

My stomach fluttered at his proximity, his words, his declaration, and the confidence of my assured safety. I looked into the earthy colors of Haedion's eyes, the warm hues of amber and honey brown, with the mossy green, and what stared back at me was *honesty*. He was pleading with me to *trust* him.

"I'm going to want answers," I muttered, relenting an inch.

"I understand." Haedion nodded. "And you'll get them."

"Fine, take me to the guest wing."

Haedion gave me a small, apprehensive smile. He bent down and scooped up my bag for me, securing the strap over his shoulder. With my fingers still laced through his, he pulled me down the entryway into the heart of the library. At the spiral stairwell, we ascended the steps past the second level, third, fourth, and didn't stop till we were nine stories up. My thighs burned, but it was second to the magnificence that seeing each level brought. Endless aisles of collectables, maps, books, and creatures in tanks extending far into the depths of the library.

On the ninth level, Haedion stepped out on the floor, pulling me alongside him.

"I'll catch up with you guys later," Bastian stretched his arms above his head with a yawn. "I'm going to bathe and sleep for eighteen hours straight. I'm just down that hallway, third door on the left. Each room has a theme, and the doors tell the story. Mine is the sun, so if you need me, my door has a giant sun on it. It matches my bright and shiny personality!" He shuffled, bag slung over his shoulder, and disappeared through his doorway.

"My room is this way as well." Haedion ushered me farther down the hallway. The polished marble floors reflected the golden firelight in the iron sconces that lined the walls. The fire, trapped in a cage, is forced to burn and glow bright regardless of its desire. Burn, burn, burn until it's so low, it will wink out and be forgotten to the world it served.

I chuckled silently. Same little firelights. We were the same.

Haedion stopped us in front of an ash grey door, where a tornado of tenebrous shadow whirled and twisted in an illusion. My head spun watching the shadows inch across, spreading their darkness, only to start over and over in an endless loop.

"This is my room." Haedion leaned a hand against the doorframe, angling himself above me. There was something different about him. I'd noticed it after he'd rescued us from the sandwraiths. Dark circles had appeared under his eyes, and his hair was messy from running his hands through it. And he'd grown stubble from the days of not shaving. But what sent a pang of concern through my core that had me reaching for his cheek were his eyes.

The eyes that had been so bright and wild, that had pulled me in on the night of the solstice and made me *want* to live, were now dull. Sure, the brilliant colors I'd come to expect when I looked at him were there, but the life in them was dim. As if he were fighting an internal battle that he was losing by the moment.

"Haedion," I whispered, my hand cupping the course skin of his cheek. "What's wrong?"

"Nothing." He started to take a step back, pulling away, but I wouldn't let him brush me off. No, not anymore. There was something here— something I'd felt since the night of the solstice. At first, I was certain that he'd played me to get me to leave Flitmoor with them. But something in my gut kept pulling me back to him. Like whatever we were made of, we recognized one another and called out, saying, "See me, please. I'm here, I'm here, I'm here."

"No." I took a matching step forward. "I can feel you. Something is wrong. It's not just exhaustion; there is more to it than that."

Haedion closed his eyes and tilted his head back. He let out a deep sigh through his nose. "There is nothing you can do to help me, Rhea. Don't worry about me. I'll be fine," he replied with a painfully forced smile that died before it reached his eyes.

With my hand still placed firmly on his cheek, I rested my other hand on his waist. The hard muscles of his abdomen tightened in response, but he didn't flinch away.

"What are you keeping from me?" I exhaled the words.

His eyes remained shut, his mouth pressed into a firm line. Frustration that had been simmering finally reared its ugly head again, and I snapped, "Fucking hell, Haedion, look at me!"

His eyes flew open, and suddenly I was pinned with my back against the wall. Haedion's face was inches from mine, his hot breath on my lips. He pushed even closer, his hips grinding against mine, and my chest pressed against his. Something tightened in my core as his hot breath rolled across my face.

"You are the problem, Rhea, all of you!" He growled, cupping my cheeks in his hands, the rough calluses on his palm scratching at the delicate skin. "Curse all the realms, I've tried so hard to stay away from you! But fuck, the way you laugh, the way you demand answers, when you're scared or when you're happy, I'm pulled into you time and time again."

He paused, his breath coming in shallow pants. "And when I finally thought I'd gotten ahold of myself when it came to you, and found where I stood, you had to go and sacrifice yourself for Bastian. In no realm I could imagine would someone do that for a near stranger. But *you* did."

My heart jumped into my throat. Any words that I had ready died on my tongue.

"Why do you have to stay away?" I whispered, my voice was so low that I wasn't even sure Haedion heard. I couldn't look away from his eyes, but the corners of my vision turned murky with shadows that leaked around us.

"I can't tell you that." Haedion leaned back an inch, the shadows disappearing with his proximity.

"Yes, you can." I insisted, moving with him.

"When you disappeared into the desert with Bastian, I wanted to kill them all right there," he said through gritted teeth. He placed one hand on my hip, pushing me back into the wall. "And I could've, would've if I wasn't..." he trailed off.

"What aren't you telling me?" I demanded, the pounding of my heart like a war drum echoed in my ears.

His lips were so close, and the familiar scent of smoke and leather wafted around us. I wanted to lean into him, see if he tasted as good as he smelled. I was completely and dangerously entranced.

As if he read my mind, Haedion leaned in, brushing his lips against mine. I opened up to him, kissing him deeper, harder. My fingers found themselves tangled in his hair as my skin sparked life, little embers dancing along my arms. I'd never felt this way before—

certainly not with Calix. With each beat of my heart, it sobbed with overwhelming relief. This was *right*.

"Ahem," an amused voice broke through our invisible bubble of connection. Haedion ripped his lips from mine, looking for the voice. At the end of the hallway stood the Necroscythe, arms crossed, leaning against the wall with a bemused smile.

"Sorry to interrupt your moment, but I need to speak to Haedion," he said.

Haedion quickly dropped his hands from my body, where they had held me so tight that I was sure I would find marks left behind.

"Of course," Haedion replied. Before he left, he paused a moment, searching my face as if memorizing it for the last time, then went down the hallway, leaving me there standing alone.

12

HAEDION

We didn't speak as we descended the nine floors of the spiral staircase, and then the additional two floors under the main level. He was leading me far away from any prying eyes or stray ears. Whatever he had to discuss, it must be important.

Once at the bottom, I was engulfed by the familiar humidity of the botanical garden. Luscious green grass and patches of flowers sprinkled across the vast space with such beauty that it would put the ones from home to shame. In the center of the garden sat the immense white willow with clumps of bioluminescent flowers of all different colors dripping from the branches.

The Necroscythe led us to the small table and chairs that sat under the tree. With a flip of his hand, a tea set with a spread of food lay in front of us.

"I'm sure you're hungry," he said by way of invitation. We sat, and I didn't hesitate before digging into the meal.

"When I sent you after the girl, I didn't expect that to happen," he mused, his fist propped under his chin in contemplation.

"What did you want to speak with me about?" I asked, ignoring the comment altogether. I wasn't going to talk about what he'd seen. I'd lost the rein of control I'd had on myself when it came to Rhea, and I wasn't sure what I was going to do about it.

"Oh, so just right to the point. Got it." The Necroscythe sat forward, preparing a cup of tea in the special way he liked it. "By now, I know you've discovered who she is."

"Of course," I said through bites.

"And your brother has contacted you, asking for your help in locating her?" He framed his words as a question when we both know the truth.

I nodded.

"So what are you going to do now?" He took a deep drink from his cup.

What was I going to do now? I had been so set on my goal when Ka'an had offered me a way home, but the last couple of days changed everything. Throughout my life, no one had changed me and made me feel the way Rhea did so quickly. Not even Eden, whom I'd tried every day to bury into the deepest depths of my memory. Since we'd found Rhea, I'd stopped waking up with the lingering feeling of Eden's blood coating my hands as I had tried, and failed, to keep her organs inside her body. The image of the light leaving her bright red eyes that used to beam at me like rubies in the moonlight, always on the back of my lids, the moment I shut them.

"I don't know." It was the truth.

"What did your brother want?" He asked, sipping the tea from a small porcelain cup that seemed ridiculous in such a powerful creature's hand.

"He made me an offer. One that I originally accepted." I wiped my mouth with the pressed white napkin, leaving behind traces of sand and dirt.

"He told me that if I found Rhea, helped her descend into the catacombs under Draconia to retrieve the Prismara of the Fae, and brought her to him, that he'd use the combined power of the stones to send me home."

"The one thing you've always wanted, but could never have." The Necroscythe hummed. "So what's stopping you?"

"At first, I considered the absolute destruction Ka'an would wreak if he possessed both stones," I hesitated, mulling over in my mind how quickly things had changed. "But now, it's *her*." I pushed back from the chair and paced away, needing to think.

"To you and your kind, she should be just another fae." He pointed out, watching me with his eyes as I paced the length of the canopy of the willow's reach.

"Forgetting Rhea and putting her aside, Ka'an can't have that much power. We were never designed to have both stones and that level of cosmic abilities. The Kirios split the powers between our two peoples for a reason," I argued. My back itched, and the umber leaked from my fingertips.

"Rhea is the difference, though. Why do you care what happens to this realm? You've experienced nothing but pain and loss here. You have the chance to go home. You've had ample chances to change the plan and give her to him now. *Make* her get the stone. So why haven't you?" He pushed, leaning forward, setting down their now-empty cup.

"Why aren't you celebrating the fact that I am fighting an internal battle on whether or not I let your realm be destroyed?" I shot back. "Do you want to see Ka'an with the power of the Kirios?"

"No, I do not. I'm simply trying to figure out if you've moved past it." He cocked his head, studying me with such scrutiny that I'm certain he's crawled his way into my memories, searching through my thoughts and seeing what we've endured since the night we left here.

"Moved past what?" I hissed, trying to find him in my mind and throw him out, his presence an uncomfortable pressure in my head.

"Moved on from the massacre of the fae. Have you finally forgiven yourself for not knowing his plan and stopping him?"

I stopped pacing in the plush green grass. My entire body goes cold with the memories, and every block I'd set up for myself was broken down. He'd found them and was anxious to see what lay beyond.

"No," I said tightly. "I will never forgive myself for not seeing what he was doing. He killed the fae. And Ka'an destroyed and potential future that could reunite the fae and vesperians with the birth of the dragon shifter. There is no going back. And I am to blame."

A wicked grin grew on the Necroscythe's face, and a light appeared in his starry midnight eyes.

"Are you certain that he killed the last dragon shifter?" He asked, his brows raised.

"Yes, of course I was there!" I snapped; the night flashed back in scenes of gore and screams.

"Gashion had just announced that Eden's best friend— his daughter— was pregnant with a son along with her sister, and we were expecting the next dragon shifter. Both of them, Alamae and Karish." The joyous laughter and clicking of glasses echoed in my ears. Eden's lips on my cheek as she'd whispered in my ear that she had something to share with me after the celebration. Her pupils were dilated wide, with happiness... and wine. Always the fae wine.

"What if I told you that you were wrong?" He stood. Rounding the table, the Necroscythe came to stand next to me where my feet had rooted to the ground.

"I'd say you were insane," I replied, coolly.

"Insane, yes. But that's only because I am infinitely old. But, my dear Haedion, that night, twenty-five years ago, Gashion told a lie." The Necroscythe declared, his eyes crinkling as he smiled.

"Why would he have done that?" I challenged. Gashion was respected, the elder of the fae. The oldest shifter himself.

"Gashion suspected that Ka'an was up to something, and on the advice from a very wise friend, he told a lie. He wanted a chance to throw Ka'an off the trail of the real dragon shifter, who had already been born and was being kept safe, away from Draconia. *She*," he emphasized, "survived simply because Ka'an never knew she existed." He shrugged his shoulders.

She.

"Gashion saved her." He added, as if I didn't comprehend the first time.

The pieces of the puzzle clicked together. The reason the Necroscythe offered to house us, feed us, and pay us. He knew Rhea was alive. Knew that she and I shared in the immense loss the night when Nador fell and was reborn into Ka'an's vision. Except I never knew about her, and she didn't know of me either. He must've known where Rhea had been all this time— that she was safe and protected. Biding his time until she discovered who she was. He must've seen it— felt her changing and sent us to retrieve her.

My chest constricted, and the room around us grew dark. The shadows emitted from me like a waterfall, circling us in a pool of night.

Eden died— they all died, and Rhea lived.

"I see you've put the pieces of the story together," he said, spinning in a slow circle, admiring the wisps of my magic dancing through his fingers.

"All this time, and you never told me she was out there?" I lashed out through gritted teeth. Rage, deep and painful, sliced through me, like the blades of the knives still strapped to my thighs.

"You weren't ready," he replied gently. His eyes softened when they finally landed on me. "Rhea needed her time to mature into herself, and you needed time to heal. It was true that Eden's younger sister was pregnant with a son— that wasn't a lie. But what Gashion withheld is that her older sister, Alamae, had given birth to a daughter in the privacy of her own residence with her husband some time before. Rhea had remained under the care of a medwitch while Alamae and her husband returned to Draconia. Being the first female dragon shifter ever, Gashion and the royal family had agreed to keep Rhea's life a secret. Again, on the advice of a friend."

That's what Eden had wanted to tell me that night after the party. My mind raced, looking for inconsistencies in the story, but everything fell perfectly into place.

"So why did you want Rhea here?" I asked, working to accept this new truth.

"By now, she's already feeling her powers. She needs someone to teach her and to tell her what she is capable of." He replied.

"And for what? To take on and destroy my brother?"

"Perhaps. If she chooses to, which I think she will, with time." The Necroscythe mused. "Prophecies are funny things, Haedion."

"You and I both know that she isn't powerful enough, even as a shifter, to kill him when he possesses the power of the Vesperian Stone." The thought made me nauseous.

"But she is fae." He walked back to the table where his steaming cup of tea waited.

"What does that matter?" I asked.

"Oh, Haedion," the Necroscythe huffed in disappointment. "Have you truly given up on the idea that good could win in the end?"

"I'm not deeming that with a response." The skin on my back tugged even more, begging to tear apart at the seams.

"Your brother wants the Prismara of the Fae. To strengthen his power and perhaps even join the realms and rule all," he mused, sitting back in their seat. The Necroscythe took a drink from his cup, and a silence filled the room.

The thought of the full power of the vesperian army and the men who created Ka'an to be exactly who he is today, coming here, would be horrific.

"We both know that can't happen," he replied, voice deep with a level of concern I hadn't heard before. "That would open up Nador to something worse than him."

I hadn't allowed myself to think of Samirah, here, in Nador.

"What do you propose then?" I asked, as I walked back to the chair and braced my hands on the back of the wrought iron design.

"We can't keep Rhea here forever. It's crucial she returns to Draconia and learns who she truly is and hears the prophecy for herself. And the sooner, the better."

"And what of Ka'an? He's going to check in with me and ask about Rhea. I'm surprised he hasn't broken down the barrier between our minds already and found us. Hell, he could already suspect where we are and be sending any number of his beasts." My hands squeeze the iron so hard it whines under my grip.

The Necroscythe watched my hands, but didn't comment. He was quiet for a moment, thinking, feeling, calculating.

"He isn't going to stop chasing her," he said at last. "But she needs to get to the catacombs and speak with the dragons herself."

"We barely got here unscathed. How do you suggest we get there and back without Ka'an finding us?"

"I have full faith in your abilities to get her there safely. Once in the catacombs, she can speak with the dragons and retrieve the Prismara of the Fae," he replied.

"That leaves the getting back here part." I scoffed, the immense challenge laying out in front of me like the unending desert where anything could go wrong.

"I know you're aware that the stones together are strong enough to open the portal between the realms, but are you not also aware that a single stone, combined with one gifted with the blood of the Kirios, can jump within their world?" He cocked his head, watching me digest the information.

"Let her go into the catacombs, get the stone, and use her blood to power it to bring us back here?" I asked, wanting to make sure I wasn't misinterpreting what he was suggesting. It wasn't a bad idea. Also, knowing she could jump within Nador gave her an out if worst came to worst with my brother.

He nodded. "That's exactly what I am suggesting," A slow, knowing smile grew on his face beneath a full, kept beard.

The idea churned slowly over in my mind. It could work. I could tell Ka'an that I had Rhea, and I'd convinced her to travel with me to Draconia to get the Prismara under a farce we would use to send Ka'an back to his realm. Our realm, my home.

I could feed him bits of truth within the lies. Even though we'd had years of distance and silence between our minds, our bond had been forged in blood and soul. It wouldn't be easy to fool him once I let him in again.

"Can you protect her if I bring her back here?" I asked. I needed to know if he was truly capable of keeping Ka'an from breaking through this fortress disguised as a library. If I was to risk it and put us all in danger, I needed to know.

"You pain me with such a question, Haedion. Have we not known each other for over two decades now?" He place a hand over where his heart would be, if he had one, looking hurt.

My eyes rolled before I could stop them. "Just answer the question. I need to know. Can you protect her?"

"If Ka'an manages to obtain both the stones of the fae and vesperians, I will not be able to hold him off long. The library will fall. But if

Rhea holds the stone of her people and gets you all back here safely, then yes, I can keep her physically safe within these walls," he confirmed.

"What do we do once we get back here?" I asked, my training demanding I stay one step ahead.

"Let's just get the prismara back here safe first, then come up with our next step. But that does bring me to my next task for you."

"Which is?" I asked through gritted teeth. Another task? We just got Rhea back here safe, no more than an hour ago.

"Rhea needs to learn to control her abilities. She will play a crucial role in all of this, and she needs to be able to manipulate her magic. You and I both know how much power flows within her veins. If she doesn't, one wrong move could have devastating consequences for her and everyone around her.

"She doesn't know what I am." My back straightened, muscles tensed so tight that I feared they might pop.

"Maybe you should tell her," he offered.

"My kind killed her people. I don't think she'd take kindly to that. Especially when she learns of my connection with Ka'an." The iron beneath my hands shatters. Pieces fall to the soft grass, landing with a soft thud.

The Necroscythe let out a long sigh. "I liked that chair." With a wave of his hand, the pieces floated up and rearranged themselves back into position. Knitting themselves together till they were whole once again.

"I believe if you give her time and let her in enough to really know you, Haedion, she will understand. But she must begin to work her magic to her advantage, and not let herself be manipulated by it. If she doesn't and her body forces her to shift before she is ready, she'll burn out." A wrinkle of stress creased between his brows as he stared, unblinking into my own eyes. When I felt his presence in the corner of my mind, I didn't shy away from it.

For as long as I could remember, I'd wanted to go home. When I was with Eden, I'd longed to bring her back with me. When she was taken, I longed to go back to grieve. And in the years since, where I wandered around Nador, I dreamt of flying among the unforgiving mountain ranges and feeling the spray of the sea on my face.

Each quest and mission that I'd received from the Necroscythe had distracted my mind enough to keep the self-loathing and pain I'd refused to address at bay. And I'd been fine with that— thrilled in fact. There was a line where those thoughts and feelings had stayed behind, and I had wanted to fight to keep it that way.

Now, Rhea had a chance, and it would be selfish of me to be a road-block in her path. I was the only one in Nador who could teach her. I'd just have to find a way to convince her to trust me when she finally learned the truth.

"I'm glad you came to the same conclusion. I suggest you all rest and prepare for the next leg of your journey." The Necroscythe nodded once again.

"I really fuckin' hate when you do that," I muttered, walking toward the stairwell. I want to get back to where Rhea was waiting.

"I have to keep it interesting, Haedion," he called, his voice growing quiet with every step. "Otherwise, we'll all lose our minds in here."

⚜

T didn't return to Rhea immediately, even though my chest ached with the desire to taste her again. Gods, how did I not know? My mind replayed the memories I'd tried so hard to erase. Of Eden, of her family, the other fae that we lived with for so many years. How did it all become such a mess?

The truth was irrefutable. No matter what angle I attempted to discredit it, it all aligned.

Now, I had to do the thing I'd put off. Contact my brother and pray that he believed me.

I closed my eyes and stepped deep into my mind, back into the dreamscape that connected our consciousness.

"Ahh, there you are. I was wondering what was taking you so long." Ka'an answered immediately. As if he'd been waiting just on the other side of the mental doorway for me.

"My issue has been resolved," I said.

"Finally, I'm glad you're back to work. But I have to say, if you cut our conversation short again and severe the connection, I won't be happy to see you the next time."

Ka'an wasn't *in* my mind; I couldn't afford to let him in, but I could sense him testing the edges, even as he kept his tone neutral.

"But back to what we need to discuss. I knew I could count on you. You were always the best, next to me, of course." He gave a cold chuckle, crossing his arms over his chest. *"What is your plan now?"*

"Draconia," I replied. *"We are making our way across the desert, through the mountain pass to Eldridge, then Draconia."* If I didn't spin the truth with the lies, he'd sense my deceit, and we would be in even more trouble. *"Then I will bring her to you in Atheria."* A lie— I held my breath.

"Hmm," he pondered my words. He tapped his chin, considering my plan. I could still feel his presence, like a cloud, floating around the boundaries of my mind.

"Are you sure she will get the stone willingly and then travel all the way to Atheria?" Ka'an pressed.

"Yes," I replied, keeping my tone even and unbothered. *"She will do as I say."*

"No, no. I will meet you in Draconia." My blood ran cold and all my senses screamed at me to run. No, no. That couldn't happen. Everything rode on this.

"I can certainly get her to Atheria, and the fact you're doubting my abilities is insulting, brother." I snapped, hoping he'd back off.

"This has nothing to do with you, Haedion," He hissed, doubling down. *"I made a mistake in letting one of these creatures survive. Do you not recall what they did to our people? I will not fail again. I want to see this fae, and soon. Samirah's creation deserves its revenge."*

Shit. Samirah. Ka'an was always unreasonable when it came to her.

"Fine," I replied, knowing any further argument was futile.

"Let me know the moment you arrive in Eldridge, and I will arrange your transportation to Draconia." Ka'an stepped backward, out of the dreamscape into his mind. *"We are close to achieving greatness, Haedion. Let's not fail now."*

Then he was gone.

13

RHEA

I stood outside Haedion's room waiting for him to return. He'd said he was going to show me to my own room before being called away by the Necroscythe, but we'd gotten... distracted.

All the realms of hell and beyond. My lips felt swollen from the kiss that had been so needy, hurried, but also desired. My head spun as I willed my heart to slow its pace.

I was still leaning against the wall, my bare skin felt clammy from the heat that had erupted in response to Haedion's touch. In his absence, I'd grown cold. Goosebumps pebbled across my arms, raising the tiny translucent hairs on end.

I could go knock on Bastian's door, tell him Haedion had been called away before he could show me where to go. Maybe he could help me. I padded softly toward Bastian's door, and as I raised a fist to knock, a deep snore permeated into the hallway.

No, no, I couldn't bring myself to wake him. I'd have to figure this out myself.

I paced the entire length of the hall, admiring each door. One was a whole ocean wave, towering high above the rest with white capped tips ready to crash down on its enemies. The next door showed flowers of all colors I could imagine, decorating a grassy hillside. The following door stopped me in my tracks. It was red, but with dimension and illusion, and it moved as though it were a live fire, crackling in a hearth. Instinctively, I reached out my hand to the golden round handle, then paused.

I shouldn't be snooping. Anyone could be in there. But I was getting colder by the second, and I longed to wrap my cape around myself and crawl under the blankets of a bed.

I walked back toward Haedion's room, my feet dragging against the shimmering marble hoping that any second he'd appear around the corner. My lids were growing heavier, and for a fleeting moment, I considered pulling my cape from my bag and curling up right on the floor.

My steps paused outside Haedion's door once again. Surely he wouldn't mind if I sat down in a chair or couch in his room, would he? Before I could reason with myself that, no, I shouldn't enter a private room without invitation, my hand turned the knob and the door swung open.

Haedion's room sat before me— a stark contrast in every way to what I imagined, but also didn't surprise me. A large four-poster bed sat on the far right wall, perfectly made with plush dark pillows to match the dark bedding. A door leading to another room sat between the bed and the farthest wall. But that wall wasn't a wall at all— it was a window. One large window ran the length of the room.

On the opposite side of the room were bookshelves that stretched floor to ceiling, filled with thick tomes and collectables tucked safely in between. A hearth, with a red-brick chimney, sat in the center of the wall of books with a sitting area directly in front. A fire simmered comfortably, as if it had felt Haedion's return and sprung to life to warm his chambers for him.

A velvet black couch was just big enough to stretch out on. The proximity to the fire kept it comfortable, but not close enough to burn if a rogue spark sprang from the embers. I placed my bag on one of the two chairs that sat adjacent to the settee, a dark wood side table next to each that matched a coffee table in the center. I retrieved my cape, slung it over my shoulders, and pulled the hood over my head like I'd done countless times. The soft, cushions of the couch called to me, and I couldn't help but collapse as the muscles in my legs gave way. I was safe here. No looking over my shoulder for Ka'an, and no running from the sandwraiths across the scorching desert. In the library, I could rest.

❦

Tears. *Why were there tears running down her cheeks?*

"Shhh, sweet baby, I know you're tired, but just a little longer, we are almost there." The woman shielded me from the powerful wind, tucking me under her cloak as she half-ran across the desert sand.

Where were we? When were we?

The beautiful woman, I knew her. I couldn't place her, but she was familiar. Dark brown hair that whipped across her face in the wind, with stark, steely eyes that begged me to remember them.

She sighed with relief as she crossed the threshold into the library. The Necroscythe, in his human form, appeared suddenly, his expression grim.

"What has happened?" He demanded, looking from me to the familiar woman.

"What you and they always feared," she cried, and more tears leaked down her dirty cheeks. "They're dead. All of them."

"Was it Ka'an and Haedion?" He asked, running his hand through his neatly kept beard.

"No, no, it was all Ka'an. When I left Haedion, he was grieving over Eden. He had no idea what Ka'an was planning. He is just as innocent as the rest of them. That poor boy."

"But you managed to save her?" He asked, gesturing to me.

She nodded. "Gashion suspected Ka'an was scheming and advised Alamae to hide her pregnancy and keep Rhea a secret. No one knew. He announced the pregnancies of Alamae and Karish, and that we were expecting the next dragon shifter, but kept the fact that Alamae had already given birth to Rhea a secret."

"At least he'd taken that piece of advice," the Necroscythe sighed. "I had advised him to spin a lie, push Ka'an's to see what he was planning. I just never anticipated that he'd kill them all."

"Is she going to remember?" The woman asked.

"She is so young, I don't believe she will," he replied, the same black eyes studying me with intense curiosity.

"Rhea cannot remember. Not one detail." The woman was suddenly frantic. "If she stands any chance at life, you must put a block on her memories. Please! I promised Alamae that if anything happened to them, I would bring her to you, then to Carina and Ragnar. They'll raise her as their own."

"Alamae and Jordi assumed I'd be able to protect her?" He asked, brows knit together in confusion.

"No, not protect. But if you can erase any memory she has of the life she was supposed to have, perhaps we can stop the progression of her powers until she's an adult. Keep her hidden. Alamae told me of the prophecy. Rhea was to join our people together again, and I hope for that future. But after what I witnessed in Draconia, I don't know how that will ever be true." The woman paled, fresh tears leaked from the corners of her eyes. "It was awful. So much blood," she whispered.

"I can put a block in her memory, prevent her from remembering the magic, the dragons, and anyone before now. But someday, her magic will appear, and it will burn the spell to ash, and I won't be able to stop it. Rhea is destined to be powerful. She will shake the earth and command the rivers of fire that flow miles below our feet. When she realizes what she is, there will be no stopping it," he said.

"Do it," the woman begged. "My sister, Marie, will be living with Carina and Ragnar as a maid to watch out for Rhea. The moment her powers begin to appear, she will know to get her out of Flitmoor and to Draconia."

"I, too, will watch for her. It is the least I could do for my dear friends. When her magic is on the brink of appearing, I will know. Such magic does not wink into the world unnoticed. It will shake the foundation of the cosmos, and it will not be something I can ignore."

"Thank you," she wept, handing me to the Necroscythe. He laid a careful hand on my forehead; his skin icy to the touch. With a smile, he whispered, "I cannot wait to see what you accomplish, my dear Rhea. We will meet again."

Darkness enveloped my vision, and I was gone.

I was comfortable. Far more comfortable than I should've been on a small sofa. My eyes flew open, and I sat upright. I was in bed, and not just any bed, Haedion's bed. My chest tightened. He must've picked me up and moved me, so gently that I didn't wake up. How long had I been asleep? The curtains on the wall-length windows were open, the night sky a cloak of midnight satin, the darkness of the night sky a comforting blanket to my senses. It was still night, and I could rest.

The sound of running water caught my attention, and my head followed the sound to the room next to the bed, where light and steam seeped from beneath the doorway. I settled back into the crisp sheets and comforting heaviness of the plush down comforter. I should get all the rest I can, but I'm overwhelmed with the familiar scent of Haedion. It surrounded me, the smell tugging at the memory of his lips on mine and the feel of his fingers as they dug into my hips. I lightly ran my hand over the spot on my skin where he'd held me. I'd been so lost in the memory replaying in my head over and over that I didn't notice when the water had stopped running and the door opened. Haedion stepped into his room, towel slung low on his waist, hair a tousled mess, the damp ends dripping tiny droplets onto the floor.

He stopped when he saw me, and a coy smile appeared on his lips.

"You didn't have to sleep on the couch," he said, sitting down on the edge of the bed.

"This is your space, I didn't want to invade," I replied, pulling the sheets tighter around me, remembering the conversation earlier, right before he kissed me. He'd been struggling with something, and when I pressed, he'd shouted at me, told me I was the problem, then kissed me. Now this? He'd tucked me so gently into his bed that I didn't even stir. It felt like we were playing a game of tug-of-war with our feelings as the flag in the middle, waiting to be pulled over the line.

"This might be my space, but you'd be hard-pressed to find something in here that I would find too personal to share." He leaned over and tucked a stray lock of hair behind my ear.

"How was your conversation with the Necroscythe?" I asked, steering the conversation away from us. Curse the Kirios.

Haedion smirked as he stood. I watched him wander over to his wardrobe, where he pulled a cream colored tunic and black cotton pants that tied at the waist.

"I will tell you after you bathe and eat," he said, returning to the bedside, holding out the clothing to me. "You'll find the water here never turns cold and never runs out. The library has a mind and magic of its own. It also has a sense of humor, so be careful what you ask it. When you're done, we can eat, and I'll answer your question."

"What do you mean, ask it?" I inquired as I clambered, ungracefully, from the sheets and stood nearly chest-to-chest with a half-naked Haedion.

"You'll see," he said, a glint of humor shining in his earthy eyes. "Although it may be kind to you. It usually is for new guests."

"Do you ever give a straight answer?" I scowled.

"It's more fun to discover and find out for yourself." He shrugged.

"Ugh, fine," I growled, snatching the clothes from his hands, sending him a glare before stalking into the bathroom.

The continued dark theme of Haedion's bedroom continued into the bathroom with all dark walls and fixtures with accents of white and silver. A huge, in-ground pool was fed by an invisible faucet coming from the wall, pouring a continual stream of steaming hot water into the tub. A tray sat next to the water's edge, filled with an array of soaps and lotions of various scents.

After making sure the lock was clicked into place, I slowly stripped my clothes off, discarding each piece one by one into a pile. When I finally stood bare, the bundle of filthy clothes disappeared. One blink, they were there, the next gone. Flabbergasted, I rubbed my eyes. Surely I was hallucinating from the stress. But when I removed my hands, and the world came back into focus, the floor was empty.

Then I remembered Haedion's words. The library had a mind of its own, with magic flowing through this place. Perhaps the library had been just as disgusted by my clothing as I had been.

I lowered myself into the deep pool of water, the heat immediately soothing the ache in my muscles. Tension, I hadn't realized I'd been carrying in my shoulders released, then my neck followed by the smallest muscles in my face dropping their strain as I submerged myself fully in the tub. A breath I hadn't known I'd been holding whooshed out of me, and with it, taking the wall I'd wrapped protectively around my mind of the horrors I'd experienced. It'd kept those things small and manageable so I could focus on the task ahead of me: surviving and getting here.

But now, we were here and I was safe. The rush of memories came at me like the continual flow of water from the faucet. The fire in Flitmoor was my fault. I'd damaged people's businesses and homes, ruined an entire celebration. Then Marie. Oh, gods, Marie. She was dead. Because of me. I'd been too weak, too small to protect her, and like a coward, I'd stood there and watched as Ka'an choked the life from her. I wanted to vomit as my mind replayed over and over the way her eyes bulged from their sockets and how her lips turned blue as she mouthed my name. She was the first victim that night of who knew how many. Did my parents survive the night? Did my sisters? Calix?

Then, when I thought we'd narrowly escaped the danger, I was almost killed by the rusalki. I looked down, and in the clear water of the tub, I could finally see the small puncture wounds where her nails had dug into my skin as she held me down against the sediment. My lungs burned as I remembered how I felt so helpless, so defeated.

Then, once again, I was rescued, just to face another set of dangers with a blade pressed to my throat, and a new set of companions whose only interest was their financial gain. And as we'd journeyed across the blazing desert, I'd sacrificed myself to the Sandwraiths. In that moment, a flip had switched in my mind. Bastian could've easily died, and I refused to let him be one more person who would suffer because of me.

Silent tears leaked from my eyes, and a sob worked its way up my throat. I wanted to scream at the unfairness of what it all was. I didn't know who I was anymore. No one knew. Where did my blood come from? What had been kept from me? Had it been to protect me from Ka'an, or keep me tame and gentle? Was that strange dream I had actually been a memory? Had the Necroscythe put a block on any memories I'd had to keep me from discovering who I was? With a frustrated shriek, I picked up the tray next to the pool and threw it as hard as I could against the wall. I stared as it clattered to the ground, the tubes and bottles lying broken, oozing various liquids across the floor, my vision blurring in and out of focus.

I couldn't be weak anymore. I had a power that ignited like sparks running through my veins jumping with excitement every time my thoughts wandered to them. With every acknowledgement, they seemed to whisper excitedly that yes, they were here, use us, please!

Where would I start, though? I wanted to learn— needed to learn how to use my abilities. If I didn't, then what was I good for? I was meant for more, and I would take the opportunity and run with it. I looked around the room and remembered where I was. I was in perhaps the most perfectly curated library in the realm, with an eons-old creature with endless knowledge. This place would be as good as any to start.

14

RHEA

I found myself staring in the mirror at my reflection once I was clean, dry, and fully clothed. I swam in Haedion's tunic that fell to my mid-thigh, and pants I had to pull tight and roll up several times to keep from tripping on the hems.

The bathroom provided me with everything I'd asked for. After I'd thrown the soaps and oils and realized I had actually *needed* them, I whispered an apology to the library and asked for more. Seconds later, the mess disappeared into the floor, just as my filthy clothes had, and a brand new tray of fresh supplies appeared in front of me.

I took my time smelling each of the scents before picking one that reminded me of the flowers that bloomed by the riverside south of Flitmoor that fed into Lake Gaia just east of the castle. The flowers, Ua Fleur, only bloomed once a year, in the spring. When their pedals opened, they captivated the area with the most wonderful scent. It was something you'd wish you could bottle up and save for the grim winters when you couldn't remember what the green grass looked like or what warm sunlight felt like on your face.

When I had finally exited the bath, two stark white towels appeared, and after I'd dried myself and changed, a hairbrush sat waiting on the edge of the wash basin. I spent my time running it through my hair, working through each tangle and knot the unforgiving desert wind had twisted into the strands.

Finally feeling clean and somewhat like myself again, my stomach growled. I cautiously opened the bathroom, finding Haedion where I'd left him, sitting on the edge of his bed. He'd replaced his towel with a dark pair of pants that matched mine and a black long-sleeved shirt.

"Better?" He asked, eyeing me up and down.

"Much," I replied, my cheeks heating under his stare.

"I'm sure you're starving. Let's eat, I'll answer your question, and then I'll show you to your room." He stood and walked to the sofa where I'd fallen asleep earlier. I followed tentatively behind, armed, crossed over my chest, watching him as he stared blankly at the empty coffee table. Just as I was about to open my mouth and ask him what he was looking at, a small feast appeared.

Meats, crackers, fruits, and breads with sauces and drinks to go with lined the table. My mouth watered as I rounded the edge of the couch, the hunger gnawing at my stomach.

"You eat, I'll talk," he said, sitting down in the armchair.

"What about you?" I asked, not wanting to be rude, but my stomach ached, urging me to put aside my politeness and eat already.

"I already ate, this is all for you."

"Alright," I muttered, distracted by the array of food. I sank into the couch cushions and tentatively began piling my plate full.

"You asked me earlier what my problem is, and when I insisted it was nothing, I told you a lie." Haedion began.

I snorted because obviously, he'd been dealing with something—anyone could see that. It didn't take a mind reader to see it. He sent me a glare as I popped a grape in my mouth and chewed slowly, motioning for him to continue.

"Ka'an wants the Prismara of the Fae. He has wanted it since he took control of Nador twenty-five years ago. He has tried and failed numerous times to retrieve it. He may be powerful, but the dragons who reside in Draconia are strong enough to destroy him, and he knows that. And now he knows you exist, the one being in the realm who has access to the catacombs."

"So it sounds like I just keep myself away from Draconia and away from the Prismara. Win-win, right?" I replied through bites of food. Another cross-country mission sounds like the worst idea I've heard. I want nothing more than to eat, sleep, and then figure out how to use my fire without burning down cities... again.

"Ka'an is never going to stop chasing you now that he knows you're alive. The Necroscythe wants Bastian and me to take you to Draconia so you may speak with the dragons yourself. There is a lot that you—we— don't know, and the answers are in the one place only you can go."

"Into the catacombs?" I asked, knowing the answer full well.

Dammit.

"Yes." He nodded. "And, when you're down there, you can get the Prismara of the Fae and, with that in your possession, we'll return here."

"Great, more opportunity to get hurt, tortured, or killed," I grumbled. The ache in my stomach was slowly beginning to fade, and exhaustion grew heavy on my lids.

"Unfortunately, yes," he echoed my sentiment. "Trust me, I'd rather stay here and help you learn how to control your abilities so we don't repeat what happened in Flitmoor or in the bunker the other night. I like my skin, I'd prefer not to have you melt it off. And the Necroscythe would be extraordinarily cross if you burnt down any of his collection that he's spent the last millennium cultivating."

"What do you know of fae abilities that you think you could help with me?" I asked, my question intending to be more curious about Haedion's knowledge of the fae, but it came out harsher than I intended. Haedion reared back, as if I'd slapped him. The air around us stilled, and a grain of guilt settled into my stomach. His lips pressed into a thin line, and I saw the Haedion from the solstice, the bunker, and tonight battling the Haedion who was blunt, rude, and unapologetic.

"I know a thing or two, Rhea." He leaned forward, bracing his forearms on his knees. "And I won't give you all the details now, that'll come later. But just know, I can help you, I can show you, and I'm willing to teach you. That will have to come after we get back here safely from Draconia. We don't have time to waste. You need to talk to the dragons and bring the Prismara here."

"Why does the Necroscythe want me to talk to the dragons so badly?"

Draconia, Draconia, Draconia, and those damn dragons and the prismara. What's a girl got to do to be able to stay and explore the library?

"He promised your grandfather that when the time came, he would help you. This is the time, and this is him helping you. There is a prophecy that is intended, just for you." He shrugged.

"My grandfather? A prophecy?" I asked, even more confused than I was earlier. "How did they know each other? Who was my grandfather?" I set down my plate, my stomach now satisfied.

"His name was Gashion, but the rest is not my story to tell," he replied.

I narrowed my eyes at him, exhaustion and indignation eating at my patience. "Fine." I stood abruptly. "I want to talk to the Necroscythe before we leave."

"Alright, but how about you get some sleep first so you can make a coherent argument?" Haedion stood also, stepping around the table toward the door leading to the hallway.

The protest on the edge of my lips died at the thought of being able to sleep. A full night's sleep. I was clean, fed, and would be able to sleep in a space saved for me.

"Hmph, okay," I muttered, following behind Haedion, who had an all too pleased-with-himself look that part of me wanted to slap off his pretty face.

He led me out of the door and to the room a few doors down from his. The door was extraordinarily similar to Haedion's; however, this door shimmers with little golden stars and layers of blues and purples that make me think of all the realms, layered on top of each other.

"If you need anything, come get me. Remember that you can ask the library for things you need. I'll find you in the morning," he said, reaching across me and pushing the door open for me.

"Thank you." I stepped inside the doorway before turning to face him. He leaned down, and I froze. With a gentle hand, Haedion cupped the back of my neck, my breathing hitching as he stared into my eyes. For a moment, I believed he would kiss me again. I *wanted* him to kiss me again. But then he dropped his hand and disappeared into his room without another word, leaving me alone.

The door shuts with a soft thud, and I click the lock into place. The room was similar to Haedion's in layout, but different in colors. Where his room was dark, mine was light—white linens, cream colored furniture, and bronze accents.

I didn't hesitate to climb into bed and pull the blankets around me, and I fell asleep before my head hit the pillow.

⚜

B*am, bam, bam*!
I jolted upright in bed, the constant pounding against the door ripping me from comfortable oblivion. For a second, I believed I was back in the huts, sandwraiths fighting to break down the door. Then I saw the night sky shone through the windows; it hadn't been long.

I was at the library, I was okay.

I jumped up, my bare feet cold on the stone floor as I flung the door open. Haedion, eyes wild, leaned heavily against the door frame, chest heaving, hair plastered against his forehead, coated in sweat.

"What's wrong?" I grabbed his arm, squeezing tight. I searched his face looking for answers, but found none. He was terrified, silver swirling in his irises. None of the awful things we'd encountered in our short time together had ever caused him to look this terrified.

"I just—," he stuttered, taking me in, looking behind me to the empty room, then back to me. He raked his hand down his face, resting it on the back of his neck as he let out a shaky breath. "I'm sorry, Rhea." Another controlled exhale. "I had a nightmare that you were dead. I just had to check. Sorry, I woke you." He rolled his neck, as if trying to calm himself. Haedion pushed himself off the doorframe, but I held on to his arm, not letting him go.

Maybe it's the complete upheaval of my life and my need for an ounce of control, or genuine desire that drove me to stop him, but I didn't want to be alone tonight. And something told me that he didn't want to be either.

"Do you want to stay with me?" I asked, chills raced up my spine, my heart skipping beats as I waited for his reply.

His brows softened in relief as he wrapped his arms around my waist, half-lifting me into the room.

He sat me down in the middle of the room, but didn't let go of me. His eyes didn't leave mine as he muttered, "I don't know what it is about you, but I can't fucking think when you're around. It's maddening. One moment, I think I have myself under control, then the next, you are my undoing." His tone balanced precariously on the edge of anger, but desire hung on every breath.

Butterflies swarmed in my stomach and spread throughout every inch of me. I took my hand and rested it on his cheek. The stubble from the hints of a beard scratched my palms.

"And I don't know what it is about you. You don't share anything about yourself, won't tell me about your past, and you go from this caring, thoughtful man to a stranger in seconds. You insist I trust you, Haedion, and gods, I don't know why I do, but I do." I rested my forehead on his chest, breathing in his scent, and my arms wrapped around his body.

"Just remember that you do. The more you learn, the harder it will be to see through the lies and messy history. We have the same endgoal. Always remember that." He rested his chin on the top of my head.

We stood like that for minutes, arms wrapped around each other, until Haedion lifted me once again, pulling me to the bed.

I scooted over on the large mattress, leaving room for Haedion, who easily settled down next to me. He snaked his arm around my waist, pulling me close to him. The scent of smoke and leather enveloped me as Haedion buried his face in my hair.

And we lay there dozing in and out of dreamless sleep, not saying anything until the sun rose, peaking above the horizon in the distance.

My hand crept out across the cold mattress, searching for Haedion when I finally woke for the last time. With the way my back and hips ached from lying on the feathery soft bed, I knew I'd been asleep for hours. I rolled over in bed, seeing my room for the first time in daylight, through clear-seeing eyes not tainted by exhaustion.

Cream-colored marble floors imbued with veins of gold shimmered brightly, reflecting the desert sun that entered through the same floor-to-ceiling windows that I'd seen in Haedion's room. Cautiously, I untangled myself from the bedsheets and walked barefoot to the window. From nine stories up, I could see miles in the distance, small rolling dunes, with freckles of vegetation standing out against the blistering white sand.

I spun in a slow circle, taking in all the details of the bedroom. This place was remarkable. An empty fireplace, with white-washed bricks framed by bookshelves already filled with texts and maps, lay waiting to be read. On the ash wood coffee table sat a steaming cup of tea next to a plateful of biscuits. Without hesitation, I popped one in my mouth. The warm, buttery layers of the cookie melted on my tongue. The tea, a perfect mixture of richness mixed with a hint of sweetness, washed it down.

A tall wardrobe sat on the side of the bed closest to the door leading to the hallway. When I opened the doors, it was filled with familiar clothing, similar to what I would wear at home. Dresses, with soft flat shoes that were perfect for spending the day wandering the library— just like I used to.

"Could I have something, maybe a little more suited to what I was wearing when I arrived?" I whispered my request to the library. I imagined the pants and tunic, I'm sure, were somewhere in the bowls of the building, being burned to ashes. I couldn't imagine even the nicest soaps or best brushes could work out the grim and sweat-caked into the threads. But I had grown fond of my pants and tunics.

With a gentle pop and soft breeze, a nearly identical set of clothing that I wore when we arrived last night appeared on the bed. Clean, perfect, but slightly different. Three iridescent buttons opened on the top fourth of the shirt, and the material was buttery smooth to the touch.

I slipped the clothing on with ease, the fit matching my body perfectly. Haedion's clothing disappeared into the floor before I could pick it up to fold it. I left my hair free of its typical confines, letting it flow in gentle waves.

Now that I was fully dressed, I tentatively inquired. "Where am I supposed to go now?" In response, the door leading to the hallway clicked open, the hinges groaning softly.

When I poked my head out into the hallway, I spotted Bastian leaning against the wall. When he saw me, his face brightened with a genuine smile.

"Good morning!" He said, offering his arm to me. "I'm here to take you to breakfast."

"I'm glad you're here." I accepted his arm as we walked toward the spiral staircase. "With ten stories, not counting the two lower levels, I had no clue where I was going to start my search for you guys."

We began the ascent, climbing the stairs slowly side by side.

"The dining room is on the tenth story. You'll see why," Bastian said.

"Have you talked to Haedion this morning?" I asked, wondering if he was aware of our new mission or if this breakfast was intended to fill him in on the plan.

"I did, after I caught him sneaking out of your room this morning." He gives me a wry side eye, his golden brown eyes glittering mischievously.

"Nothing happened!" I blurted quickly, feeling like a teenager caught kissing a boy for the first time. A laugh burst from Bastian so hard his shoulders shook, causing heat to floor my cheeks.

"Oh, trust me, I know. Haedion about tore me to shreds when I gave him a hard time about it." A dimple appeared on his cheek. "He cares for you, Rhea, and that's hard for him." He added, his voice lower. " He doesn't let many people in. Give him some grace and some time." He patted my hand.

We finally reached the top of the spiral staircase. The singular room opened before us. My eyes immediately found Haedion, dressed and seated next to the Necroscythe. What I didn't expect, however, was to find Nafre, Silas, and Eiran also seated at the table, all looking rigid and uncomfortable. Nafre's hands were balled into fists in her lap, while Eiran and Silas sat on either side of her, shoulders back and chests puffed. They would've looked menacing and confident if their eyes weren't darting between Haedion and the Necroscythe like they were waiting to see who would attack first.

"Ah, Bastian, Rhea, thank you for joining us for breakfast." The Necroscythe stood. With a wave of his hand, two seats pulled back from the table. One next to him, the other next to Haedion. Bastian dropped my arm, finding the seat next to the Necroscythe while I accepted the seat next to Haedion.

I mouthed a thank you to Bastian, who gave me an inconspicuous wink in return. Even though I was certain I was safe, the Necroscythe still made me uneasy.

"I was just filling in your companions on the next leg of your journey." He said, looking to Bastian.

"Oh?" Bastian looked from Nafre to Haedion and back to the Necroscythe, his face perfectly cheerful.

"Yes, it sounds like they will also be coming with us to Draconia," Haedion cut in, his voice tight with disapproval.

"I've hired them to act as additional security to get you all to Draconia safely." The Necroscythe beams. "They happily accepted my offer this morning."

"We will be ready to leave whenever you are," Nafre added, her demeanor so different than the woman who'd nearly slit my throat and would've willingly handed me over to Ka'an just a few days ago. Now, she sat at attention, her mouth pressed into a firm line, a subdued version of herself, ready to be a solider accepting orders.

Whatever they'd been offered, it must've been a extraordinary reward.

"We don't need extras," Haedion said, his voice monotone. His hands gripped the arms of his chair, knuckles white under the strain.

I slowly reached for him under the table, running a finger gently against his wrist.

"The more the merrier," the Necroscythe said. "Your supplies are ready for you whenever you are properly prepared to leave. Nafre,

Eiran, and Silas, I expect you to return when you accomplish your mission in Draconia."

"Yes, sir." Nafre nodded, Silas and Eiran following suit.

The Necroscythe clapped, pushing back from the table. "Wonderful, I will wait patiently for your return." And when I blinked, he was gone.

15

RHEA

N afre informed us as we began our trek that we were within a couple of days' walk of the Caverns Forest. I had to pinch Haedion's arm to keep him from snapping a sarcastic remark, earning me a glare. But he'd kept his mouth shut.

The information she found from the maps in the library had helped them compare what they'd gathered in their journeys across Nador. We all agreed to take the shortest, but most dangerous path across the desert that will lead us directly to the edge of the forest that covers the mountain range. Less coverage for our group with more chances to be spotted by sandwraiths, nomads, or hawks who could easily report to Ka'an our location. It was a risk we all agreed to take, especially with bringing three extra bodies as protection. We all wanted to get back to the library as soon as possible.

Once we hit the coverage of the forest, we would travel to the small village that sits at the bottom of the mountains to restock, then over the pass that will deposit us directly into Eldridge.

Fast, easy, and direct. Exactly what we needed when racing against time and the all-powerful ruler of Nador, who orchestrated the mass genocide of an entire race and now wants your head.

Sounded simple enough.

We walked until the sun started to dip lower in the sky, and decided then to break camp for the night.

"At least we have sufficient camping supplies this time," Eiran said to Nafre as they worked together to pitch the thick canvas tent. It was large enough to fit the three of them in one, while Haedion, Bastian, and I would share another.

"I will say it is an upgrade from some of our usual arrangements," she replied, struggling to secure one of the tent poles in the ground. With a final huff, she swung the mallet down on the stake, driving it deep enough into the stand that Eiran and Silas raised the tent.

"Although I don't think anything will compare to the library," she added, turning to face us. Haedion and Bastian had quickly secured our tent. They worked together quickly, getting it raised with bedrolls and supplies set before the trio could unravel the canvas for the tent.

"I get what you mean," Bastian said. "Once you spend time in the library, and get past the creepy shape-shifting and mind-reading, you'll never want to leave."

"And you both live there, full-time?" Nafre asked.

"When we aren't running errands or finding precious items for the Necroscythe, then yes, we live there," Haedion said, looking directly at me.

Precious items.

Haedion hadn't said much since we left the library, but he'd been my shadow, or I his. I wasn't sure anymore, but his presence and closeness were comforting.

"But, if you decided you didn't want to work for him anymore, or just didn't come back, would he send people after you? Punish you?" Silas wondered as he emerged from the tent flap.

"No," Bastian shook his head. "He isn't like that. We have free will and free rein of our lives. The Necroscythe won't punish us for using it as we see fit."

"How very interesting," Eiran muttered under his breath.

We quickly ended the conversation after that, each group finding their respective tents. Eiran agreed that he would take the first watch, then wake Haedion halfway through the night.

Sleep found me quickly, but it was short-lived. The sun rose far too quickly, and Haedion had us rising with it.

"I don't like sitting here like pond-skimmers waiting to be snatched," he grumbled as he encouraged me to pack faster so we could get moving.

"You need to get more sleep," I muttered more to myself than Haedion. Bastian stifled a laugh while Haedion walked away with a humph.

Another day goes by of our silent journey in the desert. The soles of my feet ached, and my skin hurt from the brutal, unrelenting sunshine. Eventually, just as I begin to think we will be spending another day sleeping in the desert, evidence of the forest crept into view.

Dirt, rocks, and small plants began to replace the sand, and some oddly placed large boulders greeted us as we ventured closer to the tree line. Bastian walked up to the nearest rock, pacing around it unit he found an adequate foothold. With minimal effort, he hoisted himself on top, standing cautiously, turning in a slow circle, admiring the view.

Everyone stopped to watch Bastian. Eiran and Silas plopped down on the sand next to one another, taking large swigs from their canteens while taunting Bastian.

"Do a backflip off!" Silas joked, his blonde hair caked to his forehead with sweat.

"Or a front flip!" Eiran chuckled, shouldering Silas.

"Or better yet, do you see anything interesting up there?" Haedion asked. I leaned against the boulder closest to me, — Haedion hovering just within reach.

Bastian grinned as he scanned the desert. "Nothing," he started to say before his smile melted and his eyebrows creased as he strained to look at something in the distance.

"What is it?" Nafre demanded, looking in the direction of Bastian's stare, squinting to see whatever was coming our way.

"Haedion." Bastian looked at Haedion with wide-eyed terror. "I swear to the gods I see a pack of ravagers coming this way. How the fuck are they this far from Atheria?"

Haedion was still for a moment, and for a second, I believe he's frozen in fear — his eyes unfocused and blank. Just as I was about to shake him, he blinked back into focus, eyes landing on me. Bastian jumped down from the boulder and grabbed his pack as he urged us to move.

"We've got to run." Haedion pushed me ahead of him, toward the forest edge, and we broke into a run.

"What are they?!" Nafre demanded, sprinting beside us. Each footfall sank deep into the sand, weighing me down and slowing my pace.

"Ravagers were created by Ka'an," Haedion hissed out in heavy pants. "They're bloodhounds, but bred to be bloodthirsty, carnivorous creatures. Once they catch the scent of their target, they're hard to lose. Once they taste blood, almost nothing can stop them."

Nafre doesn't respond, but matches our pace alongside us as we race for the tree line. My calves and thighs burned at the exertion, and my lungs screamed for more air. I felt myself begin to slow, and I pumped my arms harder. I sent a little prayer to the Kirios and dug deeper into myself to move faster.

"Run fast, Rhea!" Haedion snapped, looking over his shoulder at me. Just as the words left his mouth, a chorus of howls boomed through the air, and he slammed to a halt. The blood drained from his face as he stared at Bastian, and a silent communication passed between them. And I understood then: they've got our scent. We won't be able to lose them now.

Oh shit, oh shit, what are we going to do? All I had on me was the small blade Haedion gave me before I was captured by the sand-wraiths. One small knife against a murderous group of ravagers that I can only imagine will be just as horrifying as the ones I've created in my mind.

"Once you get to the tree line, find high ground. Get into a tree, on a boulder, anything," Haedion commanded. Everyone nodded their understanding, and we took off once again, arms pumping, feet pounding against the fine grains of sand.

We were almost to the tree line when the first ravager caught up. Drooling frothy white spit from his jaws, a snarl ripped from its lips. A second ravager caught up, then a third. We were twenty feet from the trees when the horrible realization came over me that we weren't going to make it. Nafre, Silas, and Eiran were slightly ahead of us, but their steps were slowing. Nafre was shouting encouragement at them, but I could see her energy waning as well. Haedion and Bastian are on either side of me. Both have daggers in hand.

"Just a little farther," I chant to myself. The warmth inside my veins, once again, begged me to use them. I should've insisted we stayed at the library a little longer, so that perhaps I could've learned more about my abilities, and I wouldn't be so useless now. Heat bloomed in my chest, just waiting for me to let down the dam I'd set up so it could rush out and obliterate anything in its path. And I wanted to, that wasn't the problem. The problem was anything in its path, and I had no idea how to direct it. I could easily hurt the group, and it was a risk I wasn't willing to take.

"Shit!" Haedion cried the moment I slammed face-first into the sand. White-hot pain shot up my leg as the Ravager sank its teeth into the thick, meaty part of my upper thigh. A blood-curdling scream ripped from my throat. I couldn't move my legs, the weight from the ravager keeping me pinned in the sand. Around me, snarls, yelps, and blades sang through the air. A scream, Nafre's maybe, pierced my ears.

With a high-pitched whine, the ravager's weight was gone, and I was suddenly face-up staring at the purple-hued twilight sky. Haedion's face appeared in front of mine, screaming at me to get up and run. But I couldn't hear him, and I'm transported back to the lake when the rusalki had me pinned deep underwater, where sound was distant and voices were carried away in the current.

I couldn't think through the pain. The blistering, angry, white-hot agony began to creep up and down the rest of my leg. My lungs couldn't get a full breath, the pain stealing the oxygen, using it to fuel its mission to spread across my body.

Haedion's face disappeared, replaced with Bastian, I think — my vision wavered, like a ripple across the pond. He scooped me into his arms, cursing as he did, and began sprinting towards the tree line.

"Rhea, just hang on. God dammit, just keep your eyes open!" He commanded, fear making the golden freckles stand out on his face.

But my eyes didn't want to stay open. Each blink was a struggle, and the pain was starting to ebb into a throbbing pulse that beat in time with my racing heart.

"We are almost there. Please, please stay with me," Bastian begged. He took a second to look down at me, and for a moment our eyes locked. His sun-warmed brown eyes blurred in and out of focus. "Haedion is right behind us. I can see some boulders ahead. When we get there, I'm going to help you up and go back to help the others."

"Okay," I whimpered. Darkness had begun to creep into the edges of my vision, blurring everything until all I saw were murky shapes.

"Bastian!" Haedion yelled, his voice tangled with an agonizing scream from someone. I couldn't tell who anymore. Bastian stopped and turned, squeezing me tight against his chest.

"Oh, shit," Bastian readjusted his grip on me before bolting again. When we made it to the nearest boulder, he leveraged me up so I could lie down on the top. The pain from the movement sent sparkles across my vision, and I felt the pull to sweet oblivion. But I couldn't let that happen. If I did, if I succumbed, I didn't think I'd open my eyes again.

"You stay here. Don't move, don't go to sleep. Put some pressure on that bite. Haedion needs help. I'll be right back," Bastian ordered.

I didn't have the energy to speak, so I gave him a weak nod. Satisfied I'd understood him, he ran back toward the group, blade drawn.

I could make out the hazy figures of Haedion and Silas— or at least I believed it was Silas, who stood side by side, slashing at the ravagers. The beasts snarled and jumped to avoid the blades. They backed up in a group and started to circle just as Bastian rejoined the fight.

Where the hell were Nafre and Eiran? My eyes moved sluggishly as I searched for them, but they were nowhere to be found. A horrible sinking feeling pulled at my gut. That scream I'd heard, I thought it had been Nafre. What if they were dead? Nausea churned in my stomach and burned the back of my throat.

A shooting pain up my leg drew my attention back to my body. Looking down at my leg, blood flowed freely out from the shredded material that used to be my pants. Tears pricked at the corners of my eyes as blood ran in rivulets down the side of the rock, like little streams cascading down a mountainside. As I examined the bite, I saw little white specks peeking through the muscle in the sinew. A sickening realization made me suppress a gag. The ravager bit down so hard that they hit bone.

If I didn't stop this bleeding, I would certainly die. The thought should've scared me, but it did the opposite. An overwhelming calm settled over me as I went on autopilot. Reaching for for my bag that managed to stay attached to me during the fight, I dug through it looking for anything I could use to tie pressure around the bite. My vision had gone so I resorted to using my feel for something—anything at all, but it feels empty. Did the Necroscythe prepare an empty bag?

Blinking some clarity into my vision, I looked inside. I could make out the edges of items scattered in the bag, but I couldn't feel them. My hands had gone numb. The numbness traveled from my fingertips, up my arms, across my chest, and raced to my head, where I'm pulled down. The pain was beginning to subside. This wasn't so bad, was it? My heart was racing, like wings of a butterfly against my ribs, keeping it trapped in a cage.

As I lay on my side, my bag and mission abandoned, I could make out the fuzzy outline of Haedion swinging a blade at one last ravager. The creature, favoring its hind leg, circled Haedion, edging closer then back, taunting him. Where were Bastian and Silas? Tears leaked down the side of my face, my arms too weak to wipe them away.

The last thing I saw before I finally gave way to the inevitable darkness was a ravager pouncing on Haedion, both hitting the ground with a horrific scream.

ↂↈↂ

I was floating. Or at least, I think I was floating. Like all those summers, I had floated across the pond with Ari, Marie sitting nervously on the shoreline waiting for us. That feeling of weightlessness, cocooned in the comfortable blanket of the sun-warmed water. This sensation was the same. My eyes felt as though there were weights attached to them, forcing them to remain closed. Oblivion whispered in my ear to join them in the pleasant nothingness. I hovered in this spot, between awareness and the darkness, where I was semi-aware that I was being carried. The warmth of Haedion's skin helps banish the chill the void brings. But in moments of weakness, where Haedion wasn't enough to keep me present, I'm swept away into the blissful abyss.

Had it only been minutes? Or had it been years in this limbo? Time was nothing.

I didn't know where we were going, and I didn't care. All I knew was the pain was gone, the mental stress and toll of the world was gone, and I simply *did not care* anymore. Perhaps this was death, just floating in space. No pain, no cares. And just as I was about to accept the pull back into the deeper depth between the folds of the realms that sparkled like stars, a kernel of pain erupted from somewhere. I couldn't tell where my body was anymore, but the pain was all-consuming. It was the same angry, white-hot blistering pain I felt when I was bitten by the ravager.

How long ago was that? This couldn't be real. Who were those people with me? I could vaguely make out their faces in between the waves of pain, like my mind wanted me to remember who they were. Then one face stopped, and played in my head on repeat. A beautiful face, with dark hair and earthy eyes that I knew were important. Smoke, warmth, and arms wrapped around me.

The pain ebbed and flowed, and I wanted to scream, but tendrils from the veil crept up and weaved their way into my mind. They climbed their way in and consumed me whole. Just when I think I'm about to implode from the pressure, I'm yanked, gratefully, back into the dark.

16

HAEDION

At least the ravager was stupid enough to impale itself on my blade when I purposely left an opening. Silas, with assistance from Bastian, took down the other ravager, leaving both of them double over, panting heavily. The silence was deafening — the only sound was the gentle breeze, and the soft hiccuping sobs from Nafre.

"Eiran," Nafre cried. She had his head resting on her lap, stroking his blood-soaked hair. His eyes were open, unseeing. I knew he was dead the minute the ravager got his jaw around his middle. I hadn't been able to move fast enough to stop him. Bastian and Rhea had just cleared the tree line, and I watched for a moment too long. I should've just trusted Bastian and his ability to protect Rhea. If I'd just been more focused, I could've saved him... I should have saved him. He'll be another name added to my list of those I'd failed.

"Haedion, we need to get back to Rhea. Right now." Bastian said, his tone urgent.

Rhea.

We both broke into a sprint, Bastian leading me to her, leaving Silas to deal with Nafre and the remaining pieces of Eiran's body. If I hadn't been furious with Ka'an for everything he'd done in the past, I was downright murderous now. My brain had skipped right over the part when he shared that he sent out ravagers out of Atheria. Why hadn't I caught on to that? My hands trembled with rage. Those vile creatures he'd created in the likeness of the beasts from Kayar that he adored so much.

My heart nearly stopped when we finally found Rhea, her body curled in on itself. Her blood was tacky on the grey rock, forming little pools of red, as more continued to ooze from the wound on her leg.

Bastian carefully slipped his arms beneath Rhea's limp body, supporting her weight as we eased her down from the boulder, inch by agonizing inch. She didn't stir, but watching her chest rise with quick, rapid breaths ignited a little bit of hope. Lying her on her side, I tore her pant leg wide to reveal the wound from the ravager's bite. A cold fear poured over me. The bite was one of the worst I'd seen. The ravager's jaw clamped too long, the poison in its saliva had seeped into her flesh. It was beginning to fester, just as the venom is designed to do. The edges of the puncture wounds had started turning the muscle and tissue a nauseating green. Small pockets of pus were also beginning to burst and ooze. If the quick work from the poison wasn't enough, it looked like the ravager had nicked an artery. If she weren't fae— the dragon shifter at that, with extraordinary strength and resilience, she would've been dead minutes ago.

"You've got to tie her leg off. Hopefully, it'll stop the flow of the blood and poison and buy us enough time to get her to a healer, or she isn't going to make it," Bastian said.

"You don't think I fucking know that?" I hissed at him. Using my shirt, I tore a long strip and wrapped it around Rhea's leg, tight enough that the flow of the blood lessened— but it was a small bandaid on a massive wound.

"I know you're beating yourself up right now," Bastian muttered under his breath as he sat beside me, waiting for instructions. "But you couldn't have used your magic. It's too big a risk and you know it."

"Shut up," I growled as I tied the final knot, securing the cloth to Rhea's thigh. He was right, though. I could've protected Rhea and saved Eiran, but at the expense of revealing what I was to the world. And that would put more than just our group in danger.

Silas and Nafre finally emerged from the tree line, both wiping at their faces, trying to rid the tears that had left salty trails down their cheeks.

"I'm sorry about Eiran," Bastian said, sitting back on his heels.

"Me too," Nafre replied. Her words come out thick, her voice warbling as she sucked in a shaky breath.

"There are more out there. I dealt a great deal with the ravagers —," I cut myself off. How would I explain that I knew these creatures and what they were capable of? Bastian knew, of course, but I couldn't trust Nafre and Silas with the truth.

"We have run into them before, near Atheria, working for the Necroscythe." Bastian finished for me. "I would guess that they caught our scent, and they split in half. One group probably went toward the library, and the other group found us. But their minds work in strange ways. They almost have one consciousness and can communicate across distances. They've got Rhea's blood in their mind now and they will be able to track her scent."

To Nafre's credit, she seemed to be able to put her grief aside and focus on the moment. It's something Samirah would've admired in a soldier.

"What if I swap clothes with Rhea? Silas, Bastian, and I can lead them away from here with the scent of her blood. We'll go the long way around the mountain and hopefully keep them away from Haedion and Rhea. The village isn't too far from here. I'm certain you can find a healer for her there."

Rhea's body lay between us. The bleeding was under control, but just for the moment. The longer the tourniquet is left on her leg, the bigger the chance that she would lose her leg, if not her life.

Dammit, I didn't want to split up. It made us all easier targets. But Rhea's clothes were drenched in her blood, and it wouldn't be long before the second group of ravagers caught up. The three of them could move a lot faster without Rhea's weighing them down. And I knew Bastian could handle this change in plan.

It's the best chance we had.

"Fine, but let's hurry. I don't know how much time we have."

Nafre quickly stripped down and, with some help from Bastian, switched her clothes with Rhea's. Silas pulled a map from Nafre's bag while they worked and showed me exactly the route they would take. It would take them three days to go around the mountain compared to our one day through the pass in the summer season. It gave me two days to get Rhea healthy enough to travel.

I just hoped it was enough.

"She's ready," Nafre said, straightening out her new outfit, which hung on Nafre in shreds. The pant leg ripped open wide, exposing Nafre's entire thigh, down to her calf, and the bottom half of the tunic dangled in shreds. She looked a mess, but certainly smelled like Rhea, who hadn't stirred during the entire time. And the longer she went without opening her eyes and giving me that scrutinizing look that I'd become so accustomed to, the more I feared she wouldn't ever open her eyes again.

"It has been some time, but last time we were in that village, there was a medwitch who worked there. She was wonderful and helped us when we got into a patch of Poison Reek. Her shop was on the west side of the village with a little blue roof. I am sorry that I cannot recall her name for you," Nafre said, stuffing the map back into her bag.

I felt myself nod, trying to take in all the information and commit it to memory, when all I wanted to do was burn my brother to the ground. What was he thinking, sending *ravagers*? He should've recalled him last night when I told him I had Rhea and we solidified a plan. This was punishment for ignoring him and cutting out conversation short. I was certain.

"I'll see you on the other side. We'll meet at the Inn. The one from last time." Bastian clasped me on the shoulder, then he looked down at Rhea. "She's going to be okay. She's a fighter. And if nothing else, she's strong-willed enough that something like a little dog bite won't be enough to stop her." He tried to smile, but it didn't reach his eyes.

Not wanting to waste another moment, I scooped up Rhea into my arms and broke into a run toward the village.

I sent a prayer of thanks to the Kirios for the first time in two decades when I rounded the corner into the village and found the medwitches' shop was right where Nafre said it would be. Sitting on the western border of the village, I found the small shop with a worn blue roof and fire puffing away, sending smoke up the chimney. The poor medwitch had a damn near heart attack when I nearly broke down her door and thrust Rhea into her arms.

She quickly recovered from the shock and jumped into action, asking what had happened. She nodded as I recalled the bite from the ravager and told her about the venom in its bite. We got to work right away. The medwitch ordered me around the shop, snapping at me to grab her supplies while she whipped together herbs in a muller. We worked for what felt like hours— she muttered enchantments under her breath while I helped pack the wound on Rhea's leg. Every once in a while, Rhea would grimace or groan softly, and each time, the muscles in my heart would constrict to the point of bursting.

"Can't you give her anything for the pain?" I snapped when a tear slipped from the corner of Rhea's closed eye and ran down her cheek. I couldn't help it; seeing her pain was like stabbing myself in my leg and twisting the knife in.

If I had to watch Rhea's face contort in pain one more time, I was afraid of what I might do. Instead of taking offense to my words, the medwitch simply slid a large dose of mirthroot tincture down Rhea's throat.

"I'd give her something stronger, but I don't want it to interfere with the other herbs. This will, if nothing else, numb her mind." She patted my hand gently, then went back to working on Rhea.

I would've given anything to switch places with her. The ravager bites are nasty and often fatal, and I would have traded places with her a million times over just so she wouldn't have to endure what I knew she was feeling right now. Instead, I just held Rhea's hand helplessly, willing the warmth and life back into her.

After what felt like an eternity, the medwitch plopped down in a rickety old chair. "She will be just fine," the woman sighed with relief, and the furrowed lines in her forehead relaxed.

I looked down at Rhea and found her face soft and peaceful. The color returned to her cheeks, with even a faint blush creeping back into her cheeks. She took deep, even breaths, as in nothing more than a deep sleep. The bleeding in her leg had stopped, and the horrific work of the venom had disappeared entirely. Her leg would certainly scar, but at least she kept the limb and her life.

"When will she wake up?" I asked, not willing to look away from her face yet. A kernel of fear wormed its way into my mind that if I stopped watching the slow rise and fall of her chest, her lungs would quit working altogether, and she'd leave me.

"It's hard to tell." She shrugged. "Her body went through something traumatic. But my guess is she'll wake by tomorrow evening. There is a small bedroom upstairs with two small beds. We can move her up there so you can stay with her, and maybe allow you to get some rest as well. Here," she groaned, pushing herself to her feet. She motioned for me to follow. "Pick her up and I'll show you."

I lifted Rhea into my arms, and I followed the woman up a steep, narrow staircase. Every step creaked as we ascended. She opened the first door on the left to reveal a bedroom with two small beds, as she said, with a bathroom directly across the hall.

"Here." She opened the door for me. "You can lay her here." She rushed ahead of me to pull back the sheets.

I gingerly placed Rhea on the soft mattress, covering her with the sheets and heavy handmade quilt. Her hair exploded across the pillow, reminding me all too much of the blood pouring from her on that damn rock. My heart rate skyrocketed once again.

She's okay, I reminded myself. Rhea was going to be just fine.

The medwitch took a step back, giving me a pointed look. "I am going to go make you a cup of tea, as well as prepare you some hot water so you can bathe." I opened my mouth to protest, but she cut me off. "You need a moment for yourself. It's one thing about caregivers, often we forget to take care of ourselves. She is fine, and I will watch over her while you tend to your needs." She took a step back, examining me with such intensity that I almost turned around.

"It's been a long time, hasn't it, Haedion?"

My breath caught in my throat. *Shit.* I recognized her the moment I stumbled through the door, but I was certain she wouldn't remember another face in a crowd from another lifetime, or rather, I prayed she'd forgotten what I'd looked like so many years later.

"Hello, Cora. It has been."

"Don't worry, we'll discuss it later. Or maybe not. I'll be back." She didn't give me a second to protest before she slipped through the door and down the stairs.

When I heard Cora hit the bottom step of the staircase, I took advantage of the moment alone and cast my mind into that cosmic space where I knew Ka'an would answer the knock.

"What the fuck were you thinking?" I couldn't restrain the anger and repulsion that laced my thoughts. *"You thought it would be a good idea to send ravagers? Even after I had told you I had the fae and the situation under control. You should've recalled them after we spoke."* I was seeing red— my rage not just with Ka'an, but with myself. If I could go back, I would have insisted he recall them instead of assuming. He'd changed in the years since Draconia, and I had been a fool.

"Oh, little brother, I didn't think that they would be anything you couldn't handle. Have you grown soft? I thought you'd keep yourself in better shape. Guess not." He was right there; his sinister laugh made my skin crawl with disgust. I bit the inside of my cheek so hard that the taste of iron coated my tongue, keeping me from spilling the words that were on my lips. Words I wanted to say so badly, but would ruin the trap I'd carefully set. He couldn't know that I fully intended to do everything in my power to keep him from getting to Rhea. And if he learned of my betrayal now, he would find me no matter where I hid.

"They're nothing I can't handle, but they nearly killed Rhea. It's made getting to our destination significantly more difficult. You understand that, don't you?"

He cocked his head and paused.

"Rhea," he said her name slowly, as if testing how it felt. *"I was right then, she was the daughter of Agnar and Carina, or was posed as. What a clever rouse they played."*

My heart dropped in my stomach. I hadn't said her name until now.

"I'm glad I disposed of them when I did. I still have the guard tracking her sisters and a few of their staff, but it's only a matter of time until they're captured and taken care of as well," Ka'an added.

"The royal family of Flitmoor?" I asked, doing my best to play dumb while my heart thrummed in my chest, aching with the pain this would

cause Rhea. Her parents were dead and her sisters were missing and being hunted. How much change and heartache could she take?

"*Yes, but forget about it now. I apologize that the ravagers made it more difficult for you to reach Draconia. I will call them off your trail and send them on a new mission. But hurry up, Haedion. She poses a danger to all that I've created, and I want the prismara and her head. How soon will you be there? We have plans to coordinate—*" I held a hand up, cutting him off.

The stairs began to creak again as the Cora started her ascent up the stairs.

"*I have to go.*" I slammed the doorway between our minds, severing the connection, and answered the gentle knock on the door.

RHEA

Ow.

Every inch of my body ached. It was a deep ache, as if I'd worked my body after spending months in bed. However, it was nothing compared to the pain I'd wrestled with in the purgatory that kept me paralyzed and forced to feel every stinging blow to my being.

How long had I been here? And where was I? The blankets wrapped protectively around me were far too warm, and the mattress I lay on was definitely too soft to be in some measly bunker in the desert. Maybe the group had carried me back to the library, where the Necroscythe and his strange magic could have played a role in saving me.

As I am pulled from the comfortable cushion of oblivion into reality, I'm met with the tranquil smell of chamomile tea and lemon. A gentle breeze caressed my cheek, like a soft kiss.

Without opening my eyes, I shifted my body. Testing the movement to see if the pain worsened. The soreness from walking across the desert, the pain from the bite, and even the discomfort from the sunburn on my ivory skin are still there, but manageable. I cracked open my lids, the feat like rolling a boulder up a hill. I scanned the room and found that I was alone. Across the room, an open window sat just above another matching bed, the twin to mine. The disheveled blankets were pulled together in a hurry. So, someone had slept here with me. Had it been Haedion? Bastian?

Soft steps sounded from outside the door, getting louder with every footfall. Panicking, I looked for the dagger I had secured on my thigh this morning. When I ripped back the sheets, I was met with bare legs and a large dressing around my thigh that covered from my groin to my knee.

This morning?

Gods, how long had it been? Where was everyone?

Before I could scramble off the bed and prepare for any type of confrontation, the door swung open, revealing a rather fearsome-looking older woman. Her thick, dark hair, streaked with silver, was pulled back into a severe bun. She balanced a tray with a mix of what looked to be herbs in small jars, white cloth ripped into strips, and a steaming pot of water on her hip.

She turned her back to me, shutting the door with a soft click. When she pivoted back around, she startled to a stop, her mouth slacking in momentary shock. She recovered quickly, and with a slow smile that spread across her face, she said, "I'm glad to see you awake. I didn't expect it to be so soon." The strange woman set the tray down on the bedside table.

"Your boyfriend will be so relieved. He's been driving me crazy with his pacing and relentless questioning. He'll be back soon. I sent him to the market to pick up some provisions to make dinner."

Warmth shot up my neck and across my cheeks. Boyfriend? Did he tell her that's who he was to me? Is Haedion the only one here? Where were the others? I had so many questions, but the words were trapped in my throat, caught on that *one* word.

"I can see I've embarrassed you. I'm sorry. I tend to assume too much. Is he not your boyfriend?" She asked, pouring a mixture of herbs into the steaming pot before closing the lid to let them steep.

"I, uh-," I stuttered, trying to clear my mind to form an intelligent thought. My head felt sluggish like wading through a thick, viscous liquid. Each attempt to grasp a clear thought was met with a dull ache behind my eyes.

"We gave you some mirthroot to help you sleep and numb your mind while I worked. You may be feeling the effects of it still. Don't worry, it'll wear off soon." She threw the strips of cloth into the pot next, closing the lid to let those soak as well. I just nodded, watching her work. Mirthroot, that explained the slowness of my thoughts. But there were holes in my memory and questions I still needed answers to. What had happened after the ravagers attacked? Was I the only one injured?

"I didn't expect you to wake till this evening. I was able to remove all the ravager venom from your blood and stop the bleeding. But you will, unfortunately, have a rather nasty scar. I've been changing your dressings every couple of hours. They are steeped in a concoction of herbs that, when brought to a boil and reapplied frequently, promote faster healing. I think you'll be pleasantly surprised at the state of the bite. I wanted to do one last dressing change, then it should be good to go."

She pulled back the bandage to reveal my leg. The last time I saw it, I'd been on the rock after Bastian left me to help Haedion. Blood had poured from the bite, the edges turning green from the venom. Any normal person should have succumbed to the injury. But, I was not a normal person, I had to remind myself.

She took her time gently removing the white cloth, tinted a light brown from the herbs, making sure not to pull at the edges of the wound as it finished knitting the skin back together. When she finally removed all the cloth, I could see my wound for the first time.

I had to be hallucinating, I decided. The bite, one that had left a gaping wound exposing fragments of bone, had miraculously healed. All that was left was a rather haggard, uneven scar. The edges of my skin were a bright pink and raised, which I'm sure would remain like that. But I am healed, stitched together by this medwitch.

"How did you do it?" I asked her. I was in awe of the woman as she worked to apply the fresh dressings to my leg.

"Haedion did a good job of applying pressure to your wound before getting you here. Herbs, tinctures, and a touch of magic also played a big part in your healing and keeping the scar from being any worse. But the biggest help was you." She looked at me with a pointed, knowing look. "Fae blood heals much faster than humans, you know."

"He told you?" I asked, wondering how much information Haedion had been forced to give up to get me the help I'd needed.

"No, he didn't have to. Your body told me. Your skin had already started to heal and stitch back together by the time he got you here. I had to cut it back open to clear out the venom so it wouldn't become infected. No normal human can heal like that. The only other time I saw anything like that was when I was a healer for the fae many years ago." She finished applying the last cloth. To hold it together, she took a dry, gauzy towel and wrapped it around my thigh.

"You were a healer for the fae?" I prodded. Someone who knew them? Worked with them? Cared for them?

She sat down on the bed across from me and didn't respond for a moment. Or did she even pause? The mirthroot she gave me to numb the pain needed to wear off soon so I could get a grip on reality instead of floating around the room, trying to hold on to her words like a lifeline.

"I was," she replied. "And you, my dear, look just like your mother. Your hair is the same as hers, but I see your farther in you as well. " A sad smile pulled at the corners of her mouth.

My mother? My father? This woman had known my parents—a million questions caught on the edge of my tongue.

"You knew them?" I blinked hard, hoping reality would even out and my world would stop spinning on its axis.

"You lie back and relax. I'm going to make you a cup of tea, and then I'll tell you the story of how I knew your parents."

Without waiting for my response, she moved quickly out the door and down the stairs. Before I could adjust myself on the pillows into a more comfortable position, she was back, a steaming cup of tea in hand. Chamomile and lemon, just as I'd suspected. She gingerly handed me the cup, taking care that I didn't spill and that it was firmly in my grasp before sitting on the bed across from me. The first warm sip coated my tongue and moved throughout my body, and instantly, I felt more awake.

"We haven't been properly introduced," she said as she folded her hands in her lap. "My name is Cora. I've lived here since the death of your family. I take care of the villagers who live here and travelers who pass through."

"I'm Rhea," I replied, with another tentative sip.

"Oh, Rhea." She placed her hand over her heart. "Agnar and Carina kept your name. I so hoped they would. When your mother was pregnant with you, your parents spent ages debating names. What would they call you? Would you have a nickname? A family name? On and on they went in circles. It was actually quite funny." Cora went quiet as if recalling the memories. "I was your mother's midwife. Her pregnancy had been particularly rough. She'd been constantly ill, spending the majority of her time in bed. Once you were born, though, she was advised to keep you a secret. Only a select few of us knew about you."

"Why?" I asked, and the information danced around me like thought bubbles. I watched to reach for each one and hold it close— examine it and commit it to memory. Pieces of who I was that I didn't even know existed to anyone anymore.

"Gashion, your grandfather, and the last dragon shifter, believed that you were in danger. Alamae and Jordi were wise to accept his advice and kept you far away from Draconia."

"The night of your parents' murder — the party," she paused, taking a deep breath, her face twisted as if trying to rein in tears. "Gashion had said he had an exciting announcement, it's the whole reason we threw a celebration. Your aunt had just fallen pregnant with a son, so we had anticipated that was the news he was going to share. We were all so excited. Your mother had just had you, and then we would have another baby, but of course, we kept you a secret." Her eyes were distant as she spoke, as if the memories were replaying in her mind's eye.

"Your grandfather rose and began to share that the next dragon shifter was going to be born and that two of his daughters were expecting children— Alamae and Karish. That's when Ka'an unleashed his dark plan. It was nothing we'd ever expected from him." Tears began to fall on sun-worn cheeks. Cora, not lifting a hand to wipe them away, continued to let them race down her face. "I don't know if he was just so proud that he was going to have two grandchildren, or if he knew a secret we did not. But your mother had already had you and tucked you away for safekeeping."

"I was there when they died, and I hid," she choked back a sob. "Like a coward, I hid as he slaughtered everyone in that room. When he left, thinking everyone was dead, with his poor brother sobbing over Eden's body, I went looking for your mother. I hoped — prayed out loud to the Kirios that I might find her alive. And, well, you know I didn't."

"You survived, though," I whispered.

"I did. I made sure I did. Alamae had made me promise that if anything happened to her or Jordi, I would take you to Agnar and Carina in Flitmoor. They'd been good friends and knew what they would have to do to protect you," Cora said, dabbing her eyes with an embroidered handkerchief from her apron pocket.

Alamae and Jordi. My parents. Their names sounded strange in my mind as I repeated them over and over. Gashion, and Eden, and Karish and shifters, and Ka'an, and a brother? He'd had a brother? Who was he? Where was he now, if he was even still alive? And what were dragon shifters? The fae had magic, yes, that I knew. But shifting magic, like the Necroscythe? It was nothing I'd ever heard of or read in the censored books from the library back home.

But how could I? If Ka'an had wanted to hide secrets of the fae, he easily did it except in the two most protected places in the world: the Necroscythe's perfectly curated library in the desert and the catacombs of Draconia.

"Ah, you're awake." Haedion's voice interrupted my hazy thoughts. He was leaning against the doorframe with Cora's bag of supplies tucked safely in the crook of his arm.

"Wonderful, you're back!" Cora hopped up and took the bag from Haedion. She squeezed his shoulder gently and whispered just loud enough that I could hear,

"I told you she'd wake up."

"You did, indeed," he gave her a soft-eyed smile of pure gratitude.

"I will give you two sometime. I am going to make a stew for dinner. Haedion tells me you need to get over the mountain to

Eldridge. As long as you stay in bed for the day, eat what I feed you, and rest, I can't see any reason you won't be ready to go by tomorrow morning," Cora commented as she dug through the bag, examining the contents.

"Thank you, Cora," Haedion said. The way he spoke to her was different. A true understanding seemed to pass through them. Not something cultivated in the hours I'd be unconscious. She patted him gently on the cheek before disappearing from my view down the stairs.

Haedion closed the door behind her and took Cora's place on the bed across from me. There were dark circles under his eyes, once again.

"You're alive," he broke the silence first.

"I am."

"So," he said, leaning back on the bed. "What do you remember?

"Not much," I admitted. "Whatever she gave me is making me fuzzy." I shook my head, attempting to clear the cloudiness from my mind. The overload of information, mixed with the trauma my body endured, with the mirthroot mixed in, my mind felt like toast left on the stove too long.

"Tell me, what happened?" I begged. I needed the spots of my memory restored.

"The mirthroot will wear off soon. She gave you a heavy dose." He sat up, bracing his elbows on his legs. "After Bastian got you to safety and returned, he helped Silas and me kill the remaining ravagers. They work in one large pack and split off into groups to hunt. The ravagers we faced were a smaller group of a larger pack. Their mind is a collective consciousness. I'm not sure how it works. But they got the taste of your blood in their mind. Your clothes were covered in your blood. There was no way I could get help for you without them catching up to us. So, Nafre offered to switch clothes with you and take Silas and Bastian with her the long way around the mountain to draw the ravagers off your scent. We are in the village just at the base of the mountain."

"You said Nafre, Silas, and Bastian. What happened to Eiran?" But

I knew the answer to my question already. Haedion looked down, playing with a loose thread in the quilt.

"I got distracted watching Bastian get you to the tree line. A ravager attacked Eiran and gutted him so fast that I couldn't do anything. He was dead before he hit the ground," he said, his voice thick with regret.

A knot formed in my throat, and guilt settled in. If it hadn't been for us, Eiran would have never been there. He'd still be alive, traveling with Nafre and Silas. Or they'd be at the library or Flitmoor or anywhere but dead. This was my fault. I wanted to cry and scream for Eiran, for the pain and loss that I knew Nafre and Silas had to be feeling. A loss that could never be replaced. I never wanted anyone to get hurt for me.

I should've never let them come with us. I should've gone on my own to Draconia.

"They knew what they were getting into when they discovered who you were. They could've backed out and left us at the library, but they didn't. They took the Necroscythe up on his offer and his bargain. Don't let his death stop you from pushing forward. Just add it to your list of those you mourn at night."

"Is that what you do?" I whispered, unable to look Haedion in the eye.

He went quiet, shoulders drooped, as if fighting the bad memories and stuffing them in a box in his mind like I did. His dark hair was long enough now that it nearly shielded his eyes. I reached out and brushed it back out of his face.

"You need a haircut," I muttered as I let my fingers play in the dark strands of his hair. Haedion grabbed my wrist; the movement was quick, catching me off guard. Or maybe it was the mirthroot dulling my reactions. He brought it to his mouth and placed a gentle kiss on my palm. My stomach erupted with tingles watching his lips caress my skin.

Before thinking could get the better of me, I slipped my hand around his neck and pulled him to me. Our lips clashed together in a mix of want and need. A groan escaped from him between breaths. The sound was intoxicating, and I couldn't get enough. I leaned back into the pillows, dragging him with me. He allowed me to pull him on top of me, settling his weight over me just enough that I could feel him, but not too much pressure to hurt my injured leg.

"Rhea," he moaned, sucking my lip between his teeth. "You are," he kissed me hard again, "going to be the death of me." Between the energy of each kiss and the mirthroot that still flowed through me, the sensation was near euphoric. I kicked free from the quilt and wrapped a leg around his waist. I wanted to be closer. I *needed* to be closer to him.

Haedion reached down and traced the exposed skin of my hip, down to my knee, all the way up my side. Chills — or maybe it was sparks— appeared on my skin where he touched me.

I could taste the smile that formed on his lips. "We should really stop, little Enya. You nearly died in my arms yesterday."

"I'm going to die if you stop kissing me." I cringed the moment the words left my mouth. No way, I just fucking said that.

I was never taking mirthroot again.

Curse the Kirios.

Haedion laughed as he pulled back. He planted a kiss on my nose and then stood. "I promise you won't die if I stop kissing you. But you could die if we don't follow Cora's instructions and let you rest." He pointed to the cup of tea Cora poured earlier. "Drink that. Nap. Heal."

I opened my mouth to protest, but Haedion sent me a dark look, as if begging me to ignore his orders. He leaned down slowly, bracing a hand on the headboard above me, trapping me against the bed. And in the lowest, most husky whisper that made me clamp my thighs together, he murmured, "If you don't stay here and focus on healing, I will tie you to this bed myself."

My mouth flopped open in shock. With a smirk, as if he knew exactly what his words did to me, he walked to the door. "I'm going to see if I can help Cora with dinner. You. Stay."

❧ 18 ❧

HAEDION

I walked along a calm sandy beach, where the waves lapped lazily against the sand. The water was lukewarm, pooled around my ankles as I went, with no clear direction in mind. In the distance, stone grey storm clouds formed against the dark navy sky — reminding me of home.

"Little brother," Ka'an's voice whispered, carried in on a phantom wind from the ocean my dreams had conjured.

"We need to talk," he said, and instantly I'm transported to the empty dream space we created, just for moments like these. Moments we needed to speak face to face when the distance separated us. The room we utilized when we were young soldiers at home, training for a war we didn't realize the intricacies of. Where we were taught to blindly follow orders, to have no feelings and desires of our own, just the main goal of the vesperians: revenge. This was different than the doorway where we could speak mind to mind. We could create here, build in here. But only in our deepest sleep.

He stood in front of me, looking the same as I'd seen him in our previous encounters the days before, but this time there was something different in his demeanor. The way his eyes scanned my face, and the way his jaw ticked. Was he becoming concerned? Or had he started

to sense my deception? Before Rhea, I tolerated my brother and acqui-
esced to his demands to help him grow his power. I did the bare
minimum to lead him to believe I wanted him to remain ruler of
Nador for the first five years of his reign. Until now, we hadn't spoken
in nearly two decades. He was not the same vesperian as he was when
we first entered our mission. But neither was I.

"What do you need?" I asked, trying to hide the tone of disgust.
The anger for betraying our plans and everything that has followed
since the massacre of the fae. For killing Gashion and Eden. For nearly
killing Rhea.

The list was growing.

"You keep cutting me off. Do you not want to speak with me? Are
you getting second thoughts?" He looked at me pointedly.

My heart began to pound wildly in my chest. "No, of course not." I
lied. "But I have to keep up the game on my end, and that requires me
to be present."

"Fine, but you should be getting close to Draconia with the girl,
right?" He clasped his hands behind his back and started to pace — the
habit he picked up from years of watching our superiors walk up and
down our formations where they picked us apart for the most insignifi-
cant flaw.

"We are a day from Eldridge. From there, we just have to hire a
vessel to carry us from Eldridge to Draconia." I confirmed, keeping my
voice steady as I watched him pace. The habit made my skin crawl. I
just had to get her to the catacombs, let her hear the prophecy, get the
prismara, and then we could return to the library, where we could keep
her safe.

"Do you have a plan to get the prismara from her without raising
her suspicions? Have you built enough trust that she'd willingly hand it
over?" He asked, eyeing me as he paced.

"I have," I nodded, knowing it was not a lie. I fully believed Rhea
would hand me the Prismara if I asked.

The thought of betraying her made my stomach roll.

"Wonderful," he said. "Don't worry about getting to Draconia. I
have already hired a vessel and crew. They will be waiting for you in
Eldridge. You will find them at the dock, just look for the largest ship.

They will transport you to the island. They've been commanded to let me know the moment she enters the catacombs. I will meet you there, and you can retrieve the prismara for me. Then we can end the line of the fae. The ones who kept us buried, who treated our kind as though we were nothing but the dirt under their feet. Failure is not something I am willing to accept again."

My heart began to pound in my chest so loud I was certain Ka'an would hear it. He had *never* mentioned he would be traveling to Draconia to retrieve the prismara in person. Curse all the realms, this was going to be a nightmare before. But now?

I had to keep myself calm and composed. Any small twitch could alert him to my plan to betray him. If he sensed anything, it could end in disaster.

"I didn't realize that you were going to meet us in Draconia. I thought you wanted me to bring the girl and Prismara to Atheria?" I inquired, keeping my tone light, but prodding just enough. I needed to see where his mind was at.

"This is too important to risk you traveling the distance with her and the stone. Anything could happen." He glared at me, but then stopped in his tracks.

"When are you going to accept my offer to help me rule Haedion?" His face softened ever so slightly. "I'm not sure I could think of a better offer. You'd have your choice of territory, your guard, anything you could want. It could all be under your control."

"You know that I was not born to be a ruler," I replied. This conversation was one we'd had so many times in the past. Ka'an was primed to rule, to take command, and follow the vision of Samirah's army. I was born to be his second in command.

"But imagine, with the girl dead, we could stay here and rule together. Samirah will continue to wait, and *we*," he emphasized the word, gesturing between us. "Can rule. We spent years following orders. But now, we have the power." A sadistic, wicked grin crept across his face. "These humans and one simple fae, they are nothing compared to us. It's our true values at our core. Power, strength, and ability. These creatures," He laughed. "They're nothing compared to us. So why don't you come join me? I know you've been holding back your own magic that I know flows within you. You can do so much more with it than you have. I have *seen* you do more."

"When we don't return, Samirah will find a way back here and see you on her throne. She'll be pissed. More than pissed, she'll burn down Nador and string you up for treason."

"I'll make decisions as I see fit if that time comes." He replied coolly.

"And I'm sure they'll be great decisions." I resisted the urge to roll my eyes. Of course, he didn't have a plan. He's continuing to lead with his narcissism and god-like vision of himself. And while he might be powerful, he wasn't Samirah.

"Very well, then. I shall see you in the throne room in Draconia. Our reunion will be one to remember."

With a wave of his hand, the dreamscape dissipated, and I'm back in bed. My eyes flew open, and I was met with the dim light of the bedroom in Cora's shop. Light from the sun was just starting to shift the sky from the midnight dark to violet blue just before dawn— I still had time.

I did my best to calm the pounding in my chest with slow, deep breaths. I slipped from the warm comfort of the quilt, quickly threw on my clothes, and slipped out the door, leaving Rhea blissfully asleep. She'd followed Cora's orders to remain in bed and ate anything we brought to her. By the time we turned in for the night, her leg was completely healed and her strength almost fully returned. One more night's sleep, and it would be like the ravager attack never happened... except the scar that ran the length of her thigh that send daggers of pain through my heart every time I saw it.

I descended the steps, each stair creaking under my feet, then I was out the front door. I angled my steps towards the tree line, away from prying eyes and far enough away that I wouldn't draw unnecessary attention.

My mind spun, and with each step I took, the spinning increased. How could I keep Rhea from Ka'an without cluing him into my betrayal? The longer he believed I was working with him and not against him, the better.

I've done my best to avoid thinking of Kayar for the last fifty years, specifically the last twenty or so. I'd worked very hard to bury the memories of the Fallen Goddess, who left Nador centuries ago to save her people from the atrocities committed by the fae. Samirah created a world where her people could escape, hide, and prepare to unleash against the fae who'd mistreated us, and kept us as slaves for centuries.

If Rhea had any clue who I was, what I could do — she'd run away. Or kill me. She should want to kill me.

She should kill me— two birds with one stone.

Once I was far enough away from the village, I stopped walking. The comment from Ka'an kept echoing in my mind. I was out of practice, and he knew it. Shaking out my limbs, I reached deep inside myself where I'd buried the shadows. They've been lurking in my veins, begging to be stretched and worked more and more. The wings that poked and pulled at the skin of my back twitched with excitement, but I couldn't let those free. Not yet.

"Alright," I sighed. Shadows and dark smoke poured from my fingertips when I mentally removed the stop I'd kept them hidden behind. Some swirled around me, and some, of their own accord, explored the surrounding landscape. They inched up into the closest pine trees, across the limbs, and rained down from the sky above me.

The release was amazing, like a mental block had been removed. With the weight gone, the thoughts flowed easily through me. Each problem, each path to a different solution, shown clearly as the day in front of me. My wings tore through my shirt, breaking free after spending months and months in confinement underneath the prison of my skin.

Well, dammit. I'd need a new shirt.

I had to get Rhea to Draconia to retrieve the prismara. If I didn't show up at the vessel Ka'an hired, he'd know something was wrong and come looking. My only hope was going to be in trying to convince Rhea not to come back from the catacombs. Beg and plead with her to have the dragons show her how to open the portal and have her return to the library with Bastian, Nafre and Silas. The prismara and Rhea would be out of his grasp. Then I'll only have to worry about dealing with my brother's wrath alone.

It's the best idea I had.

After a time, I called the shadows back in. They came, protesting as they did, disappearing back into nothing, and the magic returned to my veins.

"Hello, Haedion," Cora said from behind me. I cursed quietly. When I turned to face Cora, instead of finding anger or resentment, I saw a face full of pity and sympathy.

"Are you working with him?" She asked. She didn't need to say who — we both knew.

"I was." I had no interest or energy to hide from her when I knew she knew my truths.

"And now?"

"No."

"Why is that?" She approached, digging in a basket hanging from the crook of her elbow. She pulled out a fresh loaf of bread. Ripping it in half, she handed me a piece.

"I didn't know who she'd be to me when I accepted my brother's request to help him. He'd promised he would send me home. I didn't want to be here, watching him terrorize Nador any longer." I bit into the still-warm bread. Cora took the lead, and we slowly began our walk back to her shop.

"I always knew you were never involved with Ka'an's plan," she remarked, linking her arm through mine, leaning on me slightly as we walked. A limp I hadn't notice before became evident as we traveled over the uneven forest floor.

"How?" My brows shot up.

"Your love for Eden wasn't fake; anyone could see that. You would've never intentionally hurt her or her family. You loved Gashion and he loved you." She squeezed my arm. "But, since we are being honest, what was the mission?"

"We were instructed by Samirah to mend relations and, eventually, open the portal between the realms. We were trained to be ready for anything. But Ka'an went rogue. I don't know if it was his own idea or something more he conjured up between him and Samirah. When he realized he couldn't gain entry into the catacombs to retrieve the prismara and open the realms, he took on the role of dictator of Nador. He's punishing everyone in the realm for the sins committed by the fae against the vesperians centuries ago." I trailed off, my chest constricting at the painful memories. "He didn't tell me what he was going to do that night."

"Did you know I brought Rhea to her parents in Flitmoor?" She asked, hanging heavily on my arm for support, stumbling on the river stone littering the floor.

"No," I replied, but it didn't surprise me.

"I made a stop on the way, though."

"To whom?"

"The Necroscythe. I begged him to put a shield in Rhea's mind to protect her from anything she'd seen and from the magic. So that perhaps she could grow into an adult before her magic showed. She'd maybe have a chance." She pulled me to a halt, spinning me to face her.

"And did he?" I wondered.

"He did." She nodded. "But there is far more to him than I think any of us realizes. He never confirmed it, but I think he knew that your brother was up to something and warned Gashion before he died, in turn, saving Rhea."

My mind whirled at the possibility. The Necroscythe's life had been infinite, stating he'd been here before the fae and vesperians, before the creation of humans, and lived to see the downfall of it all and the disappearance of the Kirios. But how he could've known Ka'an was up to something without being in his presence left me questioning it all.

"Another reason I'll be in his debt forever," I muttered under my breath. He'd protected Rhea long before I could.

We walk the rest of the way back to the village in silence. The world was beginning to wake. Birds chirped, jumping between branches, and the smoke from freshly stoked fires caught the breeze, filling my nose with the scent of burning wood. Just before we reached her shop, Cora stopped and pointed to the stables down the way.

"There is a man who owns those stables. Tell him I sent you for two horses. He'll give you a good deal. Traveling on horseback will get you through the pass faster, and it'll be better on Rhea's leg. She's healed, but let's not push it."

We departed, with me in the direction of the stables and Cora toward her shop.

I was sitting at Cora's kitchen table, sipping on a cup of tea, watching her make breakfast, when Rhea finally stumbled her way down the stairs. When our eyes locked from across the room, a pink blush bloomed across her cheeks. The blood warming her cheeks did something primal to me, and all I wanted to do was take her upstairs and show her how much I needed her. I was dying to hear my name on her tongue with my mouth between her —

"Ah, there you are!" Cora said, interrupting my thoughts. "Here, come sit, come sit." She waved Rhea over to sit next to me at the small table. Cora poured Rhea a cup of tea, setting it down in front of her.

"How are you feeling?" Cora inquired as she piled the breakfast hash she'd been working on to two plates for us.

Rhea wrapped her delicate fingers around the warm mug. "My leg aches a little, but nothing like it was, and it's nothing I can't handle," Rhea said. From where I sat, I could see her tracing her new scar with her fingertips under the table. She took a sip of the steaming tea, and her shoulders visibly relaxed from the taste. A content smile bloomed on her face, with the rosiness in her cheeks — my god, what I would give to live forever with her in this moment.

"I'm so glad that it's healed so wonderfully," Cora remarked, settling down the plates of food in front of us.

"Thank you, Cora," Rhea sighed softly before digging into her breakfast.

"Yes, thank you for everything. I don't know what I would've done without you." I echoed Rhea's gratitude.

"It's my pleasure." Cora busied herself cleaning the kitchen. "Early this morning, Haedion went out and was able to secure you both horses to help you travel over the pass. Even though your leg is healed, you don't want to do too much too fast.

Rhea's smile was enough to make my knees weak.

"When do we get going?" She wondered, covering her mouth with her hand as she chewed.

"As soon as you're ready," I replied.

"I'll prepare you both lunches to eat on the way to Eldridge. It's a good thing you're traveling this time of the year. Winter months make the pass so treacherous." Cora walked up and handed Rhea a small package, wrapped in plain brown paper.

"When you get to Draconia, and the world is right again, I want you to open this."

Rhea nodded before setting the gift down on the table. I could see the tears blooming in her eyes as she pulled Cora into a tight embrace. As they stood there, arms wound around each other, I could see a piece of Rhea heal.

"You are the key to restoring the world, my dear," Cora murmured. "And I believe in you."

19

RHEA

Haedion spent the day asking me every question imaginable to pass the time. And when i'd venture to ask him about himself, he'd just smiled softly and promised he'd give me all the answers back at the library.

The waves broke against the rocky ocean terrain as we descended into the outskirts of Eldridge. A break in the trees made way for a small opening just off the trail. I guided my horse, Luna, as I'd come to learn her name, through the opening that led us to an unobscured view of the ocean. In front of us, small spits of land, covered in dark green foliage, dotted the ocean. The sight was nothing like I'd ever seen. The ocean was not quiet and gentle, listlessly lapping against the sand. It was raging and fierce, slamming relentlessly against the rocky ledges.

"I love Eldridge," Haedion said as he maneuvered his gelding, Solen, next to me. "The ocean, the landscape, the people. It's all so intriguing."

"Will I need my cape and hood here?" I asked, already reaching for my bag where I knew my cape was folded on top.

"No, not here. Your eyes are a dead giveaway to what you are, but the people here won't say anything."

"Why not?"

"Eldridge values its distance from Ka'an. The last thing they want to do is bring his attention here."

I didn't know how to respond to that. I couldn't imagine a place in Nador that wasn't under the scrutiny of Ka'an.

"I've never seen anything like this," I finally said after minutes of silence. I was so captivated by the beauty that all I could do was stare. I took my time, observing every detail of every little island in front of us, from the spruce trees to the ferns growing on the cliff edge. On the smallest island closest to us, two little amber colored eyes appeared from behind a small rock. They blinked slowly, watching me watch them. It tilted its little head to the side, and from a distance, I swore I could make out two little horns.

What *was* that?

"Haedion, do you see that?" I asked, pointing to where the golden eyes were.

"See what?" He followed my line of sight, squinting as he searched the landscape.

"Well, that's something you don't see every day," he muttered, his eyebrows creasing slightly. "We need to get down to Eldridge." He pulled on the reins, backing up Onyx, and grabbed hold of Luna's rein, guiding us away from the cliff edge.

"What was that?" I twisted in my seat, looking back over my shoulder, trying to get another glimpse of the unknown creature.

"Don't stare too long, we don't want to draw its mother's attention," he quipped, and my head snapped to face him.

"Its mother?" My head bounced between the island where the tiny eyes disappeared and Haedion.

"Yes, its mother." He tilted his head back, nervously scanning the tree branches.

"Then what is it?" I pressed.

"I've never heard of them leaving Draconia before. I know we're close, but I didn't think they left the island." He muttered more to himself than to me. "It must be you."

"Are you saying that was a dragon?" I pulled Luna to a stop. Excitement and curiosity ran through me. "I want to go back."

"Rhea," Haedion huffed, turning to face me with a look of exasperation mixed with a tone of desperation. "That was a small dragon, a baby. They get much, much larger than that. And their mother won't be too far behind. They are wickedly protective of their young. If, for a second, its mother thinks we are a danger, I don't think they will stop to think who *you* are. I know you want to see a dragon. I promise you will, but it needs to be at the right time. And certainly not a baby *without* its mother."

What he said makes sense, even if my curiosity was begging me to turn back. But what would cause them to be outside of the island?

"Why do you think they're out here?" I questioned.

He's quiet for a moment before kicking Solen forward. He says over his shoulder, "They're probably waiting for you."

৩৯৯

Eldridge was everything you'd expect from a coastal village whose livelihood was fishing, but its goal was entertaining bored sailors and taking their hard-earned coin. The moment we dropped the horses off at the stables and stepped out onto the grey cobblestone streets, I was met with the briny, salty sea air while the wheels of wagons pulled by livestock clunked down the uneven pathways toward home for the evening. As we walked, Haedion grabbed my hand, placing it on his arm, keeping me close to his side. Store owners were closing down their shops for the night just as the pubs were opening their doors. The buildings were sad mixes of grays and browns, with salt-stained wooden roofs following our journey toward the center of the city.

The deeper we wandered into Eldridge, the larger the town became. The building began to evolve from small shops and delicate neighborhoods to pubs, taverns, pleasure houses, and inns. Scantily dressed women hugged the corners, making flirtatious eyes at the men who came near, and sailors swore loudly, spilling their drinks as they laughed. This place was *so* different than home. No soldiers loomed in the dark, and no sign of Ka'an's presence. Flitmoor should've been like this, all the time. It was like a celebration every day, not just twice a year.

"How are we going to find Bastian, Nafre, and Silas?" I stood on my toes to whisper in Haedion's ear over the music drifting through the open doors of the nearest tavern.

Haedion leaned down, his nose skimming the shell of my ear. "There is an inn just down from here. Last time I was here with Bastian, we stayed there."

We walked a few more feet before Haedion jerked me to a stop. "I can't believe I forgot about this place!" He exclaimed, pointing to a small bakery, packed to the seams with patrons filtering in and out through the open doors.

"Stay here. Don't move, I'll be right back." I watched as he rushed into the crowd of people and disappeared. A small smile etched across my face. Seeing Haedion excited did something to me that I didn't expect. He seemed happy here, relaxed. I wanted to see more of this side of him.

While I waited, I found a spot against the wall across from the bakery. The noise, the smell, and the people around me put Flitmoor to shame when it came to the culture. I'd love to see the village during a celebration. Groups of people mingled and drank, and I could imagine how the city would throw a solstice celebration. The bonfires, the flags hanging between the rooftops, and the music that would filter through the roads like a song on the wind.

Movement from the corner of my vision caught my attention. A man peeled away from a group of sailors and started to walk toward me, his steps unsteady and sluggish. My stomach sank, and my heart began to thump unevenly in my chest. I could feel his eyes on me as he swaggered closer. Behind him, his friends shouted encouragement, to which he turned and made a vulgar gesture. I resisted the urge to roll my eyes and instead crossed my arms over my chest and did my best to appear uninterested.

I didn't look at him as he approached, the nauseating smell of alcohol hitting before he was even close enough to hear over the crowd. The fire under my skin started to react to my nerves, rising to the surface as if to come to my aid. Sweat beaded on my forehead, the mixture of the hot, humid summer night air combined with fire brimming just under the surface. I stared at the bakery, silently pleading for Haedion to return.

"Hi, beautiful," the man said, slurring his words. He stumbled a little as he leaned one shoulder against the wall just next to me. I balled my hands into fists to resist the urge to cover my nose and hide the gag I was forcing down.

I ignored him and willed Haedion to reappear through the crowd. *Please, please hurry up.*

"Are you waiting for someone?" He pestered, standing up straight. He moved, placing himself directly in front of me, blocking my view of the bakery.

"Yes. Now, please leave me alone." I kept my voice firm and direct as I shifted my body a step to the side. He moved with me, keeping his body in line with mine. The man leaned over me, placing one hand on each side of my body, effectively boxing me in. I was trapped.

"Don't be like that, sweeeeeheart," he slurred, catching on the word. "I just want to show you a good time." Without warning, he forced his mouth against mine. He smelled like dead fish and stale alcohol. His tongue pushed against my lips and into my mouth, as I beat against his chest. Anger ran through me like a fire through dry grass in a sun-scorched field. When he released me with a sultry smile on his face, a new sense of rage overcame me, and without hesitating, I slammed my fist into the side of his face. My knuckles screamed from the impact, but it's muted compared to the fury I felt at the violation. He staggered back, nearly tripping and landing on his ass. A few of his friends stared in shock, while the other half burst into howls of laughter, pointing and taunting their friend, who rubbed his jaw where I'd hit him.

I'm about to start for the bakery when a dark figure that moved faster than my eyes could register, picked up the drunk and slammed him against the wall. Haedion pinned the sailor so high on the wall that his legs dangled freely off the ground. He struggled against Haedion for a moment before he gave up, his eyes widening in terror.

"She told you to leave her alone," Haedion said, his voice ominously calm— which scared me even more. A midnight aura surrounded him, as though the shadows climbed out of the dark and now cloaked Haedion in their mist.

"And then you have the audacity to try to shove your tongue down her throat. Such poor manners. If I didn't have places to be, I'd kill you right here." His voice dropped lower, the threat of violence laced every syllable.

The crowd hushed, all turning to stare at the confrontation. I wasn't sure if it was the fact that Haedion had a man lifted off the ground, or if it was the tendrils of smoke that appeared to be moving around them that drew more attention. Either way, I needed to get Haedion out of here before we caused any more of a scene.

"Let's just go, Haedion. I'm fine." I yanked on his arm, silently begging him to look at me. He didn't move for a moment, as the sailor's breaths came out in ragged, fearful gasps.

"I'm- I'm sorry!" The man apologized. "I won't do it again!"

Haedion released the man with a disgusted scoff, letting him fall to the ground with a hard thud. The sailor scrambled to his feet, not waiting around for permission, and bolted toward his group of friends, who all stared dumbfounded at Haedion and me.

"We're going," Haedion snapped, wrapping his arm protectively around my shoulders as he guided me down the street.

"Haedion, it's okay," I insisted, hoping to ease the tension that he held in his shoulders, but he just shook his head, and I got the message.

We entered through the walkway of a popular pub that boasted large double doors greeted us, held open by ship's anchors. Inside, the atmosphere buzzed with energy. Small, intimate tables were half-hidden behind dark red curtains, perfect for private meetings or less formal conversations, while more public tables and a dance floor covered the rest of the space.

"Find a table," Haedion gestured absently toward the nearest alcove, not looking at me. He stalked off toward a man behind the bar counter who smiled and waved as he saw Haedion approaching.

Oh boy, he was still pissed.

"Rhea!" I heard my name moments before I was slammed into, and wrapped in an embrace. Bastian's arms held me tight as he lifted me in a spin.

Nafre and Silas stood behind Bastian, looking just as they did last time I saw them. But, I could see the loss in their eyes and subdued looks. Like they'd wanted to celebrate reaching Eldridge, but couldn't. We were missing Eiran. The thought was a bitter taste in my mouth, and guilt settled in my stomach.

"I knew you'd be okay!" Bastian exclaimed. With one more tight squeeze, he released me.

"How was your trip around the mountain?" I asked, taking a seat in the alcove they'd occupied. The three of them squished together on the bench seat across the table from me.

"It was a long couple of days," Nafre responded as she settled between Bastian and Silas, keeping her arms tucked tight together. "And we had to leave your clothes along the way. But we didn't think you'd mind. After your attack, they resembled rags more than actual clothing."

I shrugged. I didn't mind. I was just grateful that they were willing to risk themselves for me, despite the money the Necroscythe had offered.

"Did the ravagers catch up?" I asked, just as Haedion returned. He slid into the bench seat next to me, casually placing his arm behind me when a beautiful barmaid appeared, carrying cups full to the brim with cider. The fermented smell of apples overwhelmed me as she passed them around the table. She gave Haedion a flirtatious wink before rushing back off to the bar. My jaw clenched as heat climbed the back of my neck, and I impulsively placed my hand on his leg.

"We heard them about a day into the trip. I think they figured out rather quickly we'd split up and followed the scent of your clothes. That's when we left them. Silas climbed a tree and hung them by a string on a branch so your smell would carry." Nafre replied, taking a tentative sip of her cider. She pondered the taste for a minute, then her eyes grew wider. "This is amazing," she murmured to Silas.

"So, what next?" Bastian inquired, eyeing the way my hand stayed glued to Haedion's leg.

"I talked to Victor. I've arranged a crew to take us to Draconia tomorrow," Haedion replied. "Nafre, you and Silas have a room across the way at the neighboring inn. Victor didn't have space here tonight. I hope that is alright. And if it isn't, well then figure it out yourself." To which Nafre snorted her drink back into her cup.

"Ah, I did miss you the last three days, Haedion. I dare say we might become friends yet," she chuckled into her cup.

A tight grin pulled at the corners of Haedion's mouth. "I do have to thank you. You were right about where to find the medwitch in the village. Without her, I don't think Rhea would've made it."

"I apologize that we were less than friendly when we first started our journey together. I'm glad that Rhea got the help she needed, even if we couldn't save Eiran." Silas looked between Haedion, Bastian, and me.

Haedion nodded, an understanding passing between us before raising his cup and drinking deeply. The shadows that had cloaked him outside in the street had disappeared and I wanted to believe that I had imagined them, and perhaps I had. I had to get Haedion alone again tonight and ask him about what happened.

"Victor did have two rooms to rent here, so I told him we'd take those. When we are done for the night, he said he would personally escort you and Silas over to Damon's Inn."

"Victor always coming through for us," Bastian cheered. The barmaid returned then, a tray resting on her hip, stacked high with plates to share.

"In Eldrich, the custom is to order a few small dishes and share them among friends," Haedion said quietly to me. The first plate was covered in thin crackers topped with dried meat and a sauce drizzled on top. Haedion handed one to me before picking up his own and tossing it in his mouth.

"Each pub has its own flair and variety to choose from," he explained. "Typically, groups of friends jump from one place to another, share a drink and a few plates before heading to the next. Eldridge takes their nightlife very seriously." Haedion tossed another cracker in his mouth.

Bastian, Silas, and Nafre dug in, drinking, eating, and talking as the pub continued to grow more crowded. Laughter, squeals, and giggles filled the air as musicians found the small stage at the back of the pub and began to play. Men pull women out onto the floor, spinning and twirling around and around. The sight reminded me of the solstice and with it, a pang of longing formed in my chest.

"Nafre, you're coming to dance with me." Silas motioned for Bastian to move and pulled Nafre up behind him. We watched them run out on the floor and disappear into the crowd of writhing bodies.

Bastian and Haedion conversed casually while I took in the room around me. People of all types, not separated by class, body type, or race, danced and mingled together. The sight squeezed my heart so tight that I think it might burst. It seemed like this place was the only civilization left that didn't bear the scars of Ka'an's reign. I didn't understand why there were no soldiers or guards here, or why Ka'an didn't squash the joy of the people like he's done nearly everywhere else in Nador. Eldridge seemed like it was its own slice of adventure and freedom in one small coastal city. Was it the proximity to Draconia, his biggest failure and most desired prize?

Nafre popped out from the crowd near the bar. She waved at me, getting my attention as she motioned for me to come join her.

"I'll be right back," I whispered to Haedion, who let me out of the bench seat, not breaking his conversation with Bastian. Although he didn't say anything, I could feel his eyes on my back as I walked away.

"Rhea, you've got to come back with me!" Nafre giggled, a wild look of ecstasy in her eyes, and a dark rosiness highlighted her cheeks.

"Oh uh," I paused, looking back and forth between the booth where Haedion sat back, his eyes trained on me.

Nafre flashed me a wicked grin as she said, "I know what to do." She leaned over the bar, grabbing the man whom Haedion had spoken to earlier.

Nafre muttered something to him and slid a couple of silver coins across the counter. He nodded, plopping six glasses filled to the brim with an amber colored liquid. Nafre picked up two, handing one to me.

"I'm sorry about before. It had just been us three for a long time, and we had to scrape our way to get by. But you guys,—" she paused, as if searching for the right words. "You guys are different. If it's okay with you, I'd like for us to be friends."

A small smile tugged at the corners of my cheeks. A friend. An organic friend. Not one created through proximity or force, but a real friend. I'd never had one of those before.

"I've never had a friend before, Nafre," I confessed.

She nodded as she absorbed my words. "There's a first time for everything." She knocked her glass against mine. "Now let loose!" We downed the drinks in one sip. The liquor burned my nose as the liquid fire raced down my throat. The burn radiated in my stomach as it settled, and when I opened my eyes, I found Nafre smiling at me. She handed me another, and we repeated the step two more times.

"That'll help. Just give it a minute." Nafre grabbed my hand and pulled me out onto the dance floor. We found Silas dancing with a group of women who had shed a few layers as the heat from their bodies warmed up the room. Silas gave Nafre a devious smile as one woman from the group wrapped her arms around his waist, pressing her body against his.

"He's been more my brother than my own family." Nafre leaned close to yell in my ear over the pounding of the music. "He knows that I'll never be interested in him."

Nafre dragged me into the group of women who welcomed us with claps and whoops of laughter. Together we danced, and as the liquor began to hit, the room melted into a blur of shapes, sounds, and colors. The stress of what was to come floated away, and in the moment, I did not have a single coherent thought. All I felt was free. The heavy weight of the family I left behind, our people, and to stay safe all disappeared. I selfishly and purposely shoved those thoughts away as they did their best to intrude and ruin the moment. Should I be thinking about tomorrow? About entering the Catacombs of Draconia, the home of the fae, and retrieving the prismara and talking to the dragons?

Yes.

But I didn't care. Laughter bubbled up from within me, escaping in breathless bursts as Nafre spun us through the crowd. The music pulsed, a brilliant rhythm that vibrated through my body, making me feel like a living spark. The scent of sweat and spilled drinks mingled with the heady aroma of the fermented alcohol and salty air that poured in through the open doors. When I was sober in the morning, I'm sure I'd think the smell was awful. But now, it was seared into my brain— connecting it to happy, wonderful memories.

We danced for what felt like forever until Nafre took my hand and led me back to the bar. She asked Victor for two more shots of the amber color liquor and two glasses of water. We both downed the shots quickly, wanting to chase the buzz we'd been riding.

"Drink," she commanded, taking the cold cup, condensation already forming on the glass, and gulping down her drink. A small pounding started behind my eyes, but I pushed the pain aside. I wasn't about to let a little pain end our night, so I sipped the water dutifully, praying the hydration would ease the headache.

Right as I wrapped my hand around Nafre's arm to steer her back onto the floor, she looked past me, her eyes clocking in on something behind me. I turned and found myself face-to-face with someone familiar. My stomach sank. It was the man from the street. The same one who'd stuck his tongue down my throat, and whose smell made me gag. The one whom Haedion threatened to kill— and might've had there not been an audience to the spectacle.

Oh shit.

"Hi," he said, looking down at the floor nervously. "I saw you in here, and I just wanted to come over and say how sorry I am for how I acted earlier. I drank way too much and I behaved poorly."

I nearly fell over. He's what?

My mouth can't form the words through the grip that the alcohol still gripped my senses. His apology took me off guard. I'm not sure what I was expecting, but that certainly wasn't it.

"Did I not make myself clear last time?" Haedion appeared out of nowhere, his voice like a prayer promising violence.

The color drains from the sailor's face as Haedion grabbed him by the shirt, pulling him in till they were nose to nose.

"Haedion, stop!" I shouted, but he didn't look at me. His eyes had shifted from their normal earthy glow to a muted grey. The aura of darkness was back, and it wrapped Haedion in a cloak. If darkness had a prince, it would be Haedion with the promise of vengeance as his sword.

"I came over to apologize to her," the sailor sputtered, shaking under Haedion's death grip."I swear, man, that's all I was doing!" His hands held up in honest surrender, a bead of sweat dripping down the column of his neck.

Haedion relaxed the grip on his shirt, and for a moment, I thought he would let the man go. Then, he grabbed him by his throat and slammed him down on the bar counter so hard that the nearby glasses scattered, shards of broken glass skidding across the floor.

Curse all the realms. If I didn't stop him, he was going to kill that sailor. Anger, repulsion, and possessive energy radiate from Haedion in an impenetrable shield, and I was at the center of it.

"Haedion, stop!" I shook his shoulder, pleading with him to just look at me. But he didn't move; it was like trying to push a boulder up a hill. He was solid in place, unmovable— unshakeable. I don't believe he even heard me. Those grey eyes just stared straight at the man who was still lying on the bar counter with Haedion's hand around his neck. The sailor's face had gone ghostly white, his lips tinged a light blue.

"Haedion, c'mon, let the guy go. Look at him, you're making the poor guy's lips go all blue, and I'm sure that can't be good for his brain. It's getting late anyway, we should all head up for the night." Bastian said as he stepped in front of me, getting right in Haedion's face. I could physically see the internal struggle Haedion was fighting. Blood thrummed in my ears so loud that I didn't even notice that the music had stopped and everyone was staring at us, waiting to see if Haedion would let the man go or not. Heartbeats later, he finally looked at Bastian with murderous rage still written in the creases of his forehead and the sweat that dripped from his brow. But after a moment, he let go. The sailor, without hesitation, rolled off the counter with a wheezing cough and bolted for the door, not daring to look over his shoulder.

20

RHEA

What. The. Hell... was that?

Haedion watched the sailor till he disappeared from view, through the crowd that had stopped to watch the confrontation parted for him like a ship crashing through waves.

Tension poured from Haedion like a waterfall. When he finally rounded back to face us, the color had returned to his eyes. His expression softened when his gaze landed on me. Just as he opened his mouth to speak, I held up my hand, effectively cutting him off.

"Can you show me where the room is? I'm ready to go to bed." I directed my question at Bastian, who glanced between Haedion and me uncomfortably.

I was angry with Haedion. An unexplainable, alcohol-fueled rage. His blatant disregard of my wishes was enough to infuriate me. He didn't stop when I told him to in the street, and I was able to look past that. But then again, he stepped in without listening to any explanation. It wasn't the violence or the possessive need to protect me. In fact, the gesture was so attractive that a part of me screamed at me not to be angry with him.

I was though, because he didn't listen to me. Just like Calix never listened to me. How he'd always insisted he knew what was best for me and that made me want to scream.

All I wanted was to crawl into bed and sleep off the buzz I'd been riding since Nafre and I downed the liquor. My head rushed; the room was a chaos of words, music, laughter, and background noise, all blurred together with the mixed feelings I was fighting. The sensation was so overwhelming, I wanted to curl up in a ball right on the floor.

A silent understanding passed between the pair, and finally Bastian nodded once.

"Sure, Rhea. Haedion, why don't you have Victor show Nafre and Silas to Damian's Inn, and then we'll all meet up in the morning, and maybe you will be less fighty. Good as new, and sober." He gave Nafre and me pointed looks.

Nafre gave him a vulgar gesture, and a cunning smile played at her lips. "Who, us?"

"Goodnight, Nafre." I wrapped her in a fast hug, squeezing her tight. Maybe, despite everything, I might truly gain a friend in this. And that was more than I had even wished to hope for.

Bastian led me toward a small alcove on the far side of the dance floor, hidden behind a heavy red velvet curtain. He pushed it aside, revealing a hidden door that opened up to a stairwell. He didn't say anything as we climbed to the second floor, then the third floor, where he led me down a hallway, around two corners, till we reached the farthest room. Bastian produced a key from his pocket and turned the lock, opening up into a modest-sized room. The bed sat on the far left side of the room, which had a direct view of the of window. A bathroom sat just off the main room, furnished with a small basin to wash up. Steam rose from the pitchers of water, hot and ready.

"Victor always has breakfast sent up in the morning. If you need anything, our rooms are right next door. See that building?" He points out the window to an inn just across the street. "That is where Nafre and Silas will be."

"Thank you, Bastian," I sighed, exhaustion from traveling and the buzz from those last three shots began to wash over me like the waves crashing into the cliffside of Eldridge.

"No problem." He turned to leave, then paused just as he was through the threshold of the doorway.

"One more thing." He leaned against the frame. "Haedion and I have been friends for five years, and when we met, I was at my worst. He saw something in me, and I saw the greatness in him. And while he may be short-tempered and guarded, once he cares for you, he's fiercely loyal and protective. But the way he cares for you is different, and I think it scares him." He shrugged. "Try not to be too mad at him; there is more he is dealing with than you know."

"What do you mean?" I inquired. I knew Haedion had a past he wasn't sharing; that much was evident. Bastian knew, though. And whatever it may be, he was still loyal to Haedion.

He blew out a long breath, his focus on the floor as if replaying memories in his mind, trying to find the right way to explain.

"His history isn't mine to tell, but it's complicated, and he has worked very hard to get up every day and keep going. If it had been me who had suffered everything he's endured, I don't think I'd be here."

"You trust Haedion, explicitly?" I pushed, wanting to know more. What events had Haedion endured in his past that were so horrific that Bastian didn't believe he would've survived them himself?

"I do, and I will continue to do so, even if I might not understand his motives in the moment. He's lived a lot of life," he gave a low and easy laugh.

"He's lucky to have you as his best friend," I said gently. What an honor it would be to have a friend like that. To trust your decisions even if you didn't understand them, and stand by you no matter what. I used to believe I had that with Ari and Marie, but now, seeing life from outside that big castle in a small city in the corner of the world, I realized how wrong I was. There was always a separation between us, and even though they'd tried to see past what I was, they couldn't. I had been the outsider, I'd been different.

"I am the lucky one. Now you get some rest, sober up, and I'll see you in the morning. Draconia awaits!" He blew me a kiss and then disappeared down the hall.

I gave a short wave before shutting the door and instantly shedding my clothing. The sweat from dancing with Nafre made my tunic and tight pants stick to me like an uncomfortable second skin, and my hair clung to the back of my neck, overwhelming me instantly. I kicked the pile into the corner as I entered the bathroom. As best as I could, I washed myself up with the pitchers of warm water over the small wash basin. I scrubbed at the dirt that had collected under my nails, and I took a damp washcloth to wipe down the rest of my body. This was a far cry from my room at the library— but it was better than sleeping on the sand or dying of a ravager bite on the forest floor.

Once I was satisfied that I was as clean as I was going to get, I looked through the small closet that I'd missed next to the bedroom door. Tunics, far too large for me, hung in neat hangers, waiting for patrons that might never return. They reminded me of wearing Haedion's tunic nights ago, in the library. I selected an emerald green one, the same shade that represented Flitmoor. As I pulled it over my head, my thoughts wandered to home. How were my parents and sisters? Had they made it out? There had been no news, Haedion had told me he'd asked Cora while I'd been asleep, but even she had heard nothing.

I had so much I wanted to ask them and thank them for. They'd taken me in knowing that it would put their lives at risk— but did it anyway. I wanted to know about their friendship with my parents, whom I never got to know. What were they like? Who were they, really? Their position within the fae and the life they'd lived? A knot formed in my throat when the full realization hit that I'd never get to know the answers to those questions— not really.

And that understanding weakened the resolve in my anger at Haedion, and curse the Kirios, I couldn't help it as the rage slowly melted away. The kiss we shared at Cora's shop, the relief in his eyes when I'd woken up. The feeling erupted in my stomach like wings battering against the cage. He looked at me for me. Not the daughter who had been *different*, who'd been hidden and veiled her entire life. No, he looked at me for me. He'd known what I was since the beginning and didn't shy away.

Whatever he was hiding or too scared to share, it could wait, I decided. He'll tell me when he's ready. I'm still mad at him, but as I shuffled my way to the bed where the clean dark duvet cover had already been turned down, the anger had faded, nausea from the night of drinking replacing it.

As I slipped between the bedsheets, I was enveloped in a cocoon of lavender and vanilla. I turned my face into the pillow and inhaled deeply. Whatever Victor — or whoever it was that managed the inn linens had fantastic taste; the scent was incredible.

The noise from the town below continued to grow as the night progressed. Happy voices mixed with the drunk laughs and giggles of excitement made me pause. If I could just figure out a way to get rid of Ka'an—not even kill him— but just send him back to the realm where the vesperians had fled after the downfall, then maybe, just maybe, all of Nador could live like this.

This was the dream. A Nador modeled after Eldridge. This town, so perfectly untouched, is how I would reshape a world without Ka'an. But these were drunk thoughts... I could never take on Ka'an and win.

An ear-piercing shriek from the streets caught my attention. I threw back the blankets, darted to the window, and peered through the glass. Down below, a group of women stripped down to their undergarments and raced toward the bay. The first woman plunged into the water, coming up for breath with a shrill scream that echoed off the buildings. One after another, the women leapt into the frigid waters, all reappearing in a chorus of yelps and giggles. My body rocked as I watched them, the intrusive thoughts fueled by the alcohol telling me that I should join them, that the cool waters of the ocean would soothe the heat flushing my cheeks.

Knock, knock, knock.

The soft raps at the door pulled my attention away from the bay. I already knew who stood behind the door. In my mind, I could see Haedion with that dark aura that swirled around him, his jaw set, waiting to see if I'd answer.

"Please don't slam the door!" He blurted out as soon as our eyes met. I crossed my arms over my chest and gave him my best unamused look. I wasn't angry, not anymore. A little sick feeling perhaps from the liquor that was still coating my thoughts, but that didn't mean I was not going to make him sweat it a little.

Haedion just stared at me, and I wasn't sure he was even breathing.

I took a step back, motioning for him to come in. Without hesitation, he bolted straight into the room, talking so fast I could barely catch a word he was saying.

"I thought he was back to harass you. I am sure you had it handled, but I was worried that you were going to get taken advantage of. I watched you and Nafre drinking, which is fine, by the way," he added as a side note. "But I didn't want some disgusting lowlife getting it in his head that just because you are drunk and letting loose, he gets to do whatever he wants. I'm sorry if I overstepped." He doesn't take a breath as he continues.

"And I don't want you to feel like you owe me anything, Rhea. When I agreed to find you for the Necroscythe, I fully believed that you would be just another business transaction, nothing more. But now, I'd walk to the end of the world with you if that's what you wanted." He ran his fingers through his dark, disheveled hair.

I didn't have the words, my mind was empty, and all I could see was him.

"You're what I never expected to find. And if you haven't noticed, I don't always do well at letting people in, but I *want* to let you in," he finished, taking a deep, shaky breath. His eyes were clear, wide, and afraid, but full of hope and something else... longing?

"And I'm trying, Rhea. There is a lot you don't know and a lot that is to come, but if you'll let me, I want to help you."

The silence stretched between us while I fully digested his confession. He wanted to stay with me. I thought he was coming for an apology. This was more. An uncomfortable heat traveled up my spine, quickly melting away into an icy cold chill that made my bones ache.

Without saying anything, I took a step closer to him, feeling as bold as I had on the dance floor with Nafre. Haedion locked in place, watching me move with pristine stillness.

"You're forgiven," I said, standing on my toes, placing a gentle kiss on his lips. He didn't hesitate, wrapping his arms around my waist and pulling me against him. I looped my arms around his neck, dragging him even closer to me. I didn't care that I certainly smelled like sweat, alcohol, and a hint of lavender from the bedsheets. All that mattered was the feel of Haedion against me and the sounds of joy from

Eldridge outside, like a personal symphony just for us. I enjoyed it; it was so much better than the stark quietness that seemed to loom around Flitmoor at all times. Hushed voices and bodies that flinched at every loud noise.

Haedion took a step back, dragging me with him toward the bed when acid began to climb up my throat. My gut churned and rolled in warning.

Oh shit.

I pushed back from Haedion, my hand clamped over my mouth as I bolted for the bathroom, praying I would make it in time.

"What's wrong?" I heard Haedion ask me through my panicked thoughts. The door slammed shut behind me just in time for the entire contents of my stomach to reappear on the floor. Bile burned my nostrils as my body heaved again, just as another wave of sick hit the floor. My limbs felt like jelly as my knees collapsed. The coolness of the tile caressed my skin as I lay on my side, the world tilting around me. I squeezed my eyes shut, hoping that it would stop, but it didn't.

"Rhea." Haedion gently tapped on the door. "I'll be right back. You just stay there."

"Uh-huh," I whimpered through another dry heave that wracked my body, the muscles in my abdomen twitched with exhaustion from the involuntary movements.

Even if I had wanted to disobey Haedion's commands and get up, I wouldn't have been able to. Every inch of me hurt, and with how I had to keep my eyes squeezed so tight to slow the spinning, I decided the floor was the perfect place to be.

The minutes ticked by as I fade in and out of sleep, the nausea finally subsiding into a manageable level by the time Haedion returned.

"Can I come in?" He said cautiously on the other side of the door.

I peeled my eyes open, seeing the entire mess I'd made on the floor of the bathroom. Mortification ran through me. I had to get this cleaned up first.

"Give me a minute," I replied, pushing myself up. I looked around, searching for any spare towels to clean up after myself.

"I've got it, Rhea. Just open the door," Haedion coaxed.

"Nooooo," I whimpered, my head falling into my hands. The nausea was beginning to swell again, my thoughts slow and disjointed.

"Trust me, Rhea, I've seen much worse. If you come out, I'll tell you something about me. Would that be a decent trade-off?" Haedion enticed from behind the door, and I swear I could hear a faint smile.

"Fine," I answered begrudgingly, climbing slowly to my feet, making sure I was steady. The curiosity about him outweighed the embarrassment of getting sick.

The hinges of the door creaked open when I finally turned the knob. Haedion stood there, leaning against the wall, a warm, damp towel in one hand and a glass of water in the other.

"Take these, and go get in bed." He thrust both objects into my hands and side-stepped around me to open the door into the hallway, revealing the same man from behind the bar, and two others. They all gave me sympathetic smiles as they carried in cleaning supplies and ducked into the bathroom.

"Didn't I tell you to get into bed?" Haedion said, eyebrows raised in question when I stood there, mortification keeping me rooted in place.

I tried to roll my eyes, but the motion sent a stab of pain through my head but quieted and I stumbled my way to the bed. I took a few, tentative sips of water and set it on the nightstand. With the warm washcloth, I wiped my face and across my neck, where clammy sweat had my hair clinging to my skin.

I didn't want to admit it, but I felt better. When I lay down and pulled the sheets around myself, my eyelids became so heavy, I struggled to keep them open. Haedion and I had a conversation to finish; his words replayed over and over in my head.

He wanted to let me in, and I wanted him to let me in. But as I watched him chatting quietly with the men who cleaned up the mess I'd made in the bathroom, I couldn't fight the pull of sleep, and I drifted off into a restless sleep.

21

HAEDION

I waited till Rhea was snoring softly, her breaths even and deep, before I left the room, slipping out so slowly that even the latch clicked back into place silently.

Rhea was marvelous, and fuck, I wanted to finish the conversation we'd started. She'd forgiven me, then kissed me. And hell, I'm sure it would've led to more if she hadn't gotten sick. I would've happily welcomed more if she wanted. And, I still owed her a story. I'm sure she wouldn't forget.

I left the Victor's Inn, entering the calm alleyways of Eldridge. The night was calm, and the sun was minutes from rising. The last few partiers were staggering home, hoping to beat the light before it crested over the horizon. I found my way to the dock and located the crew of the transport ship. Just where Ka'an said they'd be.

"You must be Haedion," a man said, jumping from the ship to the dock. He had a heavy accident, with harsh emphasis on consonants as he spoke. His face was sun-torn, deep lines carved into his skin betraying the years spent at sea. A scraggly, unkept grey beard hid much of his face.

"I am. And you must be the captain?" I replied, reaching out to shake his hand. He shook it quickly and motioned for me to walk up

the plank connecting the dock to the ship. All business, no pleas-
antries. Fine by me.

"As you can see, we are set as requested. This is a small, three-man
crew, but don't worry, sir, we can still handle this ship. We have been
ordered to take your passengers to Draconia. Once on the island, my
crew and I will remain on board, notify Ka'an, and wait for further
instructions. How many guests will you have joining you?" The captain
asked.

"Five, including myself," I replied, eyeing the two other crew
members. They think I couldn't see them watching me as they go
about preparing their vessel? Their stares made my muscles ache with
the need to hit something. We were getting close, and I couldn't afford
one misstep. These three were quickly climbing to the top of my list of
potential issues that could arise today.

"That is two more than we were originally told," he said, his tone
clipped. He crossed his arms over his chest, sending a knowing look
over his shoulder to his small crew. "This will require more payment."

Of course, it fucking did.

"You contact Ka'an then and ask for more payment yourself," I
snapped. The captain's wide-eyed look showed that my sharp tone had
been enough to end the discussion.

"I'm satisfied with the arrangements." I turned my back on him,
headed toward the ramp leading to the dock. "I will be back with my
group later on this morning. I don't know when, so don't ask me. If you
have a problem with being on my schedule or payment, then you need
to deal with Ka'an yourself. Is that clear, or is there going to be an
issue?" When I'm back on the dock, I face the ship where the captain
stood at the top of the ramp.

"No, sir." The captain replied, his back ramrod straight at attention. This captain was a fast learner. Maybe I can keep him quiet
instead of dispatching him at Draconia like I feared I might have to.

"Good." I turned back down the dock where fishermen with sleepy
yawns start to appear, getting ready for the day. I dodge them as I force
myself to walk slowly when all I want to do is run to Rhea.

Once I'm back on the stone alleyway on the path set back for
Victor's Inn, for what I hoped was the last time, I knocked on the

door. The quiet void where my brother's presence was ever-looming jumped at the connection immediately.

"I met with the captain of the crew you hired. It's satisfactory." I told him when he appeared.

"Good." He smiled so wide, I thought the paper-thin skin of his face might tear. *"I will see you soon."*

A fresh bucket of dread flowed through my veins when I slammed the door shut, severing the connection before he could taste a hint of my confliction. Today could be the last day I spend with Rhea. Ka'an's anger when he discovers the truth would be enough to flatten the continent, and I could only hope that I could get us out of Draconia before then.

My mind raced with all the ways this plan could go awry. At the end of it, the best option was the one that made my stomach sink like a stone. I'd have to tell Rhea at the last minute to get herself out of Draconia first. Not to return for us, but go straight to the library. I know I could get the rest of us out of there— or I would tear myself apart trying.

If not, I knew I wouldn't see the light of day again once Ka'an learned the full extent of my betrayal. He couldn't kill me; we both knew that. But he could easily make me want to die. I knew the dungeons below Atheria that he created and the creatures he bred. Who and what they were capable of. I'd been present for the torture and deaths of countless people. We were, of course, bred, born, and trained by the best.

I could only pray to the Kirios that Rhea could do what I knew she was capable of and that I'd trained Bastian well enough to get Nafre and Silas out while I had my brother distracted.

The kitchen of the inn was bustling, preparing for the morning rush of guests and sailors. When I walked past Victor, he stopped me with a quick wave.

"Good morning, sir!" He said as he wiped his hand on a towel attached to his waist. "Is there anything I can get you?"

"No, no. Don't worry about me. I know you're busy getting ready for the morning rush. You always do such a great job at keeping your guests happy." The tips of his ears turned red at the acknowledgment.

"You flatter me, sir. Are you sure I can't get you anything? How about I have some pastries sent up to your room a little later? Does your guest have a favorite I can have prepared for her?"

The first memory I had of Rhea replayed in my head. When Bastian had knocked her over in line for the pastries, where she'd ordered chocolate. Gods, had I known what that night would turn into, who she'd become to me... I wouldn't have believed it. I might've flat-out rejected her then.

"She loves chocolate, Victor. Anything with chocolate would be perfect," I replied. "And maybe some mint tea? I'm sure she isn't going to be feeling her best this morning."

He gave a sympathetic nod. We'd both been in her room and seen how ill she'd been. "Absolutely, I have just the thing. I'll have it sent up a little later. Let me know if there is anything else I can do for you." He bowed his head before taking off toward the kitchen, shouting in a language I still did not understand, but I bet Rhea would. Or at least know where Victor was from.

I'd never even thought to ask and the shame of it sunk deep into my stomach.

When I slipped back through the door of Rhea's room, I found her just as I had left her. Light had just begun to filter in through the window that looked out over the bay. Rays of sunlight in orange and pink illuminated the thin clouds that covered the sky.

This place was amazing. Not just Eldridge, but the entirety of this place. I didn't know how I didn't understand it the moment we arrived in Nador from Kayar. The deep indoctrination had clouded my mind, making my thinking biased and one-tracked. I used to be *so* set on our goal. But now, as I looked over the sunrise with Rhea waiting in bed for me, I'd give anything to stay like this. Repeating this morning forever.

Fuck Ka'an, and fuck Samirah.

I'd never chosen anything for just me. It had always been for my mother— and I would do that again, but then it was Kayar, then Ka'an, then Samirah. Over and over again, I'd given pieces of myself to these people. Now I had a chance to do the right thing while also choosing myself.

I stripped down to my briefs and climbed into bed beside Rhea. In her sleep, she rolled toward me, casually tossing an arm over my waist, her light freckled skin a deep contrast against my dark tanned skin. She took a deep breath against the bare skin of my chest and buried her face in the crook of my neck. As gently as I could, I pulled her close and dozed off as the sunlight began to wake the sleepy party city of Eldridge.

22

RHEA

"Thank you, Victor. This is wonderful, beyond anything I could've expected. Please tell Damon that we appreciate everything you both do," Haedion said, his voice muted through the closed door of the bathroom where I stood in the mirror trying to braid my hair into submission. We'd spent the early morning lying in bed together, not saying anything. Just absent kisses and faint touches, looks and longing. Haedion had been so patient as I nursed the pounding headache that pulsed with every beat of my heart. It took every ounce of my will to pull myself from him and shut myself in the bathroom to clean myself up.

Footsteps grew fainter as Victor left, as the intoxicating smell of chocolate and fresh-baked bread infiltrated the room. I cracked the bathroom door.

"Everything in this place smells amazing. Gods, tell me that's chocolate," I said, stepping out into the foyer. Haedion stood shirtless, holding a silver tray stacked with pastries and a steaming teapot with two matching cups. Using his foot, he shut the door, a small pastry already stuffed into his mouth. He shot me a grin despite his mouth being full. The sight warmed something in my chest. I leaned against the wall and watched him carry the tray to the sitting area directly in front of the window, where we could easily watch the bustling bay where fishermen were already bringing back their morning catches. He placed the tray on the small table and motioned for me to join him.

"Yes, of course, there is chocolate. How could I forget your love for chocolate, little Enya? Do you want tea?" Haedion asked, placing his croissant on a plate. He arranged the table as I sat.

"Yes, please." I didn't realize at first how much had been packed onto the tray, but it was enough to cover the entire table. Croissants, cookies, chocolates, and fruit dipped in chocolate, all on small plates with hand-painted red roses. The detail was incredible— and intentional.

Haedion poured my tea, a deep, rich brown color, into a teacup decorated with water colored Shishermi flowers. The dark liquid melts the two small sugar cubes he dropped in, and cream swirled around the lip of the cup as he stirred it all together. He held the teacup towards me, kissing my lips softly before placing the cup in my hand. His mouth tasted like magic, warmth, and light.

"How did you know how I liked my tea?" I asked, drinking deeply from the cup. The warmth relaxed the sore, overworked muscles in my abdomen and back.

"That's a story I wanted to tell you." Haedion suddenly looked uncomfortable, sitting forward in his seat, forearms braced on his knees.

"Oh?" I asked, wrapping my fingers tight around the cup.

He took a deep breath, as if collecting all his thoughts. "You once asked me where I am from, and I didn't answer you. It's a long, long story, but it's also how I know how you like your tea."

"Okay?" I said, hesitantly. Where was he going with this?

"It's a long enough history that we do not have the time today for me to tell you everything, and answer all your questions that I know you will have. But if I tell you some of it, will you agree to withhold more questions until we get back to the library?"

"Yes," I blurted. I wasn't sure how Haedion had planned on letting me like he'd said he wanted to, but this felt like the first step in the right direction. He was trying, and I'd take anything he was willing to offer.

"Alright then," he stood up and paced to the window, where he watched the patrons of the fish market walk through the stalls.

"How old do you think I am?" He asked, his back still to me. I couldn't help but stare at the hard lines of his muscles, and admire the way his pants hung low on his hips.

"Oh, I,—uh," I stumbled. I hadn't considered his age. He didn't appear much older than I. His skin was still soft with youth, but had the strong jawline and scruff of facial hair that came with maturity. If I truly had to guess, no more than five years older than me.

"I'm not sure," I admitted.

"When the fae and vesperians both lived in Nador, their lives were extraordinarily long compared to the lives of humans. You, Rhea, could certainly live for centuries. Gashion had been alive for half a millennium before Ka'an killed him." He turned around, running his hand through his hair nervously.

Five hundred years? My mind couldn't even fathom the amount of life that could be lived in that many years. How much you would see, feel, hear, and experience. The books that could be read, the cities that could be explored, or the people you could meet with that gift of life.

"The reason I know how you like your tea is because I know that Cora taught Marie, because that's how your parents like their tea." He locked eyes with me, waiting to see if I followed his story.

And I didn't— not at first. Cora knew Marie? Then that dream that hadn't been a dream, but in fact a memory bubbled up. Marie *must've* been Cora's sister, who she left in Flitmoor to watch out for me.

He wasn't a fae. No, he couldn't be. His eyes were so perfectly human. But then the pieces began to click. The way the colors changed, from the bright, brilliant, earthy colors to the muted hues, then back again. And the dark aura that seemed to follow him. And Bastian's complete confidence in Haedion. His hints of there being more to his best friend than he could share.

Oh my god, he wasn't human. So what was he?

"You're not a fae?" I asked tentatively.

He shook his head. "No, but remember our deal. We do not have the time today to answer all your questions."

"Yes, yes, I know the deal, Haedion." I slammed the teacup down on the table, liquid sloshed over the edge, but I didn't reach to clean it up.

My heart rammed against the cage my ribs created to keep it safely in my chest. "Then what are you?"

"I am your opposite. The other side of the same coin. We were created from the same cosmic power." He walked back to the chair, bracing his hands on the back. He was skirting around the word, but I knew what he meant.

He was a vesperian, but how was he here?

He slowly nodded his head as if he could see the dots connecting in my mind. "I know that is how Gashion liked his tea because I had tea with him multiple times, over the years in Draconia."

"How the fuck are you here?" I stammered. When I think I have my head on straight once again and have my path laid out in front of me, something swoops in and knocks me off my feet.

"Remember, no questions." He held up a finger. "I promise you I will answer that, too. But that leads me to the next topic we need to discuss."

"What could you possibly have to tell me now?" I leaned back hard in my chair, throwing my hands up in exasperation. He casually mentioned that he isn't human or fae, rather a vesperian who, aside from Ka'an, hasn't been in Nador in well over a thousand years.

"When I spoke to the Necroscythe after he rudely interrupted us in the library the other night," he recalled, a teasing glint in his eye. "He gave me a task, and one that required me to tell you exactly what I am. He wants me to help you learn how to use your power so that you can control it, rather than it controlling you. You don't want to live in fear of it. It can be your biggest ally or your biggest weakness."

"You've got to be kidding me," I heard myself say. Every strange, unexplainable exchange I'd had with Haedion began to make more sense. I wasn't imagining the tenebrous aura trailing him. Bastian's complete faith in him and how he looked so uncomfortable when I'd questioned him about Haedion's past all tracked.

"And Bastian knows," I added.

"He does," he confirmed.

"What the hell?" I covered my mouth with my hand. His people, Ka'an, killed my entire race. I suddenly feel sick again.

"I am no different than I have been this entire time, Rhea. Now you just know the truth. I will answer any questions you have later. But please, I need you to trust me, especially as we go to Draconia today. I lived there for decades, and you're smart enough that I knew you'd have questions that I'm not ready for the rest of our group to hear yet. So when we get back to the library after you get the prismara and talk to the dragons, I will tell you everything, okay?" His voice softens, his hand extended like he might reach for me, but stops himself.

I'm torn between telling him to go straight to hell right there or thanking him for his vulnerability. He had told me he wanted to let me in, and he did, by revealing one of the most damning pieces of information about himself. He was a *vesperian*. In Nador. So many questions flew to the tip of my tongue. Did Ka'an know about him? Was he in hiding? How did he get here?

With a deep sigh, I pushed all the questions to the back of my mind. Fine, he wanted to get through today, and I could understand that, but I sure as hell would be putting him through an interrogation when we got back to the library.

"Alright, fine. Can I ask one more question then?" I asked.

"Sure, you can. I may or may not answer you, though," he smirked, but I could see the way his brows relaxed in relief.

"Why does the Necroscythe want you to teach me?"

Haedion chuckled softly, "This is why." He opened his palms as dark smoke erupted from them, throwing the room into near darkness. The smoke swirled around us, the wisps caressing the back of my neck that sent shivers up my spine. It filled up the room entirely, the smoke trailing on my skin like absent touches, lifting strands of my hair, and spinning around me in beautiful whorls of night.

"Oh my gods," I whispered, reaching out to touch the mist. It evaporated under my touch, only to be replaced by more smoke seconds later. I was in awe. The magic was so beautiful, a knot formed in the back of my throat.

"This is just a fraction of what I can do, but it's been a while," he admitted as the smoke began to recede, the room filling up with sunlight from the window.

"I understand now," I whispered, watching the magic retreating back to Haedion, like water flowing backwards up a waterfall.

"I know what it's like to feel out of control and like the magic controls you. I want to help you." Haedion stood, and he extended his hand toward me. I hesitantly placed my hand in his as he pulled me into his arms, his arms snaking around my waist.

"I'm ready to get this over with," I whispered into his chest. Draconia, the dragons, and the prismara. It was all so much. And Ka'an. What if he found us out there? Certainly, he would be anticipating that I'd return to the home of my people.

"I know," he muttered into my hair. "We just have to be quick. Get in and out and back to the library. I had Victor send a message to Nafre and Silas over at Damon's Inn. We'll meet in an hour. The crew that we secured is ready to leave whenever we are."

I nodded.

He pulled back, pushing a stray lock of hair behind my ear. "Sit, eat. You'll need your strength today."

Haedion handed me a brioche, motioning for me to eat as he talked.

"The entrance to the catacombs sits behind Gashion's throne on the floor of the dais. The dragons are supposedly hidden throughout the tunnels that run throughout the catacombs. They are vast and deep. Just like a labyrinth. When you go down there today, it will be overwhelming. The dragons have a hierarchy. You'll want to find the patriarch, tell him what you're after and why. He will know where the Prismara is and, most importantly, how to use it. Then, speak to the oracle."

"We need to get ready," he said at last. "But I have one last thing for you. Stay here and don't look." He turned, leaving me still choking down the pastry that still doesn't sit well on my sour stomach. I obeyed and didn't turn around as I listened to him walk to the hall closet across from the bathroom. When he returned, he was holding a white box, tied with a red bow, my name written on the tag.

The sentiment caused a lump in my throat that I can't swallow away. How did he have time to get me anything? I pulled gently at the bow, and it unraveled easily. Opening the lid of the box, I found an outfit, all black with buckles and loops to attach extra weapons. Knife sheaths on the ribs and thighs were hidden within the textured material that was soft but sturdy under my fingertips.

"Thank you," I whispered. The gesture nearly made my heart burst. I planted a quick kiss on his lips before pulling the outfit out of the box to examine it fully.

"I'm glad you like it." He smiled so wide, so genuine, I feared my heart might break at the sight.

"You get dressed. I'm going to go get cleaned up." Haedion placed one more gentle kiss on my forehead before walking to the bathroom and shutting the door behind him.

I quickly removed the tunic I'd been wearing and slipped into the new outfit that hugged me in all the right places. It held my waist, my hips, but moved with me so easily that running or fighting in it would be effortless.

Then I remembered my bag, where I knew I'd kept the blade Haedion had given to me before I was taken by the sandwraiths. I dug into the bottom of the bag until I found the knife, tucked between the folds of the dirty tunic that had once been Nafre's shirt. I don't know why I kept it, but something about throwing it away felt wrong.

I flipped the blade over in my hands. The short knife, handle wrapped with a deep brown leather, seemed to hum under my touch. On the metal itself was an inscription in a language I didn't recognize. Perhaps some vesperian language?

"Ready?" Haedion asked, startling me from my thoughts.

"Yes," I replied, slipping the blade conspicuously into the sheath at my ribs. It wasn't much, but something about knowing it was there made me feel a bit better.

23

RHEA

Nafre and Silas were quiet as we raced out of the bay straight into the ocean. The waves rocked the boat, making my stomach roll with each lurch. Nausea returned with a vengeance.

I sent a quick prayer to the Kirios. If we made it back to the library in one piece, I would give up drinking.

And mirthroot.

And maybe take up some daily praying to the Kirios.

My stomach heaved as we bounced along, my lips pressed together so tight that I'm sure they were white.

"We're moving fast," Haedion whispered in my ear. "It won't be long. Take some deep breaths in through your nose." All I could do was nod in response. I was too afraid I would vomit all over the deck if I opened my mouth.

Haedion, thankfully, was right. While I practiced the slow breaths to curb the nausea, Draconia came into view about thirty minutes later. The island was so much larger than any artist's rendition could depict. The castle, with spires on top of towers, disappeared high into the clouds. The stone of the castle had become grey-washed from the years of abuse of the salt water, and long rainy seasons with no one here to tend to it. Ivy climbed the walls, creating a network of dark greenery across the castle. The windows were cloudy and dark from the outside. No light, no love inside the walls that once used to house the home of the fae.

"There is an underground dock on the far side of the island. It will lead us directly into the heart of the castle," the captain yelled over the raging wind. Spray from the waves flew over the edge, covering us all in cool mist. I looked at Nafre, whose eyes locked with mine. They were bright with excitement, a new adventure. Her long braids bounce with each lurch of the ship, the gold clips twined within them caught the sunlight, making her look like an ethereal goddess.

The captain navigated us into a tunnel cut into the rocky cliffside of Draconia. Once we passed the threshold, the sunlight was quickly eaten up by the dark. The rocky waves turn calm, gently lapping at the cave walls. Goosebumps rise on my arms as the temperature plummets. Feet scurried across the wooden floor of the ship, followed by sharp commands from the captain. Seconds later, a warm glow illuminated our faces as the crew lit lanterns, hanging them around the deck on nails drilled into the bones of the mast.

The light reflected off the walls and the water as we slowly continued deeper into the heart of the island, stalactites hung from the ceiling, water dripping from the ends. Haedion, in the darkness, traced his fingers up and down my spine. I couldn't help but lean into him. He smiled at me, his eyes reflecting the silvery grey from the night before, another question added to my list.

The ship hit the dock with a thud, echoing throughout the empty chamber. We all unanimously held our breath — waiting. Would anyone, or anything, be alerted to our presence and come looking for intruders? I looked up and I was met with a maze of intricate walkways and bridges overhead. Some were made of stone, while others swung freely made of rope and boards rotten with age.

Haedion was the first to stand. Not waiting for the captain's word, he walked over to where the wooden plank that served as a walkway between the ship and the dock lay. He placed the plank down and walked off the ship, motioning for us to follow, helping us off by hand one by one.

"We will be back," Haedion said, tossing a small brown leather bag on deck. The sound of coins jingled inside when it landed. The men on the ship jumped for it, barking insults at each other while the captain tried to gain control.

"Yes, yes, fine!" The captain waved us off, not caring to look back. Haedion directed us to the nearest stone steps up from the small interior harbor to the next level. At the top of the steps, we found a larger circular room with doors leading in all different directions. Above our heads, more bridges and walkways that presumably led to more doors and rooms.

Haedion was right. Draconia was a labyrinth and more grand than I could've imagined.

"How are we ever going to find the entrance to the catacombs?" Nafre asked as she spun in place, looking up into the web that made up the heart of the castle. Silas nodded beside her, his eyes darting across the room from door to door, across each walkway as if trying to commit the sight to memory.

"Haedion knows the way," Bastian replied, sending Haedion a proud look, completely unaware of the puzzled looks Nafre and Silas shot him. They don't question it, though.

"Well, that's certainly helpful," Nafre muttered. "Lead the way."

Haedion pointed us toward the nearest door. It creaked open, the hinges screaming in complaint, rust falling like rain from the abused metal. Once we were all inside, it slammed shut. And for the first time since this morning, a sliver of fear worked its way into my heart. I imagined lying here forever as my skin faded away and my bones turned into ash.

In the alcove, we were met with a spiral staircase that circled up and up and up, with no clear end in sight.

"This stairwell will take us directly into the throne room. This place is a maze, so I suggest you don't wander. There are things alive here that live deep within the castle. When I was here before, I'd hear them clawing the walls, and screams would come from nowhere. I'd go looking for them, but never find them. But you never know what will find you."

"Maybe it's haunted," Silas said, elbowing Bastian jokingly, a laugh hanging on his words.

"Maybe so," Haedion mumbled, his eyebrows creasing as he looked up, scanning the unending stairwell ahead of us.

Haedion took the lead, starting the descent up into the castle. We climbed floor after floor until my healed ravager bite began to ache and my calves trembled with exhaustion. Just when I'm about to open my mouth and beg for a break, we reach the top. Haedion pushed the door open, and I had to cover my eyes from the blinding light.

The throne room of Draconia was the opposite of the throne room I had grown up attending back in Flitmoor. At home, thick wooden beams lined the ceilings, heavy curtains adorned the windows, with candlelit sconces hung on the walls. This throne room sat high in the castle with uninterrupted light filtering through stained glass windows, casting rainbows across the iridescent marble floor. Flecks of opal reflect in the stone, shining like diamonds.

I can't help but gawk at the stained-glass windows. Each one told a piece of a story. I immediately found the origin story of the fae and vesperians. Then more windows with more pieces of a story I didn't know all the details of. But no one did anymore— Ka'an had made sure to destroy that for the next generations. Windows filled with dragons, the Kirios, the Prismara of the Fae, and the vesperians.

Then the last window had an image of a woman I did not recognize. She was beautiful, with waist-length white blonde hair and eyes so strikingly grey that I felt like I was staring into a storm cloud. Her mouth was open, screaming in rage, the world in chaos around her. A black portal stood in front of her, the sword that Ka'an now held in her outstretched hand.

She seemed so familiar, but I couldn't place her. Who was she? I turned to ask Haedion, but found him already staring at the same image. His mouth is pressed into a firm line, his jaw worked as the muscle in his temple ticked.

Everyone silently spread out. Nafre and Silas took their time between each window, whispering under their breath to one another. Bastian bolted to one of the clear windows behind the thrones, looking out toward the sea. Haedion finally broke his stare, finding me already watching him. He held his hand out to me, guiding me toward the dais. Two thrones cut from what looked like ice, felt like ice, but were instead crystal clear stone, sat in the center.

"Someday," Haedion whispered low in my ear. "You will sit on this throne. Just as your bloodline did."

My hands began to tremble as I traced my fingers along the arm of the throne, then over the top of the back, then down the other side. The material buzzed under my touch, as if it recognized what I was and called to me.

"Wait a minute." I spun around, looking at Haedion. He cocked his head slightly, brows knitting together in confusion.

"I thought the prismara was in the catacombs under the castle. You told me the entrance was in the throne room. We're at the top of the castle. Where is the entrance?" I asked, looking around at my feet.

"I was just as confused as you were the first time I was here." Haedion stepped up on the dais next to me. "Here, I'll show you." He took my hand, guiding me to the backside of the platform.

"There," he said, pointing to the floor.

At first, I saw nothing. Just the crystal-clear stone that made up the dais.

"Look closer," he whispered, his lips brushing my ear. And I did. When I looked closer, it came into view. The light reflecting across the stone created an illusion, hiding a handle to a trap door just behind the chairs. Hidden in plain sight.

"What the hell?" I cursed under my breath as a nervous pit formed in my stomach.

"You have to jump," Haedion answered the incomplete question. "You have to jump, that's why no one can enter except the fae. It's enchanted. If you're anyone but a fae when you reach the bottom..." He paused, a coy smile on his lips. "Splat."

My stomach shot into my throat. I had to *jump*?!

My heart began to race, and my vision blurred as the adrenaline thrummed through my blood. Haedion, as if sensing my internal panic rising, grabbed me by the shoulders and whipped me around so we were standing face to face.

His finger dug into my shoulders; his stance shifted. Whatever he was about to say was vital.

"Rhea, you can do this." His eyes bore into mine, that silver flame in his iris flickering. His magic was at the surface, not hidden safely underneath the layers of protection he'd spent gods know how many years perfecting. "Now, I need you to listen to me. This is very important." He lowered his voice to a whisper. "When you get down there, you find the prismara and learn to use it. Once you do, do *not* come back up here. Open a rift and get out of Draconia. We will find you. *I* will find you. No matter where you go in Nador, I will come to you." I could feel his fear palpably in the connection between us. He was truly afraid. But his request felt like a punch to the gut.

"Why?" I gripped his face in my hands. "Why can't I come back? What happened to the plan?" Tears pricked in the corners of my eyes. Why was he doing this to me now? What happened to finding the prismara together and returning to the library as a group? Something had to be wrong. Why?!

"Please, please, trust me, Rhea." Haedion's voice cracked at the end of his plea. His eyes were wide, begging me to understand.

"I do trust you," I said, but doubt crept into the corners of my mind. "Just tell me why? Please, Haedion."

"Do as I ask. Please, little Enya. I promise you, when I find you again, I will explain everything. Go to the library, keep the prismara safe, and I will come to you. The Necroscythe will keep you safe. If you come back here instead of going home, *I* won't be able to keep you safe." Haedion trembled, leaning his forehead against mine.

I didn't want to. He'd kept this from me— this change in plan. I couldn't imagine leaving them here after what we'd endured together. This request, though, was important to him; I could feel the sheer urgency of what he was asking me in every nerve in my body. No, not just important, but he was genuinely afraid of whatever danger was ahead. Every part of me screamed to say no. How could I flee, leaving the rest of them behind?

The relief in his eyes when I finally nodded wrapped its way around my heart and squeezed tight. If agreeing to return without them brought him this much relief, I'd do it. Even if my mind screamed not to.

He kissed me then, gently, thoroughly, both of us knowing this would be our last kiss for however long. Haedion ran his hands from my waist, up my back, and ran them through my hair, coming to rest on the sides of my neck.

"If you keep kissing me like this," I uttered in between each kiss. "I won't leave, I'll come back for you."

He immediately pulled away, planting one more kiss on my nose. "Go to the library, I'll be right behind you. I will always come for you. I promise you, I will explain everything. I'll answer every question you had last night, and I'll even tell you who she is." He pointed to the mysterious, beautiful blonde woman depicted in the stained glass window.

I looked at the black hole in the floor and then back to Haedion. Bastian stood behind him, giving me a thumbs-up, his boyish grin giving me a boost of encouragement.

"You can do this, Rhea." He smiled, but it didn't reach his eyes.

A cool breeze filtered around my legs like tendrils pulling me in. They wrapped their way around my body, begging me to step off the ledge into the darkness. The air wasn't musky or stale like I'd expected, but smelled of worn books and the earthy-bittersweet scent of flames. Before the monster of doubt could dig its claws into my mind, I shut my eyes and jumped.

❧ 24 ❧

RHEA

Part of me expected to hit the ground, just like any unworthy creature who had attempted to enter the catacombs before me. The sensation of falling had been so intense that my stomach had jumped to my throat, and my lungs felt as small as pebbles. But when my feet gently touched the marble floor and the torches on the walls lit up in unison, I nearly cheered.

Holy shit, I wasn't dead!

I pivoted in place, taking in my surroundings. I was in another circular chamber, with four tunnel openings so large I couldn't help but gape. Where did I even start? I didn't know where or how to find the prismara or the patriarch Haedion had told me to locate. Even if I wanted to, how did I get out of here?

While I circled the room, I examined each tunnel opening that spread out in four directions, which I assumed to be north, south, east, and west. The beginning of the labyrinth. Maybe they led to the chambers under each wing of the castle? I cautiously walked up to one, and as I got closer, I could see a small 'S' at the top. I was correct.

"Rhea," a deep, gravelly voice boomed across the chamber, the tone echoing against the stone walls of the chamber. The consistent beat of my heart stuttered as dirt and gravel fell to the ground, stirring up a dusty cloud around me.

My eyes, still trying to adjust to the dim room, hunted the shadows looking for the source of the voice that knew my name. Then, out of the north tunnel, a dragon stepped out of the shadows, into the scarcely lit chamber. His body was deep blue, so dark it could be mistaken for black. Ridges ran from the top of his head, down his neck to his tail — a tail thick enough that one swipe could take out this entire room. I wanted to melt into the floor.

He stepped closer; each footfall sent vibrations through the floor into my very bones. I had nowhere to turn, nowhere to run, so I planted my feet, threw my shoulders back, and turned on the facade of someone who belonged here. I just hoped it was enough.

"Rhea," he said again. "Daughter of Jordi and Alamae, what is it that you seek?"

These dragons worked, in tandem, with my people to protect the treasures down here. Their oracles fed prophecies for thousands of years. They had no reason to hurt me... I hoped.

"I am looking for the patriarch and the prismara," I said, my neck craned back so I could stare the creature in the eye.

The dragon tilted his head, examining me with a predator-like gaze. After a moment, he replied. "You're finally going to do something about Samirah and those vesperians, aren't you?"

"If you're referring to Ka'an, then yes." Samirah? Who the hell was she? I committed the name to memory.

"Well, yes. Nonetheless, follow me. He turned wide, his tail scraping the wall as he turned and retreated into the tunnel from which he came. I broke into a half-run to stay by his side.

"Keep up," he snipped. "We don't have much time."

Light began to illuminate his face, and we emerged into another chamber. This one is even more grand than the first. This one bore tall walls with inlets adorned with all sorts of interesting items. Jewels, maps, books, just from what I could see at eye level. In the center of the room was another dragon. Although this one was not nearly as tall, but the respect I felt oozing from the first dragon let me know without a doubt that this had to be the patriarch.

"Go on," the first dragon said, stepping aside. I walked past him, not sure where to look. At him, the patriarch, or the priceless items gracing the walls. It was all so captivating. I could imagine it in its prime, with the fae working side by side with these creatures.

"Hello, Rhea." The patriarch's deep voice rumbles in my chest. "I'm glad you found us at last." He was a watercolor of blues, greens, pinks, and oranges across his body. Feather-like scales in brilliant shades framed his face. His eyes, even as they scrutinize my face, seem to convey an ounce of relief.

"What can we do for you?" He asked. His voice was old, but sturdy. As if he was a house built to withstand any storm.

"I came for two things. One, to retrieve the prismara and ask that you teach me how to use it." I can't help but shift uncomfortably. The magic in my veins thrummed with excitement at the proximity to such power. This place was where I was meant to be. This was my home.

"And second, I want to hear the prophecy," I added quickly before my confidence imploded from the weight of their stares down on me.

A pur-like hum rumbled in his chest. "Ah, yes," he murmured. "We can certainly help you with that. Alastor, could you bring us the prismara and also send for Agnya?"

"As you wish." Alastor, bowed his head and then, with feline-like precision and grace that I wouldn't have expected from a dragon, he began to scale the walls.

"When it comes to teaching you how to use the prismara, it's actually quite simple," the patriarch said, pulling my attention away from Alastor. "I do have something I wish to discuss with you. After the downfall of Nador, and the vesperians abandoned the realm. We agreed with the Kirios to do what we could to protect the line of the fae by blessing each generation with our magic. The gift of not only fire, but also shifting to become one of our own. " He fluttered his wings, the wind pushing my hair back.

"When it came down to it, even with our blessings, you were unable to keep yourselves safe from the vesperians and the wrath of Samirah. So, how do you, prophecy fulfiller, intend to restore balance to the world?"

My jaw slacked as I mulled over his words.

Prophecy fulfiller.

Shifter.

And that name again, *Samirah*. Who *was* she?

"I don't know how I'm going to do it," I started, my words slow and calculated while my mind tried to work through the pieces of broken history and crumbs of context I'd picked up along the way. "But I intend to rid the world of Ka'an. One way or another. Bring peace back to the realm."

"Get rid of him, or kill him?" The patriarch narrowed his slitted pupils at me.

"I, uh,—" I had no clue how to kill a vesperian. *Could* he even be killed? Haedion would certainly know.

"Yes, dear, he can be killed." The patriarch responded as if reading my mind. "It's just a complicated matter when his soul is connected to another. In killing him, you're killing his brother who you could consider partially, if not fully, innocent in Ka'an's crimes against Nador.

A brother?

The second dragon started his careful descent down the wall, a palm-sized stone in hand. Ka'an could be killed, and that information made the magic in my chest flutter in relief. But in doing so, I'd be killing another. Someone who might be innocent of Ka'an's crimes.

"Sending him back to his world could be an option for delaying the inevitable." The patriarch interrupted my unending stream of thoughts. "But you know that is opening up the world to Samirah's return, and I doubt your group is ready to take on her wrath and her legion of vesperians at her back."

Alastor returned, holding out the prismara to me, pitched between two razor-sharp claws. It was much smaller than I ever anticipated. I plucked the stone gingerly from his grasp. It was beautiful, like open flame flowing through it, dancing to unheard music inside. I could feel the power in it; it called to me, pulsing in time with my own heartbeat that filled my ears.

"You do whatever you feel is necessary to restore balance. Whether that's war, banishing Ka'an, killing him, or another unforeseen option. Know this, we will do everything to protect the knowledge and treasures that lie here," the Patriarch said. "We did, however, make the Kirios a promise all those centuries ago. We will do what we can to assist his creation. And you are the last remaining fae. The catacombs are at your disposal."

Just then, small vibrations sent small stones scattering around my feet. More heavy footfalls of another dragon entering the chamber. This one, much larger than the other two, radiated wisdom, and pure knowledge.

I turned to face her, leaving the patriarch at my back. She lowered her head, then bent each leg till she was fully settled on the floor.

"You've returned at last," Agnya spoke directly into my mind.

"I have," I answered out loud. I could feel the weight of both the patriarch and Alastor's stares on our exchange, but I can't look away from her brilliant shimmering violet eyes. "I've come to hear the prophecy. I was sent by the Necroscythe."

A throaty laugh rumbled across the room from Alastor and the patriarch. A sharp glare that I didn't miss from Agnya cut them short.

"Ah, the Necroscythe. When you see him again, send him my regards, will you?" She asked.

"Yes, of course." I nodded.

"Well, let's get into it then. You will need to be rejoining your friends soon."

"Upon the birth of the first daughter born of the dragons, the earth that was divided and the blood that was spilled will be recalled.

The soil will weep, the oceans will wail, and the sun will fight against the inevitable horizon of the end of the era, drenched in crimson. Our daughter's scream— the necessary rage— will shake the realms, her fire will purify the unrighteous, and reduce to ash the monsters within.

And with it, our people will be together again, power united."

This had to be a joke.

What the hell was that?

"You don't have much time, daughter." Agnya looked to the patriarch, who stepped around me. "You need to use the stone, now."

"But I have questions!" I exclaimed. "None of that made sense. Who is the daughter, and the fire— ?"

"The blood of the Kirios powers it," the patriarch said, cutting off my stream of questions, gesturing to the prismara thrumming in my hand. "Each time you desire to use it within Nador, you must offer a drop of your own blood as the Kirios's blood runs through your veins. A power for a power."

A small drop of my blood was enough to power the stone that could pull us through this realm with a single thought. The thought made me dizzy. I had to go, now.

"You promise Haedion, didn't you?" Agnya's voice softened sympathetically. "You promised him that you would leave once you had the prismara."

How did she know that? Ugh— I didn't have time to work through that. She was an oracle. Who knew what else that gift told her?

A knot formed in my throat at the thought of leaving Draconia alone. This was all wrong, but Haedion begged me— and I couldn't go back on my promise now.

"I did," I whispered, pulling Haedion's dagger from the sheath at my side. I positioned the blade just over the pad of my thumb, the words in the strange language I didn't understand staring back at me. Just as I laid the cool blade against my skin, the room shook. Rock and debris cascaded down around us.

"Curse him," the Oracle muttered, covering her head with a wing, extending her other to protect me.

"Curse who?" I looked between the three dragons, but I already knew.

"Ka'an," Alastor glared upward, as if he could see all the way into the throne room that sat stories above our heads.

"He's here?" The blood rushed from my face at the confirmation, horror washing over me as my worst fear manifested before my eyes. Ka'an was here. My core began to tremble, the fire within me rushing to the surface as if trying to reassure me, sooth me. But it was useless against the dread that tightened in my chest. He would kill them all because of me. Haedion knew. Somehow, he'd known that Ka'an was going to be here, and instead of calling everything off, he was willing to send me ahead to protect me. To protect the prismara and prevent Ka'an from getting his hands on it.

A calm washed over me, then. No, I couldn't leave them up there alone. I would not run. Nafre, Silas, Bastian, and Haedion, they'd come all this way, and I wouldn't let them die now.

The Patriarch extended his wing to protect Agnya's back as another thunderous boom shook the castle. "You've got two options right now. Listen to Haedion's plea and return to the library. Or return to the throne room, where your friends are being held by Ka'an and his men. It's your choice. Save yourself and maybe the world, or try to save them. What will you choose, first daughter?"

Shit, I had no time to think and endless questions.

"I will be back someday. We have more to discuss." I looked directly at Agnya, who I swear smiled.

"I look forward to it."

Before I could think about the implications of my actions, I slit my thumb and let the drops drip down the prismara. It began to glow the moment my blood connected, and I concentrated hard on the image throne room in my mind. Of the stained-glass windows and the marble floors with the thrones my family sat on before me. Where Haedion, Bastian, Nafre, and Silas were, hopefully all still alive. A tugging sensation at my core yanked me through a dark veil, and I closed my eyes as I was forced through. When I opened my eyes, I was standing just where I had imagined, in the center of the glowing, bright throne room.

I turned, searching for my friends. I had to find them. I had to save them. My eyes found Bastian, Silas, and Nafre first, kneeling in front of the dais, hands bound behind their backs. Guards stood behind of them, holding blades to their throats. Ka'an sat on the throne, one leg casually tossed over the arm of the chair. And to his right sat Haedion, whom I barely recognize. His face was unreadable. Dark circles under his eyes, his cheeks hollowed in like he'd been starved for weeks.

What had happened while I'd been in the catacombs?

And, why the *fuck* was he sitting with him?

25

RHEA

"Ah, Rhea darling. Right on time." Ka'an stood up and bowed deeply, a laugh that grated over my skin boomed across the room. The mocking sentiment was not lost on me.

"Welcome back. Thank you so much for retrieving the prismara for me." He sauntered towards me. His thin frame and grey, paper-like skin were just the same as the last time I saw him. As he neared, I could see his long dark hair floating around him as if it had a mind of its own. Inky veins started at his temples and worked down the side of his face and onto his neck where they disappeared under the tunic at his chest, pulsed in time with his steps as he got closer.

He stopped in from me, a serpentine grin plastered on his face. "If you are anything like your people, dear, then you'll do anything to save your friends, I already know. Just hand over the stone, and I'll let them go." Ka'an extended his hand toward me, palm up, waiting.

What a delusional, sick, sociopath.

My eyes glanced to Haedion, where he sat on the crystal throne, his hands braced in front of him. He didn't look fearful or guarded— he looked destroyed. Bastian had his eyes glued to him, as if begging him to just look in his direction.

No, no. I refuse to have come this far to let it end here. We'd all sacrificed too much, most of all Haedion, to let it end here. I fucking refuse. I did not lose my home, my family, Flitmoor, and most likely my adoptive family, and face horrors across Nador for it to all be a waste.

I made a show of safely tucking the Prismara into the small pocket just above my heart, patting it for extra measure. As I did, something shifted in Ka'an's eyes. The air thickened around Ka'an with something unholy. The change sent chills rippling down my spine.

He snapped his fingers, and a guard threw Nafre to the ground. He straddled her from the back, pinning her to the ground, and with his free hand wrapped her beautiful braids around his hand, arching her backward. He pushed the blade against her neck so tightly that I could see blood running down her neck. She didn't scream or fight. Instead, she angled her head to look at me. There was no fear there, only determination. We'd been here before— just weeks ago. How had I found myself stuck with my friends lives in jeopardy?

I sent a pleading look to Haedion for help. He was powerful; he'd shown me as much this morning. Maybe by some miracle, we could work together and get ourselves out of here. As if he'd sensed me, he lifted his eyes to meet mine. They were sad, his irises returned to that beautiful shade of hazel green that charmed me that first night in Flitmoor. And that's what made the room suddenly feel like it was pressing in all around me. They weren't the ominous grey that told me his magic was simmering just under the surface, ready to explode at a second's notice— they were normal, and devastated.

"Oh, he won't help you," Ka'an said, noticing my stare. "He's the whole reason you're here, you know. If it wasn't for him, you'd still be running across Nador, dodging every single creature that lives in this god-forsaken realm," he laughed — or at least I think he did. My ears were ringing so loudly that I could barely think.

Haedion didn't interject as Ka'an continued. He didn't try to deny what Ka'an said.

"My little brother was never the leader, but he was always one hell of a spy. Especially with the darkness he wields. He's nearly unstoppable."

Little brother?

Haedion went to stand, but Ka'an held a hand up, and with it, he sat back down. I had to swallow the scream that worked up my throat. My knees threaten to buckle at the embarrassment, shame, and betrayal. How could I have been so blind? Haedion knew so many things and kept me in the dark about even more with promises of answers in the future, if I just *trusted* him.

I looked to Bastian now, whose face is as pale as death. Even from a distance, I could see the ends of his hair tremble in rage, his jaw clenched as he stared Ka'an down.

"Rhea, listen." Haedion pushed himself off the throne and strode across the room, palms open

"Shut up!" Ka'an rushed over to Haedion, wrapping a hand around his throat. Haedion hissed through gritted teeth, the shadows finally making their appearance as they poured from him in waves of night. His eyes shifted then, the silvery gray wisps flicking in his iris— whether he called them or he just couldn't resist them any longer, I couldn't tell.

"I knew you and I hadn't seen eye to eye on many things, but I didn't expect you to try to play both sides of the field." Ka'an looked from Bastian to me. "When I sent you out on a reconnaissance mission across Nador, I didn't realize you'd kept him in company." Ka'an gestured to Bastian with his head, his hand squeezed tighter on Haedion's neck.

"And then, I make you a promise — to grant you the one thing you've been wanting since that day twenty-five years ago. I was going to let you go back to Kayar. And hell, I still don't know why you want to go back when I would've let you have anything you wanted here. All you had to do was get the girl here and bring me the prismara. You achieved that. But you told her to get it and not come back, didn't you?" Spit flew from his mouth as he trembled with fury.

Haedion didn't answer.

"I can feel it, through the bond, you fucking idiot. You're falling in love with that fucking fae!" Ka'an yelled, throwing Haedion back across the room so hard that he slammed into the dais, hitting the ground with a sickening thud.

"I've known this whole time, or did you forget what you signed up for when you and I completed the Euvas? You thought you could keep this from me?! You know what, I was going to keep the realms sealed just a little longer because I wasn't quite ready for Samirah to return and reduce this piece of shit realm to dust. But, you know what, we need a little change, don't we?"

Haedion struggled to his feet slowly, his hatred rolling off of him, sweeping around the boundary of the circular throne room until we are completely surrounded in Haedion's magic.

Ka'an snapped his fingers again, and a guard picked up Bastian, hauling him to his side. Bastian struggled as the guard kicked the back of his knees, forcing them to bend till he knelt at Ka'an's feet. The glare of pure loathing that Bastian gave Ka'an is one of utter disgust and pure malice.

Ka'an bent down and patted Bastian gently on the cheek, and for a moment, he paused, his head cocked to the side in contemplation.

"You know, at one time, *I* was his best friend. *We* shared everything. It was only a matter of time before you were replaced, just as I was. Haedion has no loyalty. Tch, what a shame."

Bastian tossed back his head in a hysterical laugh that was so jarring that it threw off the tension in the room. Confusion registered on Ka'an's face a moment before Bastian spat in his face.

"Go fuck yourself," Bastian declared, sending me a wink from the corner of his eye.

Ka'an reared back, wiping his face, a disgusted sound emitting from the back of his throat.

"You little prick," Ka'an growled through gritted teeth. Haedion began to move, seeing what Ka'an was about to do, but was too slow. Ka'an unclipped the sword from his side, the prismara of the vesperians glimmering in the sunlight, before taking it and shoving it through Bastian's gut.

My throat ached with the scream that came deep inside my soul, but it was lost in the roar from Haedion. Ka'an holstered the blade once again as Bastian knelt over, collapsing in on himself, his hands holding the wound at his core. Blood began to pool around him, the crimson like a pool of rubies.

Bastian stopped moving. Tears leaked down my cheeks, but I

couldn't bring myself to wipe them away. Oh gods, not Bastian. No, no, no...

"That was for your disloyalty." Ka'an pointed to Haedion, who was seething.

Haedion was feral. His shoulders heaved with deep breaths as he looked from Bastian's body to Ka'an to me, and for a moment, nobody moved. Ka'an and Haedion stared at each other in silent communication.

Then from behind Haedion, wings appeared.

I must've been hallucinating.

Black wings tore through the thin fabric, flaring to life behind him.

Ka'an began to cackle, the room shaking around us. "You haven't got the skill to fight me anymore! Put those away. When was the last time you flew, Haedion? The last time you used those useful dark shadows to do what you were trained to do? And I'm not talking the small bullshit, I'm talking about the full extent of your magic that I've seen you use to choke the life out of someone. You've spent so many years detesting what we are when you could've spent that time instead becoming better. Stronger. You pathetic waste of space. I can't believe I ever connected my soul to yours," Ka'an spat, wings spreading out behind him. While Haedion's shimmered from the darkest black at the base to a glowing white at the tips, Ka'an's were a flat black. None of the same beautiful shimmering when the light caught the fibers of the feathers like Haedion's.

The room began to tremble, and at first, I thought it was my imagination. My body and mind were working together to trick me, distract me from the blood continuing to flow from Bastian, that threatened to drown me in grief, and the sight of Haedion I was sure couldn't be real. But then Ka'an started looking at the floor — he'd felt it too. The trembling grew, and suddenly the floor exploded. From it Alastor emerged, the patriarch, and Agnya. Alastor landed next to Nafre and Silas. Using his tail, he swept the guards who stood behind them off their feet and through the stained glass windows to the raging sea below.

"Rhea, go, now!" His roar was so loud that pieces of marble broke off from the fixtures high above, falling to the ground around us.

More and more dragons filtered through the hole in the floor, and as they did, the room began to disintegrate. Ka'an screamed at his remaining guards, who had lined the walls, but I couldn't hear his commands over the crashing and bellowing screams from the dragons as they knocked the stained-glass windows from their frames, sending them down in a shower of glass.

With unsteady fingers, I pulled the prismara from the pocket. It's warm pulse ticked in time with my heart — so fast, like the wings of a bird.

"Get Bastian!" I heard Nafre yell at Silas as she bolted for Haedion. Ka'an backed up quickly, aiming for the walls as the floor beneath him began to fall away. In his distraction, Silas ran for Bastian, throwing his limp body over his shoulder and barreling toward me just as Nafre wrapped her hand around Haedion's arm, shocking him back into reality. He looked at her, absolute ruin written on every inch of his face. The powerful, confident man stripped away, leaving the raw, ravaged, grief-struck Haedion in his place.

Nafre tugged at his arm, her mouth moved, but her words were eaten up by the chaos of dragons, screams, and the pure magic that flowed from Ka'an as he struggled to gain control of the room as it crumbled away from the center— falling deep, deep into the heart of Draconia.

Whatever Nafre had snapped at him caught Haedion's attention, and he nodded. They both turned and fumbled to where Silas now stood next to me, Bastian hardly breathing over his shoulder. His eyes were closed, his golden freckled skin now littered with blood splatter. The sun-kissed blonde hair that liked to curl up at the ends was now dyed scarlet red.

"*Please*," I begged the Kirios. "Please don't take him." I sobbed through blurred vision.

"Rhea, now!" Haedion grabbed my hand and slashed a new cut across my palm. I sucked a breath in, the pain sharp but grounding. I gripped the prismara in the blood that pooled in my palm and thought of the library. Of the grand entrance with its sand-covered floor. Where I'd met the Necroscythe and where we *needed* to be.

The familiar tugging sensation at my core began; my lungs felt like they were being held in a vice grip, as I'm forced through a dark void. I squeezed my eyes shut, Ka'an's voice slithering into my mind.

"There is nowhere in this world you can go where I won't find you, little fae." I dry heave, my hands covering my ears, hoping to block out his voice in the darkness. But I can't. He's in my head.

"I would've killed you quickly once I had the prismara. I have so many plans that I wouldn't have bothered with you. But now," he hissed. *"When I find you, I will make your suffering infinite. And, Haedion..."* he trailed off.

"I have no plans of ever ending his suffering that he will endure when I find him, too."

Then he's out of my mind as we suddenly slam into the entryway of the library, just as I'd hoped.

"Bastian!" Haedion thundered as he scrambled across the floor, a fresh stream of blood oozing from his temple.

Silas gently laid Bastian on the floor, Haedion ripping open his shirt to reveal the stab wound.

"What happened?!" The Necroscythe's voice boomed across the room, my body shaking in response.

Or maybe it was because we had almost died.

Bastian could be.

"He knew all along what I was planning; he felt it," Haedion said through gritted teeth, his magic pouring from his palm that he held open over the wound on Bastian's abdomen. The shadows fell over his skin, searching and prodding the edges, gently pulling at the edges of his skin.

Bastian's breath came out in ragged, wet gasps. My knees collapsed under my weight, the prismara falling from my hand. I didn't want it, couldn't stand the feel of it against my skin.

Then, Bastian's chest stopped rising. The room fell silent. Nafre began to cry softly, Silas cursed quickly under his breath, and turned away.

"Fucking do something!" Haedion rounded on the Necroscythe, his eyes shining so bright they were nearly white.

The Necroscythe held up his palms, as if trying to reassure Haedion. But it didn't stop Haedion as he grabbed and held tight the Necroscythe.

"I lost Kayar, I lost Eden, I can't lose him, too!" Haedion roared, his voice cracking. "Please, I can't lose him, too," he begged.

"Alright." The Necroscythe pulled himself free from Haedion's grasp and lowered himself to his knees beside Bastian. He placed his hand in the open wound, where the blood bubbled through his fingers and over the sides of Bastian's stomach.

I vomited then.

Save him, save him. I chanted over and over in my mind. Bastian, the one who'd done everything to keep me feeling safe, who was unbashfully blunt and so god damn confident in his best friend. He couldn't be dead.

Through wobbly, tear-blurred vision, I watched the Necroscythe work over Bastian. The blood that dripped onto the floor suddenly stopped, hovering in place. Then, it began to work backwards, traveling back up his skin and into the wound that had started to stitch itself together at the edges.

"Holy shit," Silas gasped, his hands braced on the back of his neck.

Haedion stood above them, his face betraying every emotion that he was feeling. He looked like someone who'd had his world end before and kept going anyway, just to have it destroyed time and time again. But this loss, I don't know if Haedion could've survived this one if the Necroscythe didn't save Bastian.

The Necroscythe removed his hand from the wound, now nothing more than a thin pink scar across Bastian's abdomen.

But his chest wasn't rising. He was perfectly still, a blue shadow tracing the curve of his lips.

Bastian's eyes suddenly flew open, his chest expanding with a gasp.

Haedion crumpled to the floor, wrapping his arms around Bastian in a bone-crushing hug.

"Hey, Hae, I'm okay, I swear. I was just slightly impaled," he patted Haedion on the back. When Haedion didn't pull away, Bastian laughed, "Maybe I should die more often."

"I'd rather you not," the Necroscythe said, his face deathly pale, as if saving Bastian had drained him. His hands trembled as he sat back on his heels.

"Don't do that to me again," Haedion commanded, pulling back and looking over his best friend, his eyes returned to their glittering earthy hues.

"What happened in Draconia?" The Necroscythe asked Haedion once again, sitting down with a huff.

"Rhea got the prismara," Bastian said, giving me a wide grin. A sob of relief I'd been choking down forced its way through my teeth. I covered my mouth with my hand to stifle the cry that wracked my body with such force my ribs ached.

"Don't cry, Rhea! I was only dead for like..." he paused, looking at our surroundings. "A minute or two. I'm good now!" My laughing hiccup echoed across the chamber.

"Yes, she got it, and thank the Kirios you're alive," Haedion interjected. "But we have a bigger issue now." Haedion's expression grew grim.

"What is that?" The Necroscythe asked.

"Ka'an intends to bring Samirah here."

26

HAEDION

That could not have gone worse.

When I had instructed Rhea not to return to the throne room and to meet us at the library, I truly believed she would listen to my instructions. My heart had ached at the hurt in her burgundy eyes when I asked her. But I thought she'd felt my desperation and trusted me enough not to come back for us. Then, Ka'an showed up, and everything went to hell. It was as if he had known something I didn't. He knew she'd come back for us.

And he had been right.

That motherfucker.

Rhea wouldn't even look at me after what happened to Bastian. When the Necroscythe declared we'd meet for a debrief dinner later, we all separated to bathe and decompress in silence. Rhea had bolted straight for the stairs, leaving the prismara discarded on the floor in the entryway. I'd picked it up and carried it to my room. I pushed the door open, half expecting Rhea to be in my bed, waiting for me. But the perfectly pulled together bed and smell of fresh linens caused an unexpected pit to form in my stomach.

My body worked on autopilot as I strode into the bathroom. I stripped my clothes, my pants heavy under the weight of Bastian's blood that clung to the fibers. The library quickly filled the tub with steaming water, bordering on boiling, that soothed the ache of my muscles.

How had it gone so wrong? I'd kept Ka'an precisely on the edge of my mind, just close enough he shouldn't have been able to read my thoughts or intentions, but not too far away that he'd grow suspicious. Either I'd let myself grow so detached from who I used to be that he'd slipped through the cracks, or he'd grown his power in ways I hadn't fathomed yet.

Both options were equally as likely, and that made my stomach churn with guilt.

This had been all my fault.

Just as I'm about to crawl out of the tub, a pounding fist sounded from the other side of the bathroom door.

"Haedion, open the god damn door!" Rhea shouted.

My shoulders sagged in relief. If she was here, she must want an explanation, and I'd happily answer every question she had.

I quickly wrapped a towel around my waist a threw the door open. She's back in one of those oversized tunics, hair dripping puddles on the floor like she hadn't bothered to dry herself before coming over here. Fury, like little sparks, danced in her eyes, threatening to set me ablaze.

"Tell me. Tell me everything," she demanded, crossing her arms over her chest.

"Can we sit down?" I asked, gesturing to the sitting area where a fire crackled away in the hearth, filling the room with its warmth.

"No, I'm not doing anything else for you until you start telling me what I want to know." She pointed her finger directly in my face, heat radiating from her was so intense that I instinctively took a step back to avoid being burned.

"Fuck, Rhea," I hissed, keeping myself just out of reaching distance. "Watch where you direct your magic."

"You'd better start talking, or I'm just gonna let all this magic go that I've kept on a leash for weeks." She held her palm up where flames danced, growing and shrinking with her breath.

Where did I even begin? She'd been fed so many half-truths, would she even believe me if I told her everything?

"When Ka'an came into Nador fifty years ago, he wasn't alone. I was with him," I said.

"Ka'an and I were both individually chosen, hand-picked by arm generals in Kayar to train together, work together, and eventually we took a blood oath called the Euvas. Because of it, we can speak mind-to-mind, feel each other's intentions, and in some cases read the other's mind. It's far more complicated than that, but just so you get the idea. The one thing it does provide is strength. We can feed and provide each other with our own strength in the case one of us is weakened or injured. The caveat to the Euvas is that if one of us dies, so does the other. I can't die without killing him, and if he dies, so will I."

Rhea visibly paled.

"Before you ask, Ka'an was not always like this. He did push boundaries, had an inflated sense of self and an ego that overshadowed everything, but never did I think he'd disobey orders. He was far too loyal to Samirah." I ran my hands through my damp hair, thinking of the queen of death herself here in Nador.

"Who is she?" Rhea wrapped her arms around her middle, as if trying to hold herself together.

"Samirah." Her name tasted like ash on my tongue. "When the Kirios created the fae, Samirah created the vesperians. After the Kirios blessed both of the races with the prismaras, he stepped away— disappearing to who knows where, weakened from giving away his power. But Samirah stayed and watched their creation. Over time, a divide became apparent between the fae and vesperians. The fae believed themselves to be above the vesperians, near god-like creatures, boasting that their creator gave so much of himself for them that they were above all others. In this, they enslaved and brutalized the vesperians. Samirah decided she could not let her creation suffer any longer. She rallied the vesperians to rebel against the fae, leading a revolution. Using her cosmic power and the Prismara of the Vesperians, she opened a portal to Kayar and led her people to freedom."

"Is that the reason Ka'an burned the libraries across Nador when he took control?" Rhea's lips quivered, tears welling in her eyes.

I nodded. "What I didn't learn until later is that he had already started dismantling the line of the fae long before he carried out the genocide. He'd spent twenty-five years strengthening himself, turning humans against the fae and giving them pieces of dark magic to assist him when the time came. His followers slowly began to burn the histories and whisper rumors to spread distrust across Nador. He told of the evil history of the fae, who at the time, were anything but. So when he killed them all, it was easy for him to slip into his power."

"Why did you come in to begin with?" Fury brimmed in her eyes as silent tears rolled down her cheeks.

"Rhea, you have to understand, I was so different fifty years ago. If I knew then what I know now,—" I started.

"Don't fucking try to make excuses for yourself now, Haedion. Why did you come with Ka'an to Nador?" She seethed, venom lacing every word. The droplets of water that fell from her hair vaporated into steam around her.

"I'm not!" My hand found the doorframe, my nails biting into the wood, keeping me centered. "I just need you to understand the whole story. Please, Rhea," I begged.

I should have told her all of this a long time ago. I wish I had told her the minute I knew I would never be able to give her to my brother... when I knew I was starting to fall for her.

I didn't want to answer her question. I knew she would never forgive me. Even now, I could see it in her eyes; she's looking for a way to understood how we ended up here. The minute she understands how responsible I am for everything Ka'an has done, she'd never look at me the same again. But after everything she had been through, she deserved the truth. Even if it meant losing her.

"We were sent to get the Prismara of the Fae. It takes both stones to open the portals between realms— unless you're Samirah. Her power, combined with one of the stones, is enough to open a portal, but it's draining. She can only do it once every twenty-five or so, or risk burning herself out. She is strong enough to do it alone, but that takes her even longer to recover."

"So you wanted to open the portal so she could return to Nador?" She asked.

"Yes." I nodded.

"So what happened to that plan?" She wiped furiously at her face at the tears that fell relentlessly down her cheeks.

"My brother was— is Samirah's favorite. He is ruthless, smart, and far too much like the queen of death herself. He was chosen to carry out Samirah's mission. I, being his Euvas, accompanied him. He wasn't wrong today, I *was*," I emphasized the word. "The best spy in Kayar. I had a skillset they knew he would need."

Rhea sobbed quietly, covering her mouth to dampen the sound. My body ached to reach out to her and erase all the hurt that I've caused. I'd give anything to take it all back. To never have come to Nador, even if that meant never meeting Rhea.

"You're the reason they're dead." She looked at me, icy blue fire burning in her red eyes.

"Yes. Ka'an and I lived with your people for decades. We were their friends. Hell, we lived in Draconia most of the time. Ka'an was particularly friendly with Gashion. Towards the end, I became complacent. I enjoyed Draconia and fell in love with your people. I thought Ka'an agreed with me. We'd known that the prophecy of your birth would be the catalyst that reunited our people, and so we'd waited. Ka'an agreed not to fight to get the prismara, wait for you to be born, and let you reunite our people in *peace*." My head pounded at the memories replaying in my mind on repeat.

Lies. Every word Ka'an had said was a lie, and I'd played right into it.

"I think Gashion was getting suspicious of Ka'an. Too many unusual questions, human village uprisings— things weren't adding up. So Gashion lied. Said two of his daughters were pregnant and that we were expecting the next dragon shifter. It was a *lie* and a test. You'd already been born, and no one except a few close people, including Cora, knew. I didn't. I never knew you existed."

"That's when he decided to kill them, isn't it?" Rhea muttered, her hand pressed to her lips like she was going to be sick.

"It is," I confirmed.

I needed to get some distance if I was going to continue disclosing my biggest failure. I sidestepped around Rhea and headed for the armoire that was prefilled with freshly laundered clothes. Selecting a soft pair of grey sleeping pants, I walked right past Rhea, who just stared at the floor, eyes glazed and distant.

"Where the fuck were you?" She whispered, not looking at me.

"I was there," I said, shutting the door enough to give me some semblance of privacy to change.

"I was there, but I was distracted. I'd fallen in love with a member of the fae court. Her name was Eden." The memory didn't hit me like it normally did. Didn't slice me open and make me bleed with every beat of my heart. It was like my mind had fought against me for so long to block her from my memory that when I search for her image in my head, the edges were foggy, blurred. Her golden blond hair was dull, and the embers that used to crackle in her eyes had gone out.

"You were so distracted being love-struck by a fae, the people you were sent to infiltrate and eventually destroy, that you missed Ka'an planning the execution of my entire race. Including your what, lover?" She laughed bitterly.

"Yes." I reopened the door to find Rhea staring at the same spot on the floor.

"So you worked for your brother this entire time to get me to Draconia? Was any of it real?" Her voice cracked, the pain in her words like a slap to the face.

"Ever since Ka'an took over, all I wanted was to return to Kayar. We couldn't get the prismara, and all the fae were dead, so I was stuck. I thought all the shifters were dead. No hope for the reunification of our people. But then the Necroscythe felt your power and sent us to find you. I didn't know what you were at first; he kept that from me. But it was real, Rhea, it was all real to me." A lump stuck in my throat I couldn't swallow away.

"When Ka'an saw your magic and knew a fae lived, he told me that if I could find you, deliver you to Draconia, and convince you to bring me the prismara, he'd let me use it to go home."

"You used me," Rhea snarled, the ends of her hair glowed like live embers.

"I'm tired of lying to you. At first, I was dead set on doing whatever it took to get you to Draconia. But there was something there, from the very beginning. I knew that a part of me belonged to you. The more I fought it and tried to keep my distance, I realized I could never do what Ka'an had demanded of me. I tried to deny it, bury my feelings, but I couldn't."

"So that's why you were so distant," she whispered more to herself than me.

"I've spent nearly every day hiding the truth from you since we met." I continued. "When I say this, know I mean every word. The day my brother killed the fae was the day that I stopped living." My words were slow as I focused on each thought. I needed her to hear my sincerity.

"Since then, I've merely existed. My friendship with Bastian was genuine, and it's kept me alive when i didn't think I go could on. The night of the solstice in Flitmoor, when you danced with me, when we kissed, it was the moment I felt my heart start beating again. I will go to the ends of the earth for you. I'll transcend the realms, and if you let me, I promise that every day for the rest of my life will be dedicated to earning your forgiveness for what I've done."

"I don't know what to do." She shook her head again, and a fresh wave of tears sizzled down her cheeks.

"Neither do I," I replied.

"I need to think, and I can't do it in here." She stepped back, toward the door, her arms still wrapped tightly around herself.

"Okay," I said, doing my best to keep my voice steady and hide the hurt that seared in my chest.

"I'll,—" she stuttered, her hand resting on the door handle. "I'll see you at dinner."

Then she was gone, and with her every ounce of warmth in the room.

27

RHEA

He'd told me the truth. I could feel it deep in my bones where the fire had raged along the very fibers of my marrow. Haedion had given me the raw truth despite how much it destroyed him. I could see the haunted look in his eye as he recounted the history, not sparing the details.

And I wanted to forgive him. My soul craved to go wrap my arms around him and sob into his chest. Weep of the past coated in blood that he'd play such a significant part in. Why was it him I wanted to run to? Was it how we truly were opposites, but our souls made of the same thing?

After I bolted from his room, I'd return to mine, making sure the lock was secure before crawling under the sheets of the bed that smelled faintly of smoke and leather.

Why the hell did it smell like Haedion?

I sat up and looked at the freshly pressed sheets. Not a single wrinkle in the crisp white linens to suggest that anyone had occupied this bed before me.

This god damn library.

I flew off the bed and ripped the sheets off the bed, tossing them across the room where they crumpled into a pile on the floor.

My pressure behind my eyes pounded against my skull, and a scream built in my throat that begged to be released.

He had known all along what I was. All those moments Haedion had saved me. From the rusalki, the sandwraiths, the ravagers. It hadn't been for me, it had been for his brother, so that I could get the prismara for them. Not for me. Not to save me.

He wanted to deliver me.

Before I could stop it, the scream tore from me. A freeing, spirit-ripping scream that made my lungs burn.

I didn't remember collapsing to the ground, but the coolness of the tile floor soothed the heat radiating from me that singed holes in the tunic I'd thrown on before I'd stormed over to confront Haedion. My hands wrapped around my knees, pulling close to protect myself.

Everything hurt, like my tendons wanted to rip apart from my bones. Sparks danced behind my closed lids, searing my eyes from the inside out.

"Rhea," the Necroscythe breathed softly. A cool hand found my forehead. I squeezed my eyes shut.

"I know that you're hurting, but I'd like to talk with you, if I could?" He asked gently. "I believe I have some insight that might be useful. But first, we need to cool you down or you'll burn out," he said, voice still soft but edged with concern.

My mouth refused to move, to form the words that I was already scorching from the inside out, that the fire who'd become a part of me now wanted to destroy me. I wasn't on the *edge* of burning out; I *was* burning.

"Rhea, can you open your eyes?" He coaxed, shaking my shoulder gently. The movement sent pain down my limbs like fire licking across my flesh. No, I couldn't open my eyes, couldn't speak for fear the flames might explode from me.

"Haedion!" The Necroscythe bellowed, scooping me into his arms. He carried me into the bathroom, the floor still littered with small pools of water I hadn't bothered to clean up when I made up my mind to confront Haedion.

"Cold water, now!" He commanded, his arms still firmly wrapped around me. The library immediately reacted, water blasting from the invisible spout on the wall, the spray sizzling as it collided with my bare skin.

Somewhere in the distance, I heard a second set of footsteps race across the room.

"What's wrong?" Haedion demanded, his breath coming in fast pants.

"She's going to burn herself out. We need to get her cooled down right now," the Necroscythe said, gingerly lowering me into the tub. Steam erupted filling the room as my skin collided with the cold water swirling around the tub.

"Go down to the gardens and bring me some blossoms from the tree," the Necroscythe ordered, his hand still pressed firmly against my forehead.

The water that flowed around me ran lukewarm. It was enough to ease the burn that was all-consuming, but not enough to cross the threshold into comfortable. I was still on fire, a living spark just underneath my skin.

"You're going to suppress her and knock her out?" Haedion barked. "We just got back, I promised her I'd—,".

"You won't be able to fulfill any promises if she burns herself out. She lost out on years of preparation for what she is, and if we don't stop her, she will kill herself. She has no control. Go get it now!" The Necroscythe climbed into the tub in front of me, water splashing under him as he sat in front of me. His hands, cupping my face, held firm.

"Rhea, look at me," he demanded.

My lids protested as I cracked them open, the light on my sensitive eyes like an assault to my senses.

But I pushed through.

"Good," he sighed with relief. "Your body is trying to shift, and I am sure you don't understand. If you'd had time with Gashion, you would've learned how to control it— but right now, you have to smother the fire. Douse the magic, Rhea,"

I wanted to listen, but the roar of popping embers in my ears muted all my thoughts. Then, Haedion's face popped into my mind, pushing back the all-consuming pain.

"Where is the magic coming from?" He'd asked me that night in the hut when I'd nearly lost control the first time. That time was out of fear, the fire reacting to my anxiety. This time it was different. I was a prisoner now to my body.

The magic was a well, I remembered. In my gut, a never-ending hole of power where the fire flowed from. Last time, I'd convinced the fire to flow backwards. This time it would be different. I'd need a stopper.

I forced my lungs to expand to their fullest, breathing in the hot-damp air. Stop the flow. I imagined walking up to the stone, lined well, fashioned with a roof and bucket ready to drop down to retrieve liquid magma. Next to it sat a metal lid, the perfect size to cover the hole. I picked up the heavy lid and heaved it over the well, the magic slowing as I slid the lid into place.

Then it stopped.

The pain.

The heat.

The fire

It all stopped.

And I opened my eyes.

The Necroscythe pulled a new tunic from midair when I finally climbed out of the ice-cold tub. Haedion had returned moments after I pulled the shirt over my head, Bastian in tow with Nafre and Silas on their heels. He had a beautiful, pink blossom in his hand that he thrust over to the Necroscythe the moment he skidded to a halt.

Every movement of my eyes sent red-hot irons through the very center into my brain. I stood as still as I could, watching the Necroscythe as he held the flower in one hand, and in the other, an empty glass appeared. I must've blinked too slow, because by the time I'd reopened my eyes, the flower was gone and a liquid filled the glass, the same color the flower had been. He extended the glass to me.

"Drink," he ordered.

"What is it?" I croaked, but accepted the drink with trembling fingers.

"It's blossom tea from the willow in the gardens at the bottom level of the library. When you wake, I'll show you it myself. This tea will help you sleep, but most importantly, and dangerous for those with magic, it's a suppressant. Your magic will be a fraction of its power. So while you rest and let your subconscious digest everything that just happened, you won't have another episode like this."

It was an eloquent way of saying that he wanted my magic to stay behind lock and key while I was knocked the fuck out. And honestly, that sounded like a dream. I didn't hesitate to drink the entire cup in one breath. My throat felt like sandpaper as the warm liquid raced down my throat.

"I was going to suggest you sip it, but I like your gumption," the Necroscythe mumbled as my vision went sideways.

"Hae, she's gonna fall," Bastian lurched for me from the doorway as my knees collapsed and I was falling once again.

I didn't feel myself hit the floor.

⁂

When I woke, the sheets didn't smell like smoke and leather. Instead, the fresh scent of soap, of fresh, clean laundry filled my nose.

I sat up slowly, my limbs feeling like they moved in slow motion. I was in my room at the library, the curtains drawn back to see the dawn breaking on the horizon.

My eyes flicked around the room. In the sitting area, Bastian was asleep, head slumped sideways, mouth open, snoring softly. Haedion sat in the adjacent chair, head resting on a fist as if he'd been fighting the lull of sleep before finally succumbing.

I had to get out of there. I couldn't handle talking to him just yet.

They didn't stir as I slowly climbed from the bed and padded over to the armoire to find a loose pair of pants to slip on. As quickly as I could, I opened to door that led to the hallways, closing the door behind me with a soft click.

I felt better than I had in days. My body, still sluggish from whatever I'd drank, didn't ache with the weight of the magic. In fact, the magic was bubbling happily in the well where the power was stored—waiting, watching for a command. Perfectly under control.

When I reached the spiral staircase in the center of the library, I felt a tug.

Go up, it whispered.

And if I'd learned anything about the whispers, the half-truths, and the tugs, I knew I needed to follow.

At the top, I found the Necroscythe waiting. He sat at the head of the table, sipping from a goblet.

"It's a little early to be drinking, isn't it?" I asked, walking over to claim the seat next to him.

"When you have lived as long as I have, there is no concept of too early," he smirked. With a wave of his hand, a steaming cup of tea appeared in front of me.

"How are you feeling?" He asked, casually tossing one leg over the other.

"Better." And it was the truth— at least physically. Emotionally and mentally, I was still inside the bathtub, fighting to keep myself grounded.

"But?" He pressed, his head tilting, brows raised.

"You know everything, don't you?" I asked, wrapping my fingers around the warm cup. The familiarity of the motion was soothing against my raw nerves.

"I know most things, but I'm not all-knowing. If you are asking me if I know what Haedion is, who he is, and all that he's endured, then yes," he replied, bringing the cup to his lips.

"And yet you trust him?"

"I do."

"Why?" I pressed, shoving back from the seat and pacing to the windows where the wind ripped across the sand, bashing it against the strong hold of the library.

"Haedion was born an honorable man, guided by conviction in a world that instilled in him to fight for the wrong causes. Vesperians and fae were created with the same principles of leadership and loyalty. Samirah knew how to take those traits and create the ultimate soldier. Hence, Ka'an," he said.

"He was going to give me to Ka'an at first. How does that make him honorable?" I shot back, sending a glare over my shoulder.

"Did he get to tell you about what he left back in Kayar?" The Necroscythe inquired, his brows knitting together in uncertainty.

"Does it matter?" I turned to face the Necroscythe, who leaned back in his seat, his hands folded in his lap.

"It all matters, my dear. From who Haedion is at his core, to the mistakes he's made, to what Ka'an did to your people, to what he plans to do next. It all matters."

"That doesn't make any sense?" I pinched the bridge of my nose, trying my best to hold myself together.

"It does," he insisted. "What did I tell you about Haedion? He's honorable. He lost himself when he left Kayar, but then rebuilt himself here. Then that was torn away from him, too. The offer to return home was his weakness, and in a moment, he made a deal with his brother that went against everything he was. He believed he deserved nothing after he failed to stop the genocide of the fae. But deep down, he knew Ka'an couldn't have the prismara, and he couldn't give you over to him. And when it came to it, he fought hard against his brother."

He stood then, coming to stand next to me. "Tell me, Rhea, did you talk to the dragons?"

The dragons.

I hadn't had one second to work through the information I'd learned while in the catacombs.

"I did. Agnya wanted me to tell you she sends her regards," I said sheepishly. It felt silly, but I didn't miss the way he stood a little straighter, and the forced smile that he put on.

"Ah, yes, Agnya," he smirked, running a hand through his perfectly kept beard. "What else did she share with you?"

"The prophecy. But it didn't make any sense. It talked about the firstborn daughter of dragons," I replied. My fingers found a rough spot on my neck as I worked through the prophecy over and over again, trying to deduce what it could mean.

"Gashion was the last son born of the dragons. Only once in a generation or two, depending on the lifetime of the fae, was a male born with the gift. Upon the birth of the first daughter, the prophecy foretold the end of the conflict." The Necroscythe clarified, his brows knitted together in concentration as he studied my fingers on my neck.

"Ar—are you saying I'm a dragon shifter?" I stuttered. The skin on my neck that had started as an uncomfortable itch developed into full-on discomfort.

"I saw you shortly after the murder of your parents. I knew then what you were, so did Cora, who delivered you safely to Ragnar and Carina. They all knew what you were and that you must be protected at all costs." He grabbed my hand then, pulling me close, studying the spot on my neck that itched uncomfortably.

I rooted myself on the spot, fighting against the urge to step away out of his reach.

"It's fine," I grumbled, embarrassment tightening my chest. "Back to the subject. There is no way I'm a dragon shifter."

"No, Rhea, it's entirely possible." A smile tugged at the corner of his lips. "Come see this."

A mirror appeared on the wall, large enough that we were both captured within the frame.

"Look closer." He nudged me forward. With an exasperated huff, I stalked close to the mirror. My reflection peered back at me, looking anything but who'd I'd grown used to seeing.

My red hair hung freely down my back like normal, my deep burgundy eyes sparkling back at me, something I'd become so used to hiding over the years. The creamy tone of my skin made the exaggeration of my prominent cheekbones even more gaunt than I remembered.

Then my eyes fell to my neck. A line of what could only be described as scales ran in a line one after another from the sensitive spot where my neck met my jaw and continued down, following the curve of my throat, and disappeared beneath my shirt.

"You are the first daughter, born of the dragons, Rhea," the Necroscythe whispered, his words sent shivers up my spine.

"And you will shake the realms."

ACKNOWLEDGMENTS

I don't even know where to begin these acknowledgements. There are so many people who were critical in helping *Ashborne* become what it is today. From coming into an MFA program with an idea and a dream, through thesis, where the first draft of *Ashborne* was completed, torn apart, and then rebuilt once again. Hours upon hours of writing, revising, rewriting, and editing led to this final product. Four years ago, if you had told me that this is the path this story would take me on, I'm not sure I would've believed you.

To my wonderful **husband**, who has never once believed I was anything but capable of achieving anything I set my mind to. Could you imagine going back to that fourth-grade classroom where we met and telling our little ten-year-old selves that we'd be married with kids someday?! Thank you for growing with me. Thank you for trusting me. Thank you for going through all the long nights and even longer days by my side. I love you.

Thank you to **Samantha** for your complete, die-hard dedication to the success of *Ashborne*, for the endless voice memos you listened to, and the scenes you read and reread when I insisted they didn't work (and they did, I'm just insane). And truly, for kicking me in the ass when I needed you to (are you *sure* about the rabies?!). I love you. Thank you for being my editor...but more importantly, my best friend.

Hey, **Mom and Dad!** Look, I did it! But really, there are a million things I could thank you for, and it would never be enough. Each day, I become increasingly thankful for the life you gave me. You are the best parents, the best grandparents, the best support system, and truly, anything I ever achieve in this life is because of you. I hope you know the choices and sacrifices you made—things I didn't understand then

—are not lost on me now. If I turn out to be even a fraction of the people you are, I'll be okay. I could not have asked for better parents, and I must've done something damn good in a past life to deserve what you've given me. I love you both.

To my **darling daughters**, who watched me slave over this book day after day, remember that what you believe, you can achieve. I know that whatever you set your minds to, you can accomplish. All I ever wanted to be in life was your mom, and it remains my greatest blessing. My sun rises and sets with you both each day, and my heart beats because of you. You will never know how much I love you.

And to my **Mimi**, who has endured more than any one person should have to, thank you for being the best Mimi in the entire world. For teaching me how to sew, to knit, to make the perfect cup of tea, and for helping me with my girls and folding endless piles of laundry. I am extraordinarily thankful in ways words cannot express. You taught me how to take all the bad and turn it into good. I wish Papa were here, but I am so grateful my girls get to know their Mimi and will have those memories forever. All I ever wanted growing up was for my children to know you, and they do.

And remember, you're living till you're 120.

ABOUT JAYCIE REID

Jaycie Reid has been a soul-born bookworm and writer from the ripe age of seven years old. A lover of all things romantasy, and millennial-core, you'll find her either chasing her two little girls or hiding under a cozy blanket trying to get a few pages of her latest read in before she is once again attacked by the children (can't a girl get a minute?!).

Jaycie currently lives in Central Oregon with her husband (who she met in the fourth grade, cool right?), their girls, and one big orange fluffy cat, Leo.

Want to learn more about book two of Daughter of the Burning Throne and other book updates? Sign-up for updates at www.author jayciereid.com.

instagram.com/authorjayciereid
tiktok.com/@authorjayciereid